calls to many.  adventure; to those seeking an escape to quieter climes far from the cares of home; to those who would face the challenge of the creatures that dwell in the oceans' waters; and to those lured by fantastical dreams all their own.

Let this exciting collection of original sea tales by some of fantasy's finest sailors on the deep waters of imagination carry you off to distant realms and times with such magical accounts as:

"The Sir Walter Raleigh Conspiracy"—Was he beheaded by the king's order, or had his travels taught him a special magic with which to alter his fate?

"The Winds They Did Blow High"—Sometimes it takes a little wind-whistling to alter both the course of ships and of battle. . . .

"Child of Ocean"—She had the gift to hear the voices of the sea, and as Master Pilot the duty to always guide her ship to safety—unless she drew the one trip-token no Pilot ever wanted to claim. . . .

More Imagination-Expanding Anthologies Brought to You by DAW:

MOB MAGIC *Edited by Brian Thomsen and Martin H. Greenberg*. From gangland Chicago to corrupt old Camelot, and from AI enforcers to the Yakuza men in the shadows, the crime scenes and culprits may change but the mob always remains in control . . . here in the D.A.'s dossier of the magically most wanted. Join Mickey Zucker Reichert, Mike Resnick, Simon Hawke, Jeff Grubb, Max Allan Collins, Roland Green, Jody Lynn Nye, and other literary gangbusters as they bring to light the exploits of the criminal element in the world of the fantastic . . . cases of undying hitmen condemned to eternally repeat their crimes . . . feline detectives with a soft spot for shady ladies . . . old gods conspiring against the new kid who is muscling in on their territory . . . gangland bosses extracting revenge from beyond the grave . . . unlucky thieves and enchanted underbosses.

SPELL FANTASTIC *Edited by Martin H. Greenberg and Larry Segriff*. Fantasy is fueled by spells, from those cast by simple love potions to the great workings of magic which can alter the very nature of reality, destroy seemingly all-powerful foes, offer power or punishment, immortality or death. In *Spell Fantastic* thirteen of today's finest word wizards—including Kristine Kathryn Rusch, Nina Kiriki Hoffman, Robin Wayne Bailey, Jane Lindskold, Dennis McKiernan, and Charles de Lint—have crafted unforgettable tales with which to enchant your imagination.

WARRIOR FANTASTIC *edited by Martin H. Greenberg and John Helfers*. Alan Dean Foster, Jean Rabe, Diana L. Paxson, Fiona Patton, Tim Waggoner, David Bischoff, Janet Pack, Pauline E. Dungate, Nina Kiriki Hoffman, Kristine Schwengel, Jody Lynn Nye, Bradley H. Sinor, Bill Fawcett, Gary A. Braunbeck, and Charles de Lint let you share in the challenges and victories of those who fight to hold back the darkness. From an old arms master hired by the Sheriff of Nottingham to teach him how to best Robin Hood . . . to a betrayal of hospitality that would see blood flowing more freely than wine . . . to a band of warriors who attacked on four legs rather than two . . . here are stories of both legendary warriors and of mighty heroes drawn entirely from the imagination. All of them are memorable adventures that will have you cheering for these magnificent champions as they rescue the downtrodden and mete out justice.

OCEANS OF MAGIC

Edited by
Brian M. Thomsen
and Martin H. Greenberg

DAW BOOKS, INC.
DONALD A. WOLLHEIM, FOUNDER
375 Hudson Street, New York, NY 10014

ELIZABETH R. WOLLHEIM
SHEILA E. GILBERT
PUBLISHERS
www.dawbooks.com

First Printing, February 2001
1 2 3 4 5 6 7 8 9

DAW TRADEMARK REGISTERED
U.S. PAT OFF AND FOREIGN COUNTRIES
—MARCA REGISTRADA.
HECHO EN USA

PRINTED IN THE U.S.A.

ACKNOWLEDGMENTS

Introductions © 2001 by Brian M. Thomsen.

Oh, Glorious Sight © 2001 by Tanya Huff.

The Sir Walter Raleigh Conspiracy © 2001 by Allen C. Kupfer.

The Winds They Did Blow High © 2001 by
   Frieda A. Murray.

The Devil and Captain Briggs © 2001 by John J. Ordover.

Tribute © 2001 by Kristine Kathryn Rusch.

Midshipwizard © 2001 by James M. Ward.

Catch of the Day © 2001 by Jeff Grubb.

The Colossus of Mahrass © 2001 by Mel Odom.

Walk upon the Waters © 2001 by Paul Kupperberg.

The Sacred Waters of Kane © 2001 by Fiona Patton.

Child of Ocean © 2001 by Rosemary Edghill.

The Sea God's Servant © 2001 by Mickey Zucker Reichert.

Ocean's Eleven © 2001 by Mike Resnick and Tom Gerencer.

For C. S. Forester, Nordoff and Hall,
Robert Louis Stevenson, Herman Melville,
Dudley Pope, Patrick O'Brien, and the
many others who have so eloquently
sailed these seas before.

CONTENTS

DEITIES AND THE DEEP BLUE SEA

Sails ho, matey!
Welcome aboard!

What lays before us is a vast ocean of imagination where the annals of voyages of our past freely mix with those of places that may never have existed.

Some of the seas are filled with darkness and danger, others with magic and mayhem. The choices are yours.

Keep a watchful eye open, for no one can anticipate what we might come across when we be sailing on *Oceans of Magic*.

VOYAGES IN HISTORY

Some have chosen the oceans upon which many have traveled before, preferring voyages that have happened in our past, though in many cases events and places might not be as we remember.

From the early explorers such as John Cabot and Sir Walter Raleigh, to the warriors of the nautical skirmishes of France and England or even twentieth-century Axis and Allies, fact and fiction sail side by side, and in some cases, as with the legendary *Mary Celeste*, the two seem to blend together.

Sail on to the magical past as it might have been!

OH, GLORIOUS SIGHT

BY TANYA HUFF

WILL Hennet, first mate on *The Matthew*, stood at the rail and watched her master cross the dock, talking with great animation to the man by his side.

"So the Frenchman goes with you?"

"Aye."

"He a sailor, then?"

"He tells me he's sailed."

"And that man, the Italian?"

"Master Cabot's barber."

The river pilot spat into the harbor, scoring a direct hit on the floating corpse of a rat, his opinion of traveling with barbers clear. "Good to have clean cheeks when the sirens call you over the edge of the world."

"So they say." Only a sailor who'd never left the confines of the Bristol Channel could still believe the world was flat, but Hennet had no intention of arguing with a man whose expert guidance they needed if they were to reach the anchorage at King's Road on this tide.

"Seems like Master Cabot's taking his time to board."

That, Hennet could agree with wholeheartedly.

"By God's grace, this time tomorrow we'll be on the open sea."

Gaylor Roubaix laughed at the excitement in his friend's

voice. "And this time a month hence, we'll be in Cathay sleeping in the arms of sloe-eyed maidens."

"*What* kind of maidens?"

"You aren't the only one to have read the stories of Marco Polo; it isn't my fault if you only remember silk and spice. Slow down," he added with a laugh. "It's unseemly for the master of the ship to run across the docks."

"Slow down?" Zoane Cabatto—now John Cabot by grace of the letters patent granted by the English king—threw open his arms. "How? When the wind brings me the scent of far off lands and I hear . . ." His voice trailed off, and he stopped so suddenly Roubaix had gone another six steps before he realized he was alone.

"Zoane!"

"*Ascoltare*. Listen." Head down, he charged around a stack of baled wool.

Before Roubaix—who'd heard nothing at all—could follow, angry shouting in both Italian and English rose over the ambient noise of the docks. The shouting stopped, suddenly punctuated by a splash, and the mariner reappeared.

"A dockside tough was beating a child," he said by way of explanation. "I put a stop to it."

Roubaix sighed and closed the distance between them. "Why? It was none of your concern."

"Perhaps, but I leave three sons in God's grace until we return, and it seemed a bad omen to let it continue." He stepped forward and paused again at Roubaix's expression. "What is it?"

In answer, the other man pointed.

Cabot turned.

The boy was small, a little older than a child but undernourished by poverty. Dark hair, matted into filthy clumps, had recently been dusted with ash, purple-and-green bruises gave the grime on the thin arms some color, and the recent winter, colder than any in living memory, had frozen a toe off one bare foot. An old cut, reopened on his cheek, bled sluggishly.

His eyes were a brilliant blue, a startling color in the thin face, quickly shuttered as he dropped his gaze to the toes of Cabot's boots.

"Go on, boy, you're safe now!"

Roubaix snorted. "Safe until the man who was beating him is out of the water, then he'll take his anger at you out on the boy."

Beginning to regret his impulsive action, Cabot spread his hands. "What can I do?"

"Take him with us."

"Are you mad?"

"There is a saying, the farther from shore, the farther from God. We go a long way from shore. A little charity might convince God to stay longer." Roubaix's shrug held layers of meaning. "Or you can leave him to die. Your choice."

Cabot looked across the docks to the alleys and tenements of dockside, dark in spite of early morning sunlight that danced across the harbor swells and murmured, "Your father was right, Gaylor, you should have been a priest." After a long moment, he turned his attention back to the boy. "What is your name?" he asked, switching to accented English.

"Tam." His voice sounded rusty, unused.

"I am John Cabot, Master of *The Matthew*."

The brilliant blue gaze flicked to the harbor and back with a question.

"*Si*. That ship. We sail today for the new world. If you wish, you sail with us."

* * *

He hadn't expected to be noticed. He'd followed only because the man had been kind to him, he'd wanted to hold the feeling a little longer. When the man turned, he nearly bolted. When he was actually spoken to, his heart began beating so hard he could hardly hear his own answer.

And now this.

He knew, for he'd been told it time and time again, that ships were not crewed by such as he, that sailors had legitimate sons to find a place for, that there'd never be a place for some sailor's get off a tuppenny whore.

"Well, boy? Do you come?"

He swallowed hard, and nodded.

"Is Master Cabot actually bringing that boy on board?"

"Seems to be," Hennet answered grimly.

"A Frenchman, a barber, and a piece of dockside trash." The river pilot spat again. "He'll sail you off the edge of the world, you mark my words."

"Mister Hennet, are we ready to sail?"

"Aye, sir." Hennet stepped forward to meet Cabot at the top of the gangplank, the river pilot by his side. "This is Jack Pyatt. He'll be seeing us safe to King's Road."

"Mister Pyatt." Cabot clapped the man's outstretched hand in both of his in the English style. "I thank you for lending us your skill this day."

"Lending?" The pilot's prominent brows went up. "I'm paid well for this, Master Cabot."

"Yes, of course." Dropping the man's hand, Cabot started toward the fo'c'sle. "If you are ready, the tide does not wait. Mister Hennet, cast off."

"Zoane . . ."

Brows up, Cabot turned. "Oh, yes, the boy. Mister Hennet, this is Tam. Make him a sailor. Happy now?" he asked Roubaix pointedly in French.

"Totally," Roubaix replied. "And when you have done making him a sailor," he murmured in English to Hennet as he passed, "you may make a silk purse from a sow's ear."

"Aye, sir."

He wanted to follow Master Cabot, but the sudden realization that a dozen pairs of eyes had him locked in their sight froze him in place. It wasn't good, it wasn't safe to be the center of attention.

Hennet watched the worship in the strange blue eyes replaced by fear, saw the bony shoulders hunch in on themselves to make a smaller target and looked around to find the source. It took him a moment to realize that nothing more than the curiosity of the crew was evoking such terror.

"Right, then!" Fists on his hips, he turned in place. "You heard the master!"

"We're to make him a sailor, then?" Rennie McAlonie called out before anyone could move.

"You're to cast off the lines, you poxy Scots bastard."

"Aye, that's what I thought."

"And you . . ." The boy cringed and Hennet softened his voice to a growl. "For now, stay out of the way."

He didn't know where out of the way was. After he'd been cursed at twice and cuffed once, the big man the master called Hennet shoved him down beside the chicken coop and told him to stay put. He could see a bit of Master Cabot's leg, so he hugged his knees to his chest and chewed on a stalk of wilted greens he'd taken from an indignant hen.

The tenders rowed *The Matthew* down the channel and left her at King's Road, riding at anchor with half a dozen other ships waiting for an east wind to fill the sail.

"Where's the boy?"

"Now that's a right good question, Mister Hennet." Rennie pulled the ratline tight and tested his knot. "Off somewhere dark and safe's my guess."

The mate snorted. "We've ballast enough. Master Cabot wants him taught."

"It'd be like teachin' one of the wee folk. He's here, but he's not a part of us. It's like the only other livin' thing he sees is Master Cabot."

"It's right like havin' a stray dog around," offered another of the crew, "the kind what runs off with his tail 'tween his legs when ya tries to make friends."

Hennet glanced toward the shore. "If he's to be put off, it has to be soon, before the wind changes. I'll speak with Master Cabot."

"Come now, it's only been three days." Rope wrapped around his fist, Rennie turned to face the mate. "This is right strange to him. Give the poor scrawny thing a chance."

"You think you can win him?"

"Aye, I do."

The boy's eyes were the same color as the piece of Venetian glass he'd brought back for his mother from his first voyage. Wondering why he remembered that now, Hennet nodded. "All right. You've got one more day."

Master Cabot wanted him to be a sailor, and he tried, he truly did. But he couldn't be a sailor hiding in dark corners and he couldn't tell when it was safe to come out and he didn't know any other way to live.

He felt safest after sunset when no one moved around much and it was easier to disappear. Back pressed up against the aftcastle wall, as close to Master Cabot as possible, he settled into a triangle of deep shadow and cupped his hand protectively over the biscuits he'd tied into the tattered edge of his shirt. So far, there'd been food twice a day but who knew how long it would keep coming.

Shivering a little, for the nights were still cold, he closed his eyes.

And opened them again.

What was that sound?

"Ren, look there."

Rennie, who'd replaced the shepherd's pipe with a leather mug of beer, peered over the edge of the mug. Eyes that gleamed as brilliant a blue by moon as by sun, stared back at him.

"He crept up while you was playin'," John Jack murmured, leaning in to his ear. "Play sumptin' else."

Without looking aside, Rennie set down the last of his beer, put the pipe between his lips and blew a bit of a jig. Every note drew the boy closer. When he blew the last swirl of notes, the boy was an arm's reach away. He could feel the others holding their breath, could feel the weight of the boy's strange eyes. It was like something out of story had crept out of the shadows. Moving slowly, he held out the pipe.

"Rennie . . . !"

"Shut up. Go on, boy."

Thin fingers closed around the offered end and tentatively pulled it from his grasp.

*   *   *

He stroked the wood, amazed such sounds could come out of something so plain, then he put it in his mouth the way he'd seen the red-haired man do.

The first noise was breathy, unsure. The second had an unexpected purity of tone.

"Cover and uncover the holes; it makes the tune." Rennie wiggled his fingers, grinned as the boy wiggled his in imitation, and smacked John Jack as he did the same.

He covered each hole in turn, listening. Brows drawn in, he began to put the sounds together.

Toes that hadn't tapped to Rennie's jig moved of their own accord.

When he ran out of sounds and stopped playing, he nearly bolted at the roar of approval that rose up from the men, but he couldn't take the pipe away and he wouldn't leave it behind.

Rennie tapped his front teeth with a fingernail. "You've played before?" he asked at last.

Tam shook his head.

"You played what I played, just from hearing?"

He nodded.

"Do you want to keep the pipe?"

He nodded again, fingers white around the wooden shaft, afraid to breathe in case he shattered.

"If you stay out where you can seen, be a part of the crew, you can keep it."

"Rennie!"

"Shut up, John Jack, I've another. And," he jabbed a finger at the boy, "you let us teach you to be a sailor."

Recoiling from the finger, Tam froze. He looked around at the semicircle of men then down at the pipe. The music made it safe to come out, so as long as he had the pipe he was safe. Master Cabot wanted him to be a sailor. When he lifted his head, he saw that the red-haired man still watched him. He nodded a third time.

By the fifth day of waiting, the shrouds and ratlines were done and the crew had been reduced to bitching about the delay, every one of them aware it could last for weeks.

"Hey, you!"

Tam jerked around and nearly fell over as he leaped back from John Jack looming over him.

"You bin up ta crow's nest yet?"

He shook his head.

"Well, get yer arse up there, then."

It was higher than it looked and he'd have quit halfway, but Master Cabot was standing in his usual place on the fo'c'sle not watching but there, so he ignored the trembling in his arms and legs and kept going, finally falling over the rail and collapsing on the small round of planking.

After he got his breath back, he sat up and peered through the slats.

He could see to the ends of the earth, but no one could see him. He didn't have words to describe how it made him feel.

Breezes danced around the nest that couldn't be felt down on the deck. They chased each other through the rigging, playing a tune against the ropes.

Tam pulled out his pipe and played the tune back at them.

The breezes blew harder.

"Did you send him up there, McAlonie?"

"No, Mister Hennet, I did not." Head craned back, Rennie grinned. "But still, it's best he does the climb first when we're ridin' steady."

"True." Denying the temptation to stare aloft at nothing, the mate frowned. "That doesn't make the nest his own private minstrel's gallery, though. Get him down."

"He's not hurtin' aught and it's right nice to be serenaded like."

"MISTER HENNET!" The master's bellow turned all heads.

"I don't think Master Cabot agrees," Hennet pointed out dryly.

The breezes tried to trip him up by changing direction. Fingers flying, Tam followed.

Although the Frenchman seemed to be enjoying the music, Master Cabot did not. Lips pressed into a thin line, Hennet climbed onto the fo'c'sle.

He barely had his feet under him when Master Cabot pointed toward the nest and opened his mouth.

Another voice filled the space.

"East wind rising, sir!"

Tam's song rose triumphantly from the top of the ship.

"Get him down now, McAlonie!" Hennet bellowed as he raced aft.

"Aye, sir!" But Rennie spent another moment listening to the song, and a moment more watching the way the rigging moved in the wind.

Once out of the channel and sailing hard toward the Irish coast, the crew waited expectantly for Tam to show the first signs of seasickness, but, with the pipe tied tight in his shirt, the dockside brat clambered up and down the pitching decks like he'd never left land.

Fortunately, Master Cabot's Genoese barber provided amusement enough.

"Merciful Father, why must I wait so for the touch of your Grace on this, your most wretched of children?"

Tam didn't understand the words, but he understood the emotion—the man had thrown his guts into the sea both before and after the declaration. Legs crossed, back against the aftcastle wall, he frowned thoughtfully. The shivering little man looked miserable.

"Seasickness won't kill ya," yelled down one of the mast hands, "but you'll be wishing it did."

Tam understood that, too. There'd been many times in his life when he'd wished he was dead.

He played to make the barber feel better. He never intended to make him cry.

"What do you mean, you could see Genoa as the boy played?"

The barber feathered the razor along Cabot's jaw. "What I said, patron. The boy played, I saw Genoa. I was sick no more."

"From his twiddling?"

"Yes."

"That is ridiculous. You got your sea legs, nothing more."

"As you say, patron."

"What happened to your head, boy?"

Braced against the rolling of the ship, Tam touched his bare scalp and risked a shrug. "Shaved."

Hennet turned to a snickering John Jack for further explanation.

"Barber did it ta thank him, I reckon. Can't understand his jabbering."

"It's an improvement," the mate allowed. "Or will be when those sores heal."

"That the new world?"

"Don't be daft, boy, 'tis Ireland. We'll be puttin' in to top the water casks."

"We can sail no closer to the wind than we are," Cabot glared up at an overcast sky and then into the shallow bell of the lanteen sail. "It has been blowing from the west since we left Ireland! Columbus had an east wind, but me, I am mocked by God."

Roubaix spread his hands, then grabbed for a rope as the bow dipped unexpectedly deep into a trough. "Columbus sailed in the south."

"*Stupido!* Tell me something I don't know!" Spinning on one heel, balance perfected by years at sea, Cabot stomped across to the ladder and slid down into the waist.

Exchanging a glance with the bow watch that needed no common language, Roubaix followed. At the bottom of the ladder, he nearly tripped over a bare leg. The direction of the sprawl and the heartbroken look still directed at Cabot's back told as much of the story as necessary.

"He is not angry at you, Tam." The intensity of joy that replaced the hurt in the boy's stare gave him pause. He doubted Zoane had any idea how much his dockside brat adored him. "He only pushes you because he cannot push the winds around to where he needs them. Do you understand?"

Tam nodded. It was enough to understand that he'd done nothing wrong in the master's sight.

"What's he playing?" Hennet muttered, joining Rennie and John Jack at the bow. "There's no tune to it."

"I figure that depends on who's listenin'," Rennie answered with a grin. He jerked his head toward where Tam was leaning over the rail. "Have a look, Mister Hennet."

Brows drawn in, Hennet leaned over by the boy and looked down at the sea.

Seven sleek gray bodies rode the bow wave.

"He's playing for the dolphins," he said, straightening and turning back toward the two men.

"Aye. And you can't ask for better luck."

The mate sighed. Arms folded, he squinted into the wind. "We could use a bit of luck."

"Master Cabot still in a foul mood, is he?"

"Better than he be in a mood for fowl," John Jack cackled. Two days before, a line squall had snapped the mainstay sail halberd belaying pin and dropped the full weight of the sail right on the chicken coop. The surviving hens had been so hysterical, they'd all been killed, cooked, and eaten.

A little surprised John Jack had brains enough for such a play on words, Hennet granted him a snort before answering Rennie. "If the winds don't change . . ."

There was no need to finish.

Tam had stopped playing at the sound of the master's name and now, pipe tightly clutched, he crossed to Hennet's side. "We needs . . ." he began, then froze when the mate turned toward him.

"We need what?"

He shot a panicked glance at Rennie who nodded encouragingly. He licked salt off his lips and tried again. "We needs ta go north."

"We need to go west, boy."

His heart beat so violently he could feel his ribs shake. Pushing the pipe against his belly to keep from throwing up his guts, Tam shook his head. "No. North."

Impressed—in spite of the contradiction—by obvious fear overcome, Hennet snorted again. "And who tells you that, boy?"

Tam pointed over the side.

"The dolphins?" When Tam nodded, Hennet turned on the two crewman, about to demand which of them had been filling the boy's head with nonsense. The look on Rennie's face stopped him. "What?"

"I fished the Iceland banks, Mister Hennet, outa the islands with me da when I were a boy. Current runs west from there and far enough north, the blow's east, northeast."

"You told the boy?"

"Swear to you, not a word."

The three men stared at Tam and then, at a sound from the sea, at each other. The dolphins were laughing.

"North." Cabot glanced down at his charts, shook his head, and was smiling when he looked up again at the mate. "Good work."

Hennet drew in a long breath and let it out slowly. He didn't like taking credit for another's idea but he liked even less the thought of telling the ship's master they were changing course because Tam had played pipes for a pod of dolphins. "Thank you, sir."

"Make the course change."

"Aye, sir." As he turned on his heel to leave the room, he didn't like the way the Frenchman was looking at him.

"He was hiding something, Zoane."

"What?"

"I don't know." Smiling at little at his own suspicion, Roubaix shook his head. "But I'll wager it has to do with the boy. There's something about those eyes."

Cabot paused at the cabin door, astrolabe in hand. "Whose eyes?"

"The boy's."

"What boy?"

"Tam." When no comprehension dawned, he sighed. "The dockside boy you saved from a beating and brought with us . . . What latitude are we at, Zoane?"

Face brightening, Cabot pointed to the map. "Roughly forty-eight degrees. Give me a moment to take a reading and I can be more exact. Why?"

"Not important. You'd better go before you lose the sun." Alone in the room, he rubbed his chin and stared down at the charts. "If he was drawn here, you'd remember him, wouldn't you?"

"'S cold."

"We're still north, ain't we; though the current's run us more south than we was." John Jack handed the boy a second mug of beer. "Careful, yer hands'll be sticky."

He'd spent the afternoon tarring the mast to keep the wood from rotting where the yard had rubbed and had almost enjoyed the messy job. Holding both mugs carefully as warned, he joined Rennie at the south rail.

"Ta, lad."

They leaned quietly beside each other for a moment, staring out at a sea so flat and black the stars looked like they continued above and below without a break.

"You done good work today," Rennie said at last, wiping his beard with his free hand. He could feel Tam's pleasure, and he smiled. "I'll make you a sailor yet." When he saw the boy turn from the corner of one eye, he turned as well, following his line of sight, squinting up onto the darkness on the fo'c'sle. There could be no mistaking the silhouette of the master. "Give it up, boy," he sighed. "The likes of him don't see the likes of us unless we gets in their way."

Shoulders slumped, Tam turned all the way around, and froze. A moment later, he was racing across the waist and throwing himself against the north rail.

Curious, Rennie followed. "I don't know what he's seen, do I?" he snarled at a question. "I've not asked him yet." He didn't have to ask—the boy's entire body pointed up at the flash of green light in the sky. "'Tis the *Fir Chlis*, the souls of fallen angels God caught before they reached earthly realms. Call 'em also the Merry Dancers—though they ain't dancing much this time of year."

When Tam scrambled up a ratline without either speaking or taking his eyes from the sky, Rennie snorted and returned to the beer barrel. John Jack had just lifted the jug when the first note sounded.

The pipe had been his before it was Tam's, but he'd never heard it make that sound. Beer poured unheeded over his wrist as he turned to the north.

The light in the sky was joined by another.

For every note, another light.

When a vast sweep of sky had been lit, the notes began to join each other in a tune.

"I'll be buggered," John Jack breathed. "He's playin' fer the Dancers."

Rennie nodded. "Fast dance brings bad weather, boy!" he called. "Slow dance for fair!"

The tune slowed, the dance with it.

The lights dipped down, touched their reflections in the water, and whirled away.

"I ain't never seen them so close."

"I ain't never seen them so . . ." Although he couldn't think of the right word, Rennie saw it reflected in the awe on every uplifted face. It was like, like watching angels dance.

The sails gleamed green and blue and orange and red.

All at once, the music stopped, cut off in mid note. The dancers lingered for a heartbeat and then the sky was dark again, the stars dimmer than they'd been before.

Blinking away the afterimages, Rennie ran to the north rail only to find another man there before him. As there had been no mistaking the master's silhouette, so there was no mistaking the master.

Tam lay stunned on the deck, yanked down from the ratlines.

Cabot bent and picked up the pipe. Chest heaving, he lifted his fist, the pipe clenched within it, into the air. "I will not have this witchcraft on my ship!"

"Master Cabot . . ."

He whirled around and jabbed a finger of his freehand toward the mate. "*Tacere!* Did you know of this?"

Hennet raised both hands but did not back away. "He's just a boy."

"And damned!" Drawing back his upraised arm, he flung the pipe as hard as he could into the night, turned to glare down at Tam . . . "Play one more note and you will follow it!" . . . in the same motion strode off and into his cabin.

Hennet barely managed to stop John Jack's charge.

In the silence that followed, Roubaix stepped forward, looked down at Tam cradled in Rennie's arms, then went after Cabot.

"Let me go," John Jack growled.

Hennet started, as though he hadn't even realized he still held the man's shoulders. He opened his hands and knelt by Rennie's side. "How's the boy?"

"Did you ever hear the sound of a heart breaking, Mister Hennet?" The Scot's eyes were wet as he shifted the limp weight in his arms. "I heard it tonight, and I pray to God I never hear such a sound again."

Cabot was bent over the charts when Roubaix came into the cabin. The slam of the door jerked him upright and around.

"You are a fool, Zoane!"

"Watch your tongue," Cabot growled. "I am still master here."

Roubaix shook his head, too angry to be cautious. "Master of what?" he demanded. "Timber and canvas and hemp! You ignore the hearts of your men!"

"I save them from damnation. Such witchery will condemn their souls . . ."

"It was not witchcraft!"

"Then what?" Cabot demanded, eyes narrowed, his fingers clenched into fists by his sides.

"I don't know." Roubaix drew in a deep breath and released it slowly. "I do know this," he said quietly, "there is no evil in that boy in spite of a life that should have destroyed him. And, although the loss of his pipe dealt him a blow, that it was by your hand, the hand of the man who took him from darkness, the man he adored and only ever wanted to please, that was the greater blow."

"I cannot believe that."

Roubaix stared across the cabin for a long moment, watched the lamp swing once, twice, a third time painting shadows across the other man's face. "Then I am sorry for you," he said at last.

He would have retreated again to dark corners, but he couldn't find them anymore, he'd been too long away. Instead, he wrapped shadows tightly around him, thick enough to hide the memory of the master's face.

* * *

"He spoke yet?"

"No." Arms folded, Rennie stared across at the slight figure who sat slumped at the base of the aftcastle wall.

"Ain't like he ever said much," John Jack sighed. "You give 'em yer other pipe?"

"I tried yesterday. He won't take it."

They watched Cabot's barber emerge from below and wrap a blanket around the boy murmuring softly in Italian the whole while.

John Jack snorted. "I'd not be sittin' in Master Cabot's chair when that one has a razor in his hand, though I reckon he hasn't brains to know his danger."

"I don't want to hear any more of that talk."

Both men whirled around to see Hennet standing an arm's length away.

"And if ya stopped sneakin' up on folk, ya wouldn't," John Jack sputtered around a coughing fit.

Hennet ignored him. "There's fog coming in and bow watch saw icebergs in the distance. I want you two up the lines, port and starboard."

"Ain't never been near bergs when we couldn't drop anchor and wait till we could see."

"Nothing to drop anchor on," the mate reminded them. "Not out here. Now go, before it gets any worse."

It got much worse.

Hennet dropped all the canvas he could and still keep *The Matthew* turned into the swell, but they were doing better than two knots when the fog closed in. It crawled over the deck, soaking everything in its path, dripping from the lashes of silent men peering desperately into the night. They couldn't see, but over the groans of rope and canvas and timber, they could hear waves breaking against the ice.

No one saw the berg that lightly kissed the port side.

The ship shuddered, rolled starboard, and they were by.

"That were too buggerin' close."

Terror wrapped them closer than the fog.

"I hear another! To port!"

"Are you daft? Listen! Ice dead ahead!"

"Be silent! All of you." Cabot's command sank into the fog. "How long to dawn, Mister Hennet?"

Hennet turned to follow the chill and unseen passage of a mountain of ice. "Too long, sir."

"We must have light!"

The first note from the crow's nest backlit the fog with brilliant blue.

Cabot moved to the edge of the fo'c'sle and glared down into the waist. "Get him down from there, Mister Hennet."

Hennet folded his arms. "No, sir. I won't."

The second note streaked the fog with green.

"I gave you an order!"

"Aye, sir."

"Follow it!"

"No, sir."

"You!" Cabot pointed up at a crewman straddling the yard. "Get him down."

John Jack snorted. "Won't."

The third note was golden and at its edge, a sliver of night sky.

"Then I'll do it myself!" But when he reached for a line, Roubaix was there before him.

"Leave him alone, Zoane."

"It is witchcraft!"

"No." He switched to English so everyone would understand. "You asked for light, he does this for you."

The dance moved slow and stately across the sky.

Cabot looked around, saw nothing but closed and angry faces. "He sends you to hell!"

"Better than sending us to the bottom," Rennie told him. "Slow dance brings fair weather. He's piping away the fog."

Tam stopped when he could see the path through glittering green/white palaces of ice. He leaned over, tossed the pipe gently, and watched it drop into Rennie's outstretched hands. Then he stepped up onto the rail, and scanned the upturned faces for the master's. When he found it, he took a deep breath, and jumped out as hard as he was able.

No one spoke. No one so much as shouted a protest or moaned a denial.

The small body arced out, farther than should have been possible, then disappeared in the darkness. . . .

The silence lingered.

"You killed him." Hennet stepped toward Cabot, hands forming fists at his side. "You said if he played another note, he'd follow his pipe. And he did. And you killed him."

Still blinded by the brilliant blue of the boy's eyes, Cabot stepped back. "No . . ."

John Jack dropped down out of the lines. "Yes."

"No." As all heads turned toward him, Rennie palmed salt off his cheeks. "He didn't hit the water."

"Impossible."

"Did you hear a splash? Anything?" He swept a burning gaze over the rest of the crew. "Did any of you? No one called man overboard, no one even ran to the rails to look for a body. There is no body. He didn't hit the water. Look."

Slowly, as though on one line, all eyes turned to the north where a brilliant blue wisp of light danced between heaven and Earth.

"Fallen angels. He fell a little farther than the rest, is all; now he's back with his own."

Then the light went out, and all the sounds of a ship at sea rushed in to fill the silence.

"Mister Hennet, iceberg off the port bow!"

Hennet leaped to the port rail and leaned out. "Helmsman, two degrees starboard! All hands to the mainsail!"

As *The Matthew* began to turn to safety, Roubaix took Cabot's arm and moved him unprotesting out of the way of the crew.

"Gaylor," he whispered. "Do you believe?"

Roubaix looked up at the sky and then down at his friend. "You are a skilled and well-traveled mariner, Zoane Cabatto, and an unparalleled cartographer, but sometimes you forget that there are things in life you cannot map and wonders you will not find on any chart."

The Matthew took thirty-five days to travel from Bristol to the new land Cabot named Bona Vista. It took only fifteen days for her to travel back home again and for every one of those days the sky was a more brilliant blue than any man on board had ever seen and the wind played almost familiar tunes in the rigging.

THE SIR WALTER RALEIGH
CONSPIRACY

BY ALLEN C. KUPFER

LONDON, 1st Day of November, 1618.
    Sir Walter Raleigh was surely dead.

I, Robert Defoe, must at least surmise, being a rational man fully in control of my faculties, that the body which I saw before me *was*, indeed, that of Sir Walter Raleigh.

This cell in the Tower has been secured since his arrival, except when I entered or left the chamber. Any other entrance or escape would have been impossible. Yet . . . could that freakish form which I saw before me in reality be the famed poet, courtesan, and explorer?

Allow me, as Aristotle once suggested, dear reader, to begin at the beginning. Although I must write *these* words first: *I record this information because, given the circumstances of this highly peculiar, shocking case, I fear for my life.* Hopefully, in the succeeding paragraphs, you will come to understand why.

But . . . to the beginning.

Less then a fortnight ago, I made the acquaintance of one Sir Roger Kent, who impressed me with his courage and his dedication to our King James. He was a rather statuesque man, who, standing at a height of at least five-foot-ten, towered over most men. His figure was an imposing one, and his demeanor, while not exactly threatening, seemed to tolerate no nonsense. Indeed, rumors had circulated over the last few days that the man had even slain a sea dragon in the waters of the New World.

Imagine my utter shock three days ago when I heard that he was dead. His faithful first mate—a young officer by the name of Henry Wilmot—approached me on that day as I was leaving one of my audiences with Raleigh and slipped a small pamphlet into my hand, taking great care so as not to be seen. He seemed quite agitated, and, if I dare say so about one of His Majesty's seamen, considerably frightened. "Read this," he whispered to me. "Then secure it." After I tucked the booklet under my jacket, he and what I assumed to be other members of the crew of the *Buoyant Moon*, Sir Roger's ship, left the proximity of the Tower in great haste.

But *again*, perhaps, I get ahead of myself What, you must be asking yourself, dear reader, does all this nonsense have to do with the renowned Sir Walter? I shall try to explain.

Several of the King's armed guard summoned me to the Court ten days ago. Since my field of endeavor and study has been the practice and execution of the laws of our land, I would not, under usual circumstances, be surprised by a summons of this type. But as the messengers were *armed*, and the darkness in the sky was of that kind one only sees in the night in the hours immediately following midnight, I was taken quite aback. I was given just five minutes to dress and then was led—perhaps *marched* is the more appropriate word since the guard on either side of me whisked me along, their hands under my arms—to a chamber of the Tower where sat several of the King's counselors and the great Monarch himself. I can recall that on the trip there, the guards would answer none of my questions, and, upon reaching the Tower, I feared that *I* might, at any moment, be losing my head for some untold crime.

The King's Councillors, after establishing my identity, my profession, and, I hesitate to add, my dire poverty, ordered me to accept the appointment of defense counsel to a prisoner they expected to be delivered into their midst forthwith. I was told I would be paid handsomely and all my debts would thus be erased; I was assured that my client had not, as one council member said, "a hangnail of a chance of being found innocent," and I was being hired merely to give the legalities an air of authenticity; I was commanded to swear absolute secrecy in all matters relating to, or involved with, this case.

First, I was asked if I understood the gravity of the matter. I nodded agreement in answer. I was then asked if I understood that I was *not* to pursue the matter of the prisoner's innocence in an earnest matter. Again, I nodded that I did. Finally, I was made to swear before all present, that the secrecy of this matter was of the utmost importance—for matters of national security—and that my knowledge of it would go with me, untold, to the grave. Again, I nodded.

"Otherwise," my great Monarch, James I, said, "you will need two graves: one for your body . . . and one for your head!"

The pride I felt that the King had spoken to a humble citizen like myself, I must admit, was overshadowed by the fear that made my body tremble.

For the next two days I bided anxiously at home, awaiting the Royal Summons. But none arrived. On the third day, however, I was escorted to the Tower, then blindfolded and led up a seemingly neverending, narrow staircase. When finally the desired destination was reached, I heard the high-pitched squeal of a cell door opening, was told to stand still, and the blindfold was removed. As my eyes adjusted to the faint light, one of the guards said, in a most blatantly sarcastic manner, "Meet your client, the noble Sir Walter Raleigh." Then the guards laughed as they locked the cell behind me.

When finally my eyes adjusted and I saw the man before me, I let out a scream of fear. For there stood, within an arm's reach of me, a ferocious savage of the kind I have heard exists in far corners of the Americas. He was completely naked; his body was painted; he was filthy; and his thinning hair fell almost to his waist. My heart pounded as he extended an arm toward me, but, truly I nearly fainted when I heard him utter in a sickly voice, "You are here to save me, are you not?" Then he cackled like I have heard the New World heathens do, wildly, insanely, all the while scratching his genitals.

Having heard his voice and words in English, and realizing that the man before me, strange as it may seem, was an Englishman, my shock turned to disgust. "Have you no sense of decency, sir?" I said. "I can see your garments piled there in the corner of the cell. Why do you stand there naked?"

"We all shall someday stand naked before the eyes of God," he answered, then cackled again. "Is that not a paraphrase from your Bible?"

Again, I was surprised. " 'My' Bible? Have you rejected the word of God as well as clothing?" I asked.

"I have rejected nothing; I have simply *accepted* more," he responded cryptically. "Please sit and have no fear of me."

Reluctantly, nervously, I did so.

I will spare you, dear reader, the reproduction of every line of dialogue that passed between this bizarre visage of Sir Walter Raleigh—because it *was* indeed he—and myself for the next few hours. I will merely tell you that we spoke for a total of nine hours over the next three days. The content of what he related to me seemed to me then to be amazing yet undeniable facts. At this first meeting, for example, he told me that he had been living in Guiana, a much-desired area of the New World, for many years. He had, he said, come to love the land and in particular, the peoples, customs, and what he termed "the sense of magical possibilities" of that part of the world. And so, he rejected his initial purpose for sailing there—to explore and exploit the land and people for the sake of England—and remained with the primitive people he had learned to respect.

I left that first discussion with Sir Walter utterly amazed and considerably confused. On my way out, I was introduced to Sir Roger Kent, whom I have mentioned earlier and relate more about in this narrative soon. When I opined that I thought it was a damned shame that Raleigh had gone mad, Kent put his hand on my shoulder and said, sternly, "I, too, thought him mad. As I stand here now, I would *not* testify thus. He is many things, perhaps a traitor among them, but mad he is not!"

I noticed two of the king's councillors overheard Sir Roger's words and looked at one another curiously, but thought nothing of it at the time, so I thanked Kent for his thoughts and made my way—escorted, of course—home.

The next day I was instructed to prepare my case, for Raleigh would be tried in two days and secretly beheaded the day after that. I met again with Raleigh that day. Unlike the previous day's conversation, this one was filled with the ravings of a lunatic. He related tales of wild beasts and terrifying monsters that lurked in the lush jungles of Guiana. He told of priests (of a pagan sort) who were able to merge their intellects with their carnal selves to such an extent that their skulls ceased to exist and their orifices of the senses—by that, of course, I mean ears, eyes, and nostrils—merged with their torsos. In effect, he said, these shamans were so "at one" with their total beings and with the "soul" of nature itself that their faces (for lack of a better word) could be seen squarely in their torsos.

Needless to say, I was even more certain this day that Sir Walter had lost all grip on reality. My attention began to drift as he continued, though I did hear some of his account of his attempts to learn the mystic philosophies and magical practices of his beloved Guiana tribesmen. Perhaps he sensed that I was growing weary of his fantastical verbal meanderings. I remember he reached out his hand and pressed his thumbs against my eyelids. . . .

A guard shook me awake. I realized I had fallen asleep. When I gazed at Sir Walter, he was all smiles and declared, "You have slept for at least an hour. Do you now see what I have learned? That was a mere parlor trick compared to what I am now capable of."

"Time to go," ordered the guard, snapping me back to full consciousness.

My head felt as though it were filled with goose down. As I followed the guard downstairs, I wondered if indeed Raleigh had somehow induced me to sleep. But after giving the matter further consideration, I determined that falling asleep was perfectly natural given the stress and sleepless nights I have endured since being summoned by the monarch.

The guard this day did not even escort me home, not that I wished the ruffian to perform that service. He merely turned me out into the public courtyard with the following reminder: "Be prepared to return tomorrow."

It was immediately after he shut the door behind me that I was accosted by Henry Wilmot, Sir Roger's junior officer, the man I mentioned earlier in this account. It was at this point that he slipped the booklet to me.

What I did not mention before—this narrative writing is a chore, I now realize, best left to the likes of Sir Philip Sidney & Co.—was that when I arrived home, after making certain that I was alone and unwatched, I opened the book and saw the words *The Private Journal of Kent* on the first page. Further, there was a slip of paper tucked inside which read, "Kent was murdered last evening by the King's guards, his eyes plucked from their sockets. Others of the *Buoyant Moon*'s crew have also been found dead and eyeless or not found at all. I fear that all involved with the capture and imprisonment of Raleigh are in danger of their lives." The note was signed: "A friend."

This "friend," I determined, must be Wilmot. But why had Sir Roger been murdered, if indeed that was true? Why would the King order the execution of a faithful officer of his naval forces? Or were Raleigh and his infernal magic somehow responsible?

No, I reasoned, that was ridiculous; it was to put credence into the madman's ravings.

Nervously, I sat at my modest desk and opened the journal. I now relate to you, dear reader, selected segments—in chronological order—of the late Kent's written entries:

1617: December the 3rd

At the behest and command of His Majesty, James I, I this day sail forth to the new world to find and capture the traitor, Sir Walter Raleigh, who has abandoned his King and his country. I have been informed by His Majesty that the traitor, after receiving the funding and support to expedite his exploratory and commercial voyage, remains in the territory called Guiana and fancies himself a member of the primitive heathen community. . . .

*   *   *

1617: December the 5th

His Majesty has explained to me the nature of my endeavor; furthermore, he has impressed upon me that it must be conducted with the utmost discretion abroad and with the utmost secrecy on our beloved native soil. The King's councillors have explained that should the unschooled masses of our citizenry learn that a gentleman, one who has been intimately acquainted with our current leaders and even more intimately acquainted with the dearest Queen, Elizabeth, God rest her soul, has forsaken his King and taken a place among heathens, it would suggest to the feeble masses that they, too, might reject the current God-appointed leadership of our nation and our way of life. Therefore, I am to capture the traitor alive, if possible, and return him to our nation, not for public condemnation and punishment, but for secret execution, once our Ministers have extracted from the traitor all the information of the peoples, resources, and Co. regarding this land of Guiana and surrounding areas. I have been told that the ordinary citizenry of our nation must never know of Raleigh's affront to his King, for it is dangerous knowledge for the masses to have. . . .

1617: December the 29th

This morning, as the purple skies brightened, several of my men noted a most peculiar fact: our maintopsail was cleft completely in two! It is virtually useless. The main topgallant, just above it, and the mizzen topgallant staysail directly behind it, are fully intact and whole. What might have occurred overnight is a mystery. Wilmot suspects that perhaps one of our crew—several of whom are here not of their own free will—damaged the maintopsail

during the night, hidden by the darkness. How he might
have accomplished this nasty feat without the cooperation
of other men on the night watch . . .

It is my deepest hope that members of my own crew,
whom I treat with as much friendship and respect as is
possible aboard any vessel, are not of that particular sort
of criminal who would engage in this sort of mutinous sabotage. . . .

Although the sail has been taken down and is in the
process of being repaired—if indeed we have the capacity
to repair it—this tragedy will add weeks to our voyage. I
pray to our Lord Jesus Christ, whose day of birth we cel-
ebrated (in a modest way) several days ago, that our stores
hold out.

1618: January the 14th
An incessant roaring of the winds and icy rains has
plagued us for several days. At times, Nature has been so
ferocious that we can barely see the ocean waters at all.
Our navigator, Patrick Swift, informs me that he believes
we are well across the Atlantic, but neither he, nor the
other navigators on board, is absolutely certain of our latitude. Due to this, we have reduced sail greatly; the winds
fortunately continue to push us in a westerly direction.

The Buoyant Moon has taken on much water from the
continuous downpour; so much so that several seamen at
a time have been assigned to disposing of the collected
water. My men are cold; they are exhausted; they feel that
God has abandoned us. Some believe that as we venture
closer to heathen shores, the Christian God has turned his
attention away from us in protest. Hunger will cause the
best of men to form such heretical, wild thoughts. . . .

We continue to sail at not over four knots, at least until

*this storm dissipates. For now our sails are stiff as wood
and our rigging completely frozen. . . .*

1618: February the 4th

*We sail this day with the first glorious sight of land in
many weeks. If I am correct, we are north of the islands
on which Columbus allegedly landed (for one of the bodies of land within sight is indeed an island), but far south
of the tobacco colony Raleigh established (again, with
royal funding) in the territory known as Roanoke Island.
The land we seek is yet farther west. I pray we reach it
soon; nearly one-fourth of my crew has died from mal-
nutrition or scurvy; another one-fourth is gravely ill;
and the majority of those still alive have been engaging
in mutinous whisperings, according to Wilmot, who is
dedicated and loyal to his captain. I thank God for his
presence. . . .*

1618: February the 15th

*I have just consulted both navigational charts and the
treatise on this New World that the traitor himself writ several years ago. I am certain we sail south on the river
known as the Ooroonoko. The climate and foliage, I must
admit, is precisely as the traitor described it. There are
myriad insects about in this hellish heat and dampness;
some are the size of a man's fist. A swarm of these insects
attacked us last evening. One bit through a helmsman's
eyelid, causing the eye to swell and ultimately burst from
its socket. Many of the other men were bitten or stung by
these devilish insects. For at least several hours last
evening, one could not walk anywhere on board the ship
without hearing the disgusting sound of crunching under-
foot. . . .*

*   *   *

1618: February the 16th
One of my crew, who sailed with Raleigh on his earlier voyage, tells me the countryside is very familiar to him. He has also informed me that anon we will be forced to leave the ship, for the waters of the river will become too shallow. Wilmot is above, recruiting men for the journey on foot, which I have been assured is not more than ten miles. . . .

Forgive me, dear reader, *but* I must explain that Kent's penmanship here takes a turn for the worse in his journal. Therefore, I pray you will allow me simply to present his notions to you, as I was able to make sense of the variable bits and pieces of legible handwriting. For to attempt to present them as I have been doing will, no doubt, cause annoyance: the quotations will be peppered with lacunae, gaps in logic, and diverse other irritations. I therefore relate to you Sir Roger's journal notes, filtered through my own sensibilities.

After a day's journey on foot, several dozen natives captured Sir Roger's band of men. Kent states that he put up no resistance, for the sailor who had been with Raleigh on the earlier voyage assured Kent that these natives' costumes (what little there were of them) and face markings, derived from some sort of berry or plant and hideously odious, were identical to the tribe with whom Raleigh had negotiated.

Kent's crewman had been correct. Before long, Kent & Co. were brought before the native elders. One of these high priests, without the slightest hesitation, brought forth to his lips some manner of pipe or straw and from it blew a small, colorful dart, which struck one of Kent's men (named Joseph Crane) full in the throat, piercing the skin on his neck. Within seconds, Crane's face grew a dark pur-

ple and several of the veins in his neck and face inex-
plicably burst, spilling blood onto other crew members as
well as the ground. Horrified and weaponless, Kent expected subsequent executions. But no more were to follow.

From one of the huts emerged two men, one of them
obviously white and almost as obviously Sir Walter Raleigh.
He was filthy. His clothing consisted of no more than a
cloth around his waist and a beaded headband. He gave
every appearance of having somehow become a savage.
But, Kent reports, Raleigh said something incomprehensi-
ble to the shaman with the dart-pipe, the shaman nodded,
and no executions followed. At least in this way, Kent determined, Sir Walter had retained some small shred of decency and Englishness.

Again, I ask the reader's indulgences if I move the story
along quickly by omitting some details and hastening
through others. At Raleigh's behest, the men of the *Buoyant Moon* were from that moment well treated by the tribe.
They were fed; they were given shelter; and their weapons
were returned to them. Neither Kent nor any of his crew
spoke of his true motive for being there. Instead, they won
the affection of Raleigh, who believed what Kent had told
him: King James had sent the expedition to renegotiate
with the peoples of Guiana. Sir Walter, though skeptical,
told Kent that he would act as interpreter for his adopted
people and that he would so serve as a barterer acting in
their interest.

A few nights hence, Kent and his crew pounced upon
Raleigh in the dead of night, bound and gagged him, and
whisked him away. They had to silently kill several of the
tribesmen who served as guards. A chase ensued, but with
a minimum of loss of life of his crew, Kent, the next day,
brought Raleigh aboard the *Buoyant Moon*, and the vessel

set sail northward. The natives' crudely-constructed canoes could barely compete and were soon left far behind.

Once safely distant from the tribe, Raleigh, still in native garb, was untied and permitted to walk freely upon the ship's deck. According to Kent, that evening Sir Walter, or Okeeshwa, as he insisted on being referred to, stared out over the river, occasionally making a gesture with his hands. And from time to time he would stare up at the moon and chant some heathen incantation.

Kent, in a noticeably erratic handwriting, describes the next hour in detail, hard to believe as it may be. First, he writes, various spots on Raleigh's chest began to palpitate. Then a cold wind whipped across the deck of the vessel, knocking one man overboard. As many of the crew, including Sir Roger, peered over that side of the vessel, there rose from the water a sea monster of the manner which our other explorers have referred to as sea lizards or *all-I-ga-tors*. Its length, Kent is certain, was at least the length of six or seven normal men, its width at least the length of one and one half men. It crashed into the side of the ship, doing much damage to the appearance of the vessel, though, luckily, little to its construction. In its jaws was the unfortunate man who had gone overboard. He was still alive and screaming in agony until the mighty beast snapped its jaws shut, cutting the man in half, both halves dropping into the sea.

The crew had readied and aimed two cannons at the monster, which again leaped at the side of the vessel. Kent ordered the men to fire, but, while doing so, noticed the ghastly purple glare in Raleigh's eyes; he seemed unmoved by any of the commotion or danger. Finally, the guns fired. The monster was hit in the side, which barely dented its thick skin, but the second shot entered its open jaws, striking it, it seemed, in the throat. Bleeding, it turned away from the *Buoyant Moon*, never to reappear.

Raleigh congratulated Kent on his victory, but warned the captain that he had learned much of the occult and the mystic during his time with his adopted people. Sir Roger had no patience with Raleigh's ravings; the traitor was stripped, tied, and blindfolded for much of the journey back to our beloved homeland. And while he dared not believe the traitor had the power to summon beasts from the water, he surmised that it was better not to tempt fate.

There is so much more contained in Sir Roger's journal. But I shall not burden the reader with them, so that I might hasten to the conclusion of *my* accounts.

I visited the prisoner again the next day, but this time I viewed him somewhat differently, influenced, no doubt, by both Roger Kent's journal ... and his death. I could scarcely believe that our monarch would have had one of his faithful naval officers put to death. But upon entering the prisoner's cell, I greeted him, prepared to attempt to compile some sort of defense for him; but he greeted me with these words, spoken slowly and seriously: "Kent has been killed, you know. His eyes were cut out of his face." I was taken by surprise. Had one of the guards told Raleigh of this news? That seemed highly unlikely.

"How do you know that?" I asked.

"I can see and hear and *sense* many things," was his reply.

"Are you responsible?" I continued.

He seemed genuinely troubled by the question. "I am not. Your sovereign monarch ordered his demise."

"That's preposterous," I added, though secretly I suspected the same. "Why would the King do such a thing?"

"Because Kent saw and knew too much. He knew the truth."

"What *truth* is that?"

"The truth of my being. My powers. My knowledge. Powers and knowledge that no alleged civilized Englishman will ever know until he abandons the shackles of his society. For only when one is merged with the forces of nature can one obtain true power, true knowledge."

"I do not understand," I insisted, truthfully.

"You *can*not understand. Yet you know I do possess these gifts."

"I . . . I do."

"Then you must help me." He stood up. "I am not, regardless of what our esteemed King thinks, a traitor of any kind. For posterity it will be recorded that my voyage ended in failure and I was beheaded here in this prison, tomorrow."

"We still have a chance," I said. "I am compiling . . ."

"There is *no* chance," he interrupted. "I am to die. I *will* die. It must be thus. Besides my alleged traitorous activities, I am considered a danger by the King. He will prevent any of his subjects ever seeing me, what I have become. In this Christian land where Catholics are seen as revolutionaries, imagine, if you can, what I must symbolize. I am the ultimate subversive. I must die."

I gathered my wits and stated, "I have read Sir Roger Kent's journal of his voyage to find you. He implies that you had the power to summon a beast from the river waters. Why do you not now use these powers to secure your own freedom?"

"My powers are not limitless, and whatever powers I use are, in fact, nature's powers that I usurp. In Guiana, the necessary ingredients—herbs, flora, and the like—are readily available and the aura of the land itself is not tainted with deceit and hypocrisy, as it is here."

"So you cannot free yourself?"

"No, not physically. However, I swear to you that King James shall never have the privilege of beheading me."

"What do you mean?" I inquired.

"I say nothing else, friend," Raleigh concluded. "You waste your time here. Prepare your case at your own quarters."

Completely confused and not a little insulted, I turned to leave the cell. But Raleigh's hand alighted on my shoulder and he whispered, "Protect yourself, friend," he said. "Do not allow Kent's fate to be your own."

I was relieved when I exited the Tower. The sunlight, the fresh air—if that is what it may be called in London—served to reinvigorate me. Then, suddenly, approaching me were two of the King's Guard carrying a body on a common stretcher. I stopped to allow them to cross my path. But as they passed in front of me, the coarse blanket that covered the corpse came loose and slipped off the body's head. I was able to see the deceased's face. It was the face of Henry Wilmot; I recognized it even with its ghastly white color and empty eye sockets.

Wilmot dead also, I thought, as I entered my abode. But why? And why so cruelly? Then I reconsidered some of Raleigh's words. *He saw too much. He knew too much.* Was the removal of the eyes some *symbolic* death stroke? Was it meant as a warning to others who . . . ?

I then realized the intention of Raleigh's warning. *I, too, knew too much*, even if, in fact, I hadn't *seen* anything. He was trying to tell me my life was in peril!

Agitated and unable to calm down, I poured myself some port from the one bottle I possessed. I drank it quickly and locked my doors. Then I drank some more.

It seemed like only moments later when I heard a banging at my door. I opened it, and one of the two guards informed me that it was time to present my case before the King and his justices. I had, I came to realize, slept for nearly three-quarters of a day! I begged the guards to give me a few minutes to assemble my notes and papers, but they allowed only seconds. Hastily, I grabbed what I could and was escorted to the Court.

I shall not deaden my reader's senses by describing the trial of Sir Walter Raleigh. I shall only say that its unfairness was characterized by this fact, most typical of the proceedings in general: the defendant was not even allowed to appear at his own sentencing because he was considered a danger to all present! I, as his Defender, was permitted to make three statements, lasting no more than a total of two and a half minutes. I was then commanded to "remain seated and silent." The sentence of death by beheading was given, and I and several of the jailers ascended the stairs to Raleigh's cell while the King was escorted to the Executioner's Offices to await the condemned.

We reached Raleigh's cell, and the door was opened. But there was an ungodly sound emanating from Sir Walter's lips. As I looked closer—dear reader, perhaps it was the great amount of port I consumed the day before, but—I thought I saw Sir Walter's standing body, arms outstretched, begin to twitch and shake slightly. And as the sound grew louder, his head sank—for I know not else how to explain what I saw—sank and merged into the trunk of his body, which turned a bright crimson, so bright that I was forced to close my eyes for a few seconds. When I reopened them, the unclothed body of Sir Walter lay strewn on the floor, headless. Lifeless eyes stared from his chest. Colorless lips remained silent and unmoving below them.

I thought I had gone mad, I was certain of it until I heard one of the jailers say, "Sweet Lord in heaven! He has no head!"

I must have fainted because when I came to hours later I was again in my house, in the very chair in which I had fallen asleep the day before. My first conscious thought was that I had dreamed the entire episode. But reason told me otherwise. Raleigh had indeed learned from the people of the Oorinoko region. At his life's sunset, he finally achieved the mystical state of oneness so valued by that tribe.

And, I realized, Raleigh's satirical gifts, which once were so evident in his verses written for his beloved Queen Elizabeth, were still intact. For, indeed, as he had professed to me, *"King James shall never have the privilege of beheading me!"*

*   *   *

London, October 2nd 1713.
                    Journal Entry Number 763.
As I sit here reading this fanciful account written by my great-uncle Robert, who, family rumor has it, was put to death by assassins of good King James I, I note the gentleman's haphazard narrative technique and also his sincere, if a bit strange, revelations. Perhaps what he wrote here long ago is the truth, even though by all *accounts Raleigh was beheaded in 1618, with many witnesses present. I shall keep my ancestor's written work, for it contains some information on the area known as Guiana, which is the setting for my current prose work-in-progress,* The Life and Strange Surprising Adventures of Robinson Crusoe. *To add some small sense of verisimilitude to my work—based to some degree on the adventures of Alexander Selkirk, who was stranded for a time in that God-forsaken part of the uncivilized world—I must somehow acquaint myself with the pamphlet, writ by Walter Raleigh,*

entitled The Discovery of Guiana, *mentioned in my uncle's work.*

Although from all accounts my great-uncle Robert was not much of a barrister, I fondly wish he were here to assist me in getting out of this debtor's prison in which I am now incarcerated. At any rate, I shall keep his narrative private. I need no further trouble with the lawkeepers.

Daniel Defoe

THE WINDS
THEY DID BLOW HIGH

BY FRIEDA A. MURRAY

I SET out to call upon my friend Captain Boughton three days after the great spring gale blew inland. It had played havoc with new growth in field and orchard, and many a chicken coop was swept away. Fallen trees and high-running creeks added to the hazards of travel.

The local windwitches sniffed out the storm's spell-caused origins, and said it would be better to let it blow out than to try countermeasures.

Thus, on a morning of pale but steady sunshine, and after assuring the vicar that I would assist with local relief, I rode for Abbottsford. Captain Boughton is a retired post captain, and he was the most likely man in the district to know the provenance of this unnatural storm. Besides, there was Miss Boughton to think of, and I was doing quite a lot of that. She is a dark, elegant lady with never a hair out of place in the worst of winds. Some wind magic of her own, I fancy, though she has never mentioned it to me.

When Fenton admitted me to the morning room, I found I was not the only visitor. Seated in an armchair not designed to accommodate his swordbelt was Captain Northcott of the Customs Guard. I had a slight acquaintance with him, and now recalled that he was distant kin to the Boughtons.

"What brings you so far into Somerset?" I asked when greetings had been exchanged. Actually, Abbottsford has a toehold in Devon, but it is a far haul from Bristol, never mind Cork, the usual ports for the Irish coast.

"Prize disposal," he replied, with the smile of a sailor to whom the winds have, for once, blown good fortune. (That was one advantage of the Customs service, although a Naval man's chances of prize money are quite fair these days. With the French royal family exiled to Switzerland and Austria, and France being governed—for all practical purposes—by the salon witches of Paris, port taxes are an ungodly mess. Any sloop master can take a cargo out of Brest and dispose of it profitably in who knows how many isolated coves between Bournemouth and Land's End, without even the bother of taking it to Ireland. Not that smuggling in Ireland—a land without law or civilized behavior—need surprise any, but shame though it be, far too many of my own countrymen regard smuggling as merely vulgar, not criminal. I have heard that these crews refer to themselves "honest *tradesmen*.")

Captain Boughton spared me the offense of being inquisitive by giving a positive *roar* of laughter. "Prize money! That's like saying there's water in the sea, Cyril. You have made your fortune out of this."

"A snug competence, anyway," answered Captain Northcott. "And I fear many of you have paid for it."

"The storm—what do you know of it, Captain Northcott?" I asked. "We were told that it was spell-caused—"

Both captains looked a trifle stiff, and I was beginning a disjointed apology, when Miss Boughton entered the room, every hair in place as usual. Her dress-spencer was dark blue, but I am no connoisseur of the female toilette, save to note that Miss Boughton was always elegantly turned out.

Her entrance, followed by Fenton with a tea tray, turned the attention from my less than felicitous enquiry, but I felt that she greeted me less warmly than in the past.

She then turned to Captain Northcott.

"Now, cousin," she said, "the tale, the whole tale, and nothing but the tale, if you please. I've spent the morning on our accounts and most of yesterday inspecting the damage to our land and people, so I should like to know what lies behind it all. If you have no objection," she finished, turning to me.

"I should be most happy to hear anything Captain Northcott has to say," I replied.

"French contraband has been getting worse these three years and more," began the Captain, fortified by tea. "If we see anything smaller than a sloop of war off the French coast it's probably running contraband. The cruisers still in service are running coastwatch." He grimaced.

"Just whom does the present government think would take the trouble to invade?" asked Captain Boughton disgustedly. "Prime Minister Pitt would toss all his port into the Thames if the question were raised in the House."

"There is always talk of the royal family's return," I said. "John Romsey, who was just posted to the Ambassador's staff in Lisbon, wrote me that such rumors are rife there at both the court and in the city."

"There may be something to those rumors, this time," said Captain Northcott. "Word reached me that Prince Metternich could buy enough of those Directors, as they call themselves, to support Austria in the restoration of the French crown."

(The exiled queen was a Habsburg by birth, but even so, the thought of a powerful Imperial presence at Versailles, even with a restored French monarchy, left me slightly uncomfortable.)

"What of Hanover, were that to occur?" asked Miss Boughton, and I realized the source of my discomfort.

"Pitt would prefer neither more nor less pressure on our German allies," replied Captain Northcott. "But there is no shortage of Habsburg princesses, and the Act of Settlement binds the English crown only."

"So we watch," he concluded. "That is about all the French navy is *officially* doing now. Those Directors will barely allocate funds for coast guarding, and I've encountered French contraband runners who split the take with line captains for ship maintenance. Of course," he added, "you may be sure that the line captains will return the courtesy one way or another."

"Have you heard of outright piracy by the French fleet?" I asked.

"Or what's left of it," he smiled. "No, but—" he paused.

"Three years ago," he continued, "you'd have found neither wind-whistler nor wave-singer aboard a French ship of the line, any more than in our own. Now they must be pressganging them. Lieutenant Sommers—he rides out of Plymouth—told me he's seen at least three vessels this season making for the coast quite easily while the Plymouth patrol was becalmed. And last fall," his smile was rueful, "I was hovering off the Scillies when a schooner came reaching past against the current. Under normal winds she'd have been driven onto Land's End."

Miss Boughton refilled his cup and passed the biscuits.

The captain continued. "But she made it through and headed for Cork, most likely. I couldn't stop her. The crew was nervous enough, seeing that wind in her sails, and whistling a counterwind could have wrecked us both. It was no time to risk being made a scapegoat."

He paused again, but only to refill. It seemed that the captain had come to terms with his ability to whistle the wind, if he was willing to speak so easily of it before the comparative stranger that I was. I knew that it had cost him his naval career; Lieutenant Northcott had been quietly requested to transfer to the Customs service because that ability made his superior officers uneasy. Not only the officers; the crew would have found him the natural scapegoat whenever something went wrong.

The unspoken prohibition was much weaker in the Customs service, which appreciated a whistler's ability to keep His Majesty's vessels away from coastal hazards, though even there it was wise to be circumspect.

"Speaking of which, or witches," said Captain Northcott, "I have heard—talk only!—that some of these vessels are shipping female wave-singers."

(I grant you that having a singer on board can be useful at sea, but breaking the ban on women crew? Any captain in His Majesty's navy who permitted, or even failed to prevent such would be tossed overboard to remove the ill luck. So would the woman, unless she could show that she had been brought aboard by force. Even women passengers have to walk softly once on board, and not a few vessels marked their quarters with a taboo line.)

"Is there trouble in Ireland, Cyril?" asked Captain Boughton quietly, although his face reflected the shock we all felt.

"When is there not trouble in Ireland! Show me the Irish merchant who does not carry on as if we were cutting off his hand by asking him to pay his duty! And the pressed men—brawlers every one of them! They take pride in wearing out the belaying pins!"

"There is little wealth in Ireland and a great distaste for duties of any sort," I said, "unless you count it a duty to inconvenience His Majesty's government."

"Yes, certainly, but have you noticed anything that might be French influence, Cyril?"

"Well, we have seen more French vessels headed for Cork—or its vicinity," the captain added dryly. "But as Mr. Handforth said, there are not that many wealthy men in Ireland. And as for a *revolution à la francaise*—I defy the most zealous pamphleteer or the most seductive salon witch to bring *that* about! A fight they might get—a bunch of yokels with pikes and clubs singing songs of the Old Pretender—they'd be fighting each other before the day was out. We'd only have to stand back and watch."

"And make sure things didn't get out of hand," said Captain Boughton. "But trouble in Ireland could occupy us at a critical point."

"I don't think so," said Captain Northcott. "French interference in the West Indies, now, that could be serious."

"Ireland's closer, though."

"Cousin," said Miss Boughton, "Irish heads may be harder than ship timbers—and indeed, with so many holy, or haunted, wells—you can't always be sure of the water in the font, or the priest—"

"Not to mention," said her brother, "the spells they use for their home-brewed. Will you touch the liquor in Cork, Cyril?"

Miss Boughton gave a quelling look at her brother and turned again to Captain Northcott. "Was it an Irishman, cousin, who blew three sheepfolds into kindling and drowned the best stud bull on our lands when the cattle bridge broke?"

"Most practical cousin," said Captain Northcott. "You must accompany me to Cork when next the *Helena* needs refitting. Your appearance alone will charm the Supply Major, your most excellent sense will stun him, and he will do anything you ask."

"Do thou likewise," ordered Miss Boughton, but with a smile.

"Aye aye, Ma'am. A fortnight ago, we were in Falmouth to restock. Contrary winds—natural—had kept us in the Channel, but we had a good chance of meeting a supply ship from Plymouth.

"The luck favored us. Captain Graham of the *Portsmouth* was most accommodating, and we got the latest reports. The *Anne* was refitting at Plymouth, including new pumps, and would be heading for the West Indies under Sir William Gordon in two days, weather permitting. And Cherbourg had been unusually busy for the season."

"The Directors hold Normandy as firmly as they can," said Captain Boughton. "Brittany, now—"

"The Bretons have been a law unto themselves since before there was France," said Captain Northcott. "Let's not complain, though. They help our men as often as not—when they aren't trying to slip a cargo past us, that is."

"And you—" prompted Miss Boughton.

"I was glad to hear it. The crew had been getting restless."

I could imagine that it had been. Coastal patrol is one of the more boring jobs in His Majesty's forces at sea, and has been known to lead to mutiny (usually for insufficient shore leave) or once in a while, to throwing the captain overboard as a scapegoat. Of course, if the captain was not the source of any bad luck, the crew is guilty of murder, subject to both court martial and the vengeance of the sea, which does not respect murderers.

"We headed southeast; there was no harm in taking a look before heading back to our station. The wind was against us, but light, so I whistled just enough breeze for a steady course."

The captain's cheerful expression did not alter as he

mentioned this detail. His crew must be fairly comfortable with a wind-whistling captain, and he must have gotten a fair amount of practice if he would whistle in anything but a dire emergency.

"I thought to allow three days, weather permitting. It held, and about two hours before sunset on the second day the lookout spotted a heavy mass of sail. I scrambled up to take a look myself. They had to be French, and they were too many for us, though for the most part they were mostly single-masters.

"Still, no matter what they were carrying, we couldn't let a French fleet, however small, out of the Channel."

(Naturally not.)

"I remembered the *Anne*. She should have left Plymouth on the outgoing tide, and with the present winds she should be headed for the Lizard, but not too fast. If we could get her south in time, her twenty-two guns should let us deal with whatever the French were trying to ship.

"We went about, double-quick. We were with the wind now and I plotted the *Anne*'s course. We had to be north of that, but not so far as to miss both her and the fleet, before I tried to whistle her about.

"The wind rose about sunset, but I doubled the lookouts and told the galley to keep tea handy. We ran before, so neatly that I had to consider a wind-whistler with the French ships. Shortly after midnight I had us lie to." He grinned. "We weren't facing heavy weather then, but we were about to.

"I checked the chart again, promised that any lookout who failed in his duty would be thrown overboard, handed sealed orders to my second, and had the quarter boat lowered."

The captain was about to whistle a counterwind, a much more dangerous maneuver than strengthening one already blowing, or calling one in a calm. But with any wind, there is always the danger of getting more than you can handle. So the captain had the ship lie to, and left her. The better for the ship, and possibly the worse for the captain.

"The wind was blowing west and a little south, so true that I knew another wind-whistler had to be behind it. Sir William must have been quite happy. I faced west, and then—"

Then he whistled the spell that would turn the wind. Whistlers won't discuss that; it's supposed to be *very* unlucky. Besides, Captain Northcott had worked out spells to be used at sea. If some idiot on land tried one of them, who knows what might have happened?

"It wasn't easy. I felt as if I were dueling, which I was, of course. The wind rose and dipped, and so did the boat. I told the men with me that we were facing another whistler, and they gritted their teeth but stayed at the oars. Finally we felt the wind begin to shift. I gave the order to return, while I sat in the stern until I was sure the wind was blowing easily east by south. Then I emptied the waterskin and another, plus half a bottle, when we got back to the *Helena*."

Another hazard: you can't stop to eat or drink in the middle of a spell. Captain Northcott must have been near fainting for want of water before he allowed himself to unstopper the waterskin.

"It was about four in the morning when we got back. I checked the chart again and ordered an intercept course for the *Anne*. I reminded the lookouts that my threat still held but that the first man to sight the *Anne* would receive a guinea. I left orders to wake me at once if the wind shifted, and turned in.

"I'd just finished breakfast when the 'sail, ho' sounded.

It was the *Anne*. I noted the sailor's name and put on my best kit to pay a call on Sir William.

"You've met him, cousin, so you know what he's like." Captain Boughton chuckled. "Still, I doubt that you'd have been pleased to see me yourself, under the circumstances."

"I'd have given you a first-class dressing, for the good of the service, of course. But then, I'd know you had probably had something to do with the contrary wind. Did he know you?"

"Not at first. He recognized my name, when I was finally able to give it.

"'Cyril Northcott, Captain of His Majesty's Customs vessel *Helena*,' I told him, and he turned from pepper to ice in an instant.

"'What are you doing *here*, Captain Northcott?' he asked.

"'There're about ten French single-masters, cargo unknown, headed out toward Land's End,' I told him. 'In the name of His Majesty's Treasury, I request the assistance of His Majesty's ship *Anne* to search and if necessary seize these vessels.'

"The ice started melting. Sir William invited me aboard, and we pulled out our charts and got to work. He was ready to roar again when I admitted to whistling the counterwind, but he was none too happy about another wind-whistler in the area."

(Naturally not. What prudent captain wants to be hard by a duel between wind-whistlers?)

"We considered the probable course of the French convoy. They might, of course, round Finistere and head out into the Atlantic, but considering the struggle I'd had the night before, they were probably trying for Land's End. In that case there was a better than even chance they were headed for Ireland.

" 'How close do you think they'll come to the Lizard?' he asked.

" 'They'll try to give the coast plenty of room in any case,' I said. 'But that's the best point—from here—to stop them.'

"The wind had shifted again, and was now blowing from the east, but cautiously. It felt as if a normal wind were being helped.

"We checked our charts again, and agreed on rendezvous and reconnaissance. But before I left the cabin Sir William said, 'Captain Northcott, I would rather meet this convoy under *normal* conditions, if you please.'

" 'The wind's blowing our way, now,' I replied. 'I don't anticipate the need for further efforts on my part.'

"The quarter boat took me back to the *Helena*, and we set out for the rendezvous point. I rescinded the threat, but had the lookouts maintain a sharp watch for both the *Anne* and the French. The wind rose, without changing direction, during the afternoon, so we made good time.

"The *Anne* made the rendezvous later than expected, close upon nine in the evening. They had seen no French ships. Sir William was determined to wait, as I had done earlier, no more than three days. I had the men rest and eat well, but told the ship's carpenter he would get his share after the *Helena* had been thoroughly inspected. I also ran our sharpshooters through firing drill.

"Then we waited. The *Anne* lay to closer in, while we rode a shallow arc. There was enough moon to show multiple sails. Still, we'd seen no others since we ran to whistle up the *Anne*, and I was obliged to consider that the convoy was heading for Finisterre after all. But the wind blew steadily from the east.

"Around ten the next day we heard 'sails, ho' from the lookouts. When I could spot them through my glass from the quarterdeck, I sent the sharpshooters into the shrouds with orders to take out the wind-whistler, and had the guns cast off.

"As they came on, we could finally distinguish what we had to stop. There were seven single-masters and one two-master, all with fore and aft rigs and mounting four-pounders, and a schooner with twelve six-pounders. They all flew the tricolor.

"We had to take out the schooner. The *Anne* might be able to handle the rest of the convoy, but we were damned close to being outgunned.

"The glass showed the schooner—the *Lyons*—had her guns run out. She probably couldn't see the *Anne*, which was trying to work her way into a position between the convoy and the Lizard. The wind had slowed a bit—it felt all natural for the moment—but it was still against the *Anne*, except to drive her onto the Lizard.

"The wind-whistler might be in the schooner, but was more likely to be in the two-master, which seemed to be rearguard. I passed the word up, and had our guns run out.

"Just as well. The *Lyons* fired, but she hadn't the range on us. That meant we couldn't reach her either—we both mounted six-pounders.

"'Hold her steady!' I yelled down. Wind and wave were bringing us closer, and if we could get a shot at her masts—!"

"Wind and wave—the wind continued slow, enabling the convoy to keep together, but the waves were not subsiding. The convoy had shipped a wave-singer as well as a wind-whistler! What *was* it carrying?

"'The masts!' I yelled. All our guns on that side fired, and the mainmast collapsed. That should keep them, and that pestilential singer, out of action long enough for the *Anne* to come up, I hoped. Where was she?

"In the meantime some of the single-masters were turning their four-pounders on us. We had the range, but they had the numbers. They were not trained in squadron tactics, however, and one vessel in the convoy had its mast shot down by another. We worked our way broadside of the convoy, aiming for masts, and looking for the *Anne*. *Where was she?*

"In trouble, we found. We had disabled the *Lyons*, and the *Anne* had her range, but the wave-singer was trying all too effectively to force her onto the Lizard. With almost all hands occupied in keeping her off the rocks there was no time for accurate gunnery, and if the wind came up—!

"We were now northeast of the *Anne*. I had to keep the *Anne* offshore, and that meant an easy west wind. It would also counter the convoy—until the French whistler got into action. Well, it was time we got close enough to take him out.

"I swallowed a mouthful of water and whistled. The wind came at once, and in less than ten minutes the *Anne* had worked her way back out. She took a little longer to fire because the gunners had to cast off again, but as we worked our way to the rear of the convoy we could see her smoke-cloud.

"I had to hold the wind steady, but the men worked in better harmony than many musicians I've heard. Since we wanted prizes, we shot to disable, which meant we had to watch for last-ditch heroics. But they were effectively becalmed—my sharpshooters took out every lookout on the two-master to be sure of getting the wind-whistler. I knew when he fell because I could sense the gale he'd let build up about to break loose. I sent it northeast, away from us. No, it wasn't an Irishman, cousin, it was a Frenchman.

"By five in the afternoon all the tricolors had been struck.

The cargo was the usual: wine and brandy, tea, silks and laces, guns, gold, documents.

"But such quantities?" I asked. "Why? Where was it going?"

"I can't discuss that."

"What about the crews?" asked Captain Boughton.

"They were French citizens, as they call themselves. They will be paroled on French soil—in the French West Indies, or possibly in New Orleans."

"And Sir William?" asked Miss Boughton.

"It was a good thing he had new pumps. He took in quite a bit of water fighting those waves. But his share will make a handsome addition to his fortune—and I certainly can't complain about mine! Still, he was glad to see the last of me. He was due to *continue* to Kingston yesterday."

"When do you take the *Helena* out again?" she asked.

"Lieutenant Marsden will take her out next week. I've been ordered to stay in Bristol to attend to—certain matters. I'll be there about a month, I think. After that, we'll see."

"We shall," she said with a smile.

I thought about that smile as I rode from Abbotsford, and resolved to increase the frequency of my visits. In fact—the vicar would *not* approve, but perhaps I would make discreet inquiries about a love spell. . . .

THE DEVIL AND CAPTAIN BRIGGS

JOHN J. ORDOVER

THE old salt said:

If in the year 1926, Father Dominicus of the island of San Pedro (and the mission of the same name) had not discovered the following account and promptly destroyed it, the mystery of the *Mary Celeste* would not have come down to us as a cautionary tale of the vagaries of the sea. Instead, the ill-fated vessel would have been merely a supporting player in the tragic story of another legendary ship.

The account was in the scrawled hand of one Captain Benjamin S. Briggs, once commander of the deserted vessel. Father Dominicus had pulled Captain Briggs nearly drowned from the rough waters on the south side of San Pedro. His heart full of Christian charity, the priest took Briggs into the mission and gave him the room next to his, where he nursed him back to as much health as was possible.

Despite the holy man's careful ministrations, Captain Briggs' senses never did fully return to him. He slept by day and spent his nights writing feverishly and swearing vengeance against the devil for what he had done to him and his family. Captain Briggs' nightly conversations with the unholy one only motivated the good Father to greater acts of caring, since clearly before him was a soul in great need of solace.

When Captain Briggs died several months later, having never swerved from his nightly attempts at communication with demonic forces, Father Dominicus can be forgiven for taking but a quick glance at the Captain's scribbled parchments, noting the contents, and placing them directly into the fire. If he had not, though, this is what might have come down to us:

My name is Benjamin Spooner Briggs, and I was once the captain of the *Mary Celeste*, but then I once had a family and once believed myself to be a man committed to the infinite power and mercy of our Lord God.

It had further been my belief that the sea was a rough master but not a cruel one, and that while it had its challenges, they were no greater than those posed by a tall mountain or deep cave; that its challenges, while real and difficult to overcome, were in their totality within the sphere of what men call the natural world.

I had no patience for tales of mermaids or sea monsters or great serpents that tore ships apart. I thought them merely the drunken ramblings of poor sailors seeking to excuse their follies with wild tales. Legends of phantoms of the sea, whether those of drowned men or cursed ships, also had no power to move me.

On taking command of the *Mary Celeste*, I made myself aware of her history. She had once been called *Amazon* and had acquired an unsavory reputation as a ship prone to misadventure. To me, such talk was nonsense. What I thought I had learned on three previous commands was that a ship is only as prone to accident as her captain and crew are.

So what I saw before me was merely a wooden half-brig, just over one hundred feet tall and perhaps a bit under three hundred pounds. She had been launched in Nova Scotia and had just finished a stem-to-stern repair, and lest you think me careless because of what befell me and my crew, let me put that from your mind. I walked the ship and checked every seam myself, ran my hand over every yard of sail. All was fine save one small thing.

Above the bed in my cabin, which I had made suitable to accommodate my wife, Sarah, and my daughter, (ah, if only my love for my wife was not so strong that I could not bear to go to sea without her, how different my fate might have been!) some unworthy craftsman had carved a blasphemous seaman's prayer: "If God sees fit to sink us, let the Devil keep us afloat." At the time I was both a meticulous and God-fearing man, and so had the wood that bore the carving torn out and replaced. But the prayer stayed with me just the same.

As for the crew, it was a varied one. My first mate was Albert Richardson, a stout man with a friendly twinkle about him and a reputation (despite his height of only five-feet-two) of wrestling grizzly bears to the ground, a notoriety he neither encouraged nor denied. If he was not as ready to command a ship as I was, then the difference was not one that could be easily measured.

The second mate I knew little of, and as he was a Dane and spoke only his own tongue I would learn little more save his name, Andrew Gilling.

The rest of the sailing crew were German and consisted of the two Lorensons, older and younger, and Martens and Gondeschall, all of whom spoke English to one extent or another and knew sailing as if they had been raised onboard ship. Our steward and cook was an American, Edward Head, and he knew his job as well.

We left New York Harbor on November 7, 1872. I said good-bye to my son Arthur, who was left behind to continue his schooling and so avoided the fate that befell the rest of us. We sailed out on a bright morning, bound for

Genoa with cargo of 1701 barrels of American Alcohol, shipped by Meissner Ackermann & Co., the purpose of which was to fortify wine.

The day was brisk but clear, the ocean itself calm and welcoming, and the strong southwest wind could not have better suited us if we'd ordered it carved by a master crafts-man. First Mate Richardson, gauging the ship's speed by tossing wood chips over the bow and counting the seconds until they drifted past the stern, judged our speed at a good eight knots. It was as promising a beginning to a voyage as I had ever had.

We were not twenty-four hours out from land when an odd rasping sound was heard echoing throughout the ship. Flotsam, I supposed, and I ordered all hands save Richard-son, who was at the wheel, to the sides of the ship. Noth-ing could be seen port or starboard, yet the rasping continued. One of the Lorensons—I cannot now remem-ber if it was the younger or the older—suggested that per-haps our cargo was shifting and the ship was merely echoing the sound in some way. When I descended to the hold to check Lorenson's theory, I discovered to my horror that the rasping was coming from beneath the ship.

Those of you who place stock in legends of the deep will perhaps misunderstand the source of my fear. My first thought was that somehow we had strayed into water far shallower than we had anticipated, or run afoul of some uncharted undersea mountain peak. The prospect of a hull torn open in midsea is one that should (and does) chill the heart of any sailor.

I ran back up to the deck and ordered the sails dropped and the ship slowed as much as possible. The crew obeyed with alacrity. First Mate Richardson, once the ship was se-cured, queried me on the reason behind my actions, then agreed with them wholeheartedly. The ship's progress halted, and we drifted lightly on the current. Yet despite this, the rasping sound did not stop—in fact it grew louder.

Suddenly the ship rocked to port, throwing the men off their feet. Then it rocked back the other way, or not so much rocked as tilted to starboard sharply enough to send us all sliding along the deck toward the ocean depths. There were screams in the air, and cries of fear, my own as well as the others. The ship held its pivot for a long moment, then with a sickening sense of release fell back into the water and righted itself. The air became deathly calm.

The rasping had ceased as well. Long moments passed with nothing reaching my senses save the normal salt smells and sounds of the sea. I shook the fear out of myself and determined that it was no mountain or shallow bottom we had experienced. I knew not what it was, but nonetheless preferred to have it at a fair distance from my ship. So as I had before given the command to stop, I now reversed myself and ordered the ship ahead with all possible speed.

The sails were set and the ship readied for speed in less time than it takes my unsteady hand to write about it. The wind was with us, the sails filled brightly, and the ship moved forward at a goodly speed, or so we thought.

It was Richardson who determined that we were not moving at all. The sails were pulling at us well enough, but something was anchoring us in place, something below us that we could not see.

Through Richardson I learned that Gilling was the best diver among the men. We arranged through signals that he should be lowered over the side to discover what it was that held us in place. I took no chances with my crew's life, and Gilling went over with a stout rope tied around him, so that we could haul him back from any misadventure.

After his first dip he signaled that he had not been able to dive deep enough, so we gave him more slack on the rope and some heavy metal scrap to pull him down quickly. Gilling disappeared beneath the surface, and only moments elapsed before we felt a huge tugging and pulling on the rope that, we thought, was our signal to pull Gilling up as fast as we could.

At first he seemed heavier than we could account for—the rope strained as we pulled. Surely, we thought, if he had signaled us for rescue, he would have dropped the iron he was carrying?

All at once the weight on the rope was not what it had been and it went loose in our hands. We reeled in as quickly as we could.

Gilling's body had been bitten in half, as if by a fish that took part of one's bait as it slipped the hook. What remained was his head and arms, and part of his chest. Sea water and blood mixed together and ran out of his body from holes no man was ever meant to have.

We dropped the line, and poor Gilling's body fell back into the ocean. We recovered ourselves, then raced over to the side to see if there were any remains of Gilling that could be hauled aboard and returned to his loved ones.

Instead a horrendous sight faced us. A gigantic creature with a maw the size of a whale and pale blue tentacles that spread out from its face like maggots fleeing the sun. It had gigantic eyes, one on each side of its wedge-shaped head, and sharp tusks protruding from around its mouth. There was blood on its lips, Gilling's blood.

The creature tilted its head and searched the water. On spying Gilling's remains it made quick work of them, then turned to look at us.

My pistol, the only weapon on board, flew into my hand of its own accord, and I quickly readied it and discharged it into the face of the horror that floated before me. There was no noticeable effect. The creature moved to the side of my ship, and then began to haul itself out of the water and up toward the deck.

What had shown above the water was only the smallest part of the gigantic body of this creature. As it pulled itself up, the ship rocked under its weight, and I determined that its goal was to capsize us and feast on our bodies. My men stabbed it with knives, attempting to carve off its fleshy hooks and return it to the depths. It was of no use. The ship tilted farther and farther.

As we fought for our footing on the wet and slimy deck, the creature's tentacles seemed to grow longer and more massive before our eyes. In long curving arcs, three of them reached out to pluck men from the deck and carry them through the air, screaming, to the creature's cavernous mouth. Four more slid their searching way around the deck, sliding down into the hold and the galley—I saw the most unfortunate Edward Head dragged out and swallowed— even smashing through my cabin door, behind which my beloved Sarah and our precious daughter, just two years old, had taken refuge. In seconds my wife's cries, mixed with those of our daughter, joined the agonized shouts of my men to create the most horrifying din I had ever been unlucky enough to be subjected to.

We were at our last moments. How much better to have died cleanly before the unfortunate, unfaithful words had left my mouth! But at the time I thought only of saving my family, my crew, and, yes, myself as well.

"If God sees fit to sink us," I prayed, "let the Devil keep us afloat."

The moment I finished that dark invocation, I saw a tall ship appear alongside us. (How it had gotten so close without my noticing I was in no condition to consider, nor did

I notice at the time that the schooner made no wake against the water, and seemed to be sailing in the face of the wind itself. That its masts were blackened and its sails the color of blood also escaped my harried eyes.)

I saw at least two dozen well-armed sailors, their clothing pale in the sunlight reflected off the water. Before I thought they were close enough, they leaped bodily the distance between my ship and theirs and joined with my few remaining men in the fight to loosen the creature's hold on us and on my ship. The captain of the other ship bellowed out an order in a deep-throated voice, and a barbed iron harpoon sailed out from his vessel and shot deep into the flesh of the creature that had set upon us.

More of his crew began heaving on the iron line chain the harpoon trailed, and surely enough, the two-front war these saviors—for so I thought them at the time—waged began to turn the tide toward us. A second harpoon was fired, and then a third, and all around me the creature's tentacles were being hacked to pieces by the strong arms and sharp daggers of the men of this unknown ship.

Before long, the creature had been pried from my ship and pulled back into the water. As soon as it was clear, the captain ordered his men to cut the harpoon lines—and the creature, belching black blood the whole time, sank again beneath the waves.

Before I knew it, the men from the other ship had somehow returned there, leaving First Mate Richardson and myself to count the dead. It was not a pleasant job, nor sadly a long one. Besides Richardson and myself, we found the only survivor to be my young daughter Sofia, who sat crying for her mother, for my beautiful wife could no longer answer our daughter's call.

When we had consigned to the sea all those whom the sea monster (for what else could I call it?) had not claimed

already, I sat on deck with Richardson, Sofia sleeping rest-
lessly in my lap, and tried to understand how all this had
befallen me. A motion from the other ship shook me loose
from my misery. With gestures, a sailor made clear that we
were expected to come aboard the silent ship that had saved
our lives.

I stood, little Sofia in my arms, and dusted myself off
as best I could. I felt little in the mood for socializing, but
how could I reject the man whose presence had saved what
little I had left? I shouted back a time a few hours hence.

That night Richardson, Sofia, and I boarded our last un-
damaged boat and rowed away from the *Mary Celeste*, not
knowing that we would never walk her decks again.

I knew that all was not right before we even set foot
on the ship. For one thing the ship was of a kind that I
knew to be at least a hundred years old, if not one hundred and fifty. Yet it looked as if it had left the shipwright's
only weeks before. Moreover, as it was coming on late
evening and the sun had dipped below the horizon, I saw
that the ship's sails were not merely dyed red but gave off
their own eerie red phosphorescence.

Despite the crimson glow, I could see Richardson's face
grow pale with fright, as if he recognized the ship we now
stood on board as a greater nightmare than the one it had
saved us from. What could create such fear in a man I
knew to be so brave?

The ship's crew, also pale despite the ruddy light, stood
in silence as the captain stepped forward and addressed us.
He, too, was dressed in a style that had been fashionable
over a century earlier. His voice, when he spoke, was that
of a man driven by forces beyond his ken.

Whatever his greater concerns, the captain spoke to us
as colleagues rather than refugees. He spoke of the bond

among seamen to come to one another's aid, and how on rare occasions when men called out to his tormentor—that was the word he used, tormentor—he would stray from his endless course and do what was right.

He said that while his ship could not make port, he would take us within sight of land and allow us to make our own way in the small boat that had brought us from our ship to his.

I asked of my ship and cargo, and offered to share our stores with him in gratitude for our rescue, but he waved me aside, saying he and his men had no use for such things. As for the ship, he could not and would not let us return to her. She was as cursed as his ship now, he said. Let her sail herself without a captive crew.

I saw that Richardson, for all his fears, understood who this strange captain was and what strange ship we had boarded. I, who had spurned the myths of the sea, had no such knowledge. All I could do was thank the captain for my life and my daughter's life, and agree to his conditions.

At a nod from the captain, the ship set noiselessly to sail. A crewman led me, my daughter, and Richardson to an empty cabin on the foredeck.

Once my daughter was asleep on the wall-mounted bed, Richardson pulled me aside and explained what ship we were on, and who the captain was. (I must relate that even with the reality underneath my feet I refused, at first, to believe him.) Angry at what I thought his foolishness, I stepped out of the cabin and back onto the deck. The sea I gazed out at was as it had always been. Had it really been only hours since I was sailing calmly over the water, the confident master of a ship of my own, with a wife I loved dearly by my side?

As I stared out over the water, I felt the whispered presence of some crew walking behind me. I turned, intend-

ing to amuse them with Richardson's wild notion about
their ship. Then I recognized one of them, and my heart
stopped momentarily in my chest.

It was one of the Lorensons, again I do not recall whether
it was the younger or older of the two.

*I had seen this man die before my eyes, yet here he was
among van Der Decken's crew.*

I knew, then, that it was true, that Richardson was right,
that we were aboard the most cursed ship of all, the *Flying Dutchman*, and that my prayer to the devil was what
had brought it to us.

The scope of the ship's tragedy hit home to me, and I
wished fervently that there was something I could do for
these poor men, spirits doomed to sail for eternity aiding
only those who cry out for the dark one. I resolved, when
I got to land, to see what church, nay what magician, could
be consulted for a way to lift the curse that kept the *Flying Dutchman* on the mains. They had saved me and my
daughter. Perhaps I could save them.

At that point Gilling wandered by, his spirit-body whole
where his flesh and blood body had been torn to pieces.
Then the thought struck me. Those who had died on the
Mary Celeste were now here, on this ship. That meant that
somewhere my wife's spirit wandered these decks.

I rushed to speak to the captain about summoning her
before him, so that I might speak with her one last time.
He only laughed at me. A woman on his ship? he said.
Never. It was bad luck, after all.

I wondered how a man cursed for eternity could still
worry about the state of his luck. I replied that surely
women sometimes die at sea, like men do, and that surely
their spirits too would find themselves with him.

He allowed that that might be true, but that if it were,

any such spirits would stay well away from him and his crew.

But his acquiescence gave me hope of seeing, of conversing, with my wife one last time. If I had to search the ship from top to bottom a thousand times, I would find Sarah and be reunited with her for one last moment. With that I made my second request of the devil that day. I asked the captain that I not be sent away with Richardson and my daughter, but that I be allowed to remain on board until such time as I found my wife's spirit.

He stared at me, with eyes that dug right to my soul. Then he agreed to take me on for a term, though, he said, that it might be longer than I could ever dream.

I put my daughter into Richardson's care, and told him of my son back in New York. He swore to me that he would raise Sofia as his own, and do his best to find and care for my son Arthur as well. We released him near the southern coast of America, and I watched as he paddled his way toward shore.

When he was out of sight, the ship turned and headed back to sea.

I could tell much of what the ship did as it traveled and I searched. For me it felt like only months were passing, yet from the occasional passenger we took on I found that time was passing far more quickly than that. Their clothing became strange and their ships stranger still. The world I returned to, I knew, would be nothing like what it had been. My daughter would be grown, perhaps with a family of her own. But still I searched for my wife, anticipating the happy day when I would find her.

Find her I did, but it was not a happy day. I had finished a thorough search of the ship and was ready to begin yet another. The captain was not on deck, and there were questions I had for him about the construction of the ship

and where any secret smugglers' rooms might be. I went
to his cabin, and heard a familiar feminine voice coming
from within.

Bursting with joy, I threw open the door, only to find
my wife Sarah locked in an embrace with Captain van Der
Decken himself. She stared at me with no recognition for
a long moment. Then as if a past life were coming back
to her, she said my name, questioningly, and I acknowl-
edged who I was.

Sarah broke off from the captain and stood before me,
her spirit-body as beautiful as her living body had ever
been. She addressed me calmly, in loving but distant tones.
She had loved me strong and well while she was alive,
Sarah admitted, but now death had parted us and our fates
were no longer intertwined. Her death at sea had sent her
here, to this ship, and here was where her story would continue.

I stood stunned. There was no hope then, I thought, of
Sarah and I being reunited even in the next life.

Unless I, too, died at sea.

If I hesitated even a moment, my resolve would weaken.
I turned, threw myself from the room and over the side of
the ship.

It is simple to be brave in a moment, hard indeed to
keep that bravery through an entire act of self-destruction.
As sea water forced the air from my lungs, I found that I
was, involuntarily, fighting for my life with all possible
strength. Once again, my fear of death drove me to the
prayer I had sworn I would never more invoke: "If God
sees fit to sink me, let the Devil keep me afloat."

The water sucked me down quickly, and all was black
until I came to not on board the *Dutchman* with my Sarah,
but here in this mission where the kindly Father Domini-

cus explained to me that God had saved me from drowning and delivered me into his hands.

To live, but without Sarah? It was not God, I knew, who had saved me, but the devil who had kept me afloat.

I find that I have only short moments of clarity before rage at myself and my cowardice overwhelms me once again, and that time is now once again fading.

At least I have completed my story, for what good it might do others.

The devil brought me life when that was what I desired, but then denied me death when release was what I sought. I no longer seek either, but want only vengeance against the unholy one, which I have little hope of achieving in this life or in the next. Little hope, but perhaps now, enough faith.

Captain Briggs died shortly after his account was completed. Father Dominicus buried him in the small graveyard behind the mission. For the rest of his long life, the good Father prayed daily for the captain's soul . . . or at least so I've heard.

TRIBUTE

BY KRISTINE KATHRYN RUSCH

W E were on the Pacific, a long stretch of nowhere, gray upon gray, going on forever.

This was early in the war, our backsides still blistering from the pounding the Japs were giving us. I was a newly minted lieutenant with a job I hated: I was the one who read all the outgoing mail and censored it even before it left the battleship.

I'm sure our boys knew someone read the mail. I'm sure all of them knew it was me. But we didn't discuss jobs much. I was just one of a handful of ranking paper-pushers on a vessel where most guys got their hands dirty. I like to think I was more uncomfortable than they were; after all, I knew more about any of them than they would rightly tell me.

... Judy, hon: dreamed about you three nights running. Finally Sanders, my bunkmate, told me to think purer thoughts—guess I was moaning suggestively in my sleep ...

... Martha, remember that night down on Wisconsin Point? Sometimes I think I still got sand in my drawers ...

... And, Ma, don't say nothing to Carl about when I'm coming home. No sense in disappointing the kid. I just have a hunch things ain't gonna go the way we planned ...

Hopes, dreams, and fears, all hand-scrawled, all personal. Sure, the guys knew someone would read them, but even on this, their first mission—maybe especially on this, their first mission—they were scared and homesick, that rush of emotion that led 'em to join up forgotten back at the first day of camp.

I was a more grizzled vet. I joined up in '39 for a variety of reasons. My folks were gone, my sweetheart married another. I'd left Connecticut angry and lost. There was a war brewing; we all knew it, and I thought if I joined early, I had a better chance of surviving.

Hard to convey how naïve we were. Fresh out of Seattle with a stop in Hawaii. We looked at those charred ships still decorating Pearl Harbor, saw some of the survivors moaning in the remaining hospitals, and felt patriotic all over again.

But out in the middle of a gray ocean, nothing around us but water and sky, it was easy to forget how badly we wanted revenge. Nights spent listening to the engines chug along—the only thing between us and a watery grave— and we knew we were heading into the unknown. It didn't matter how right our mission was. Our lives had changed, and we still weren't used to it.

We weren't part of any fleet. We thought we were supposed to join one at Pearl, but those orders got changed. Of course, we didn't learn about the change until after we stopped, refueled, and steamed ahead on our own.

We felt as if the battles were being fought ahead of us, as if we were struggling to catch up. Some of the ensigns sat watch on deck, worrying about Jap suicide missions. Those worries got into the letters too—and I'd cut them out, using thick black ink on both sides of the paper, so that no one could read what the boys were saying. Sometimes I literally cut the pages and taped the remains together. That way the folks at home wouldn't know if little

Johnny was fighting in the Pacific or the Atlantic, and they wouldn't know how frightened he was.

But I did. The fears stuck with me, haunting me in different voices when I lay down on my bunk. I ranked a cabin—smaller than the head, but private just the same—because of the secret nature of my job. I guess the brass was afraid I'd confide in my bunkmate or talk in my sleep, so they censored me in the only way they could—by letting me have my privacy.

In my privacy, there wasn't a lot to think about except what I read. How Hastings hoped his newborn daughter was doing well, Carmichael worrying about his wife, who'd never lived alone; and all those investments LeMeu was making from abroad. Still, when the strangeness started, I didn't think much of it. I was concentrating on the gossip, wandering how scrawny guys like Daemer managed to get a date at all, let alone five different women whom he claimed undying love for.

Muriak, I think, was the first one to mention the ship. *Like a pirate ship*—he'd written in his sprawling prose—*lots of masts and riggings. Only there had to be an engine, too, because she kept up with us. Always dogging us in our wake.*

I cut the reference without much thought—except to note the superstitious way he talked about her. I even remember thinking of warning him—a man wasn't allowed to talk about anything that referred to the war (no wonder so many of those letters ended up pornographic: they didn't have anything else they could write about)—but I changed my mind soon enough. If I warned every guy who crossed the line, I'd have no job to do. Or worse, they would all remember that I was the man who read their mail, and knew exactly what they wanted to do to their sweethearts (often in painfully graphic detail) when they got home.

I'd been too visible already on this trip. I'd done my duty, and while it had been the right thing, it had bothered everyone—including me. Still, I paid attention. I had to.

Muriak had first watch most nights, and it seemed that sitting alone in the dark got to his head. At least that was what I thought. If there was a ship dogging us, like he wrote about, he would have reported it to the captain— that was part of his duty. I checked, discreetly, and he never had.

The second reference came in DeBeyr's daily letter to an old friend of his in Princeton, a guy who was an unhappy 4-F. *Seems Blackbeard is tailing us*, he wrote. *Wonder what we should do if he boards.*

I cut that, too. Even though it was fanciful, it read like code—and that wouldn't be a good thing to fall into enemy hands.

Then the very next letter, Briscoe's, had this: *A lot of guys have seen a ghost ship. I think it's the effect of staring at nothing all day. You can't know how depressing it is, staring at sea and sky with nothing to show you the horizon. When there's emptiness all around you, you start making stuff up to fill it.*

The black pen inked out that section, too, wise as it was. My stomach clenched, though. Not because I was censoring—believe it or not, I got used to that pretty quick—but because of his tone and the idea that some of the recruits were going slowly, steadily mad.

I read Briscoe's letter just before lunch. I finished it (he wrote to his sister every day even though, before he shipped out, they weren't close. *Just need someone sympathetic to talk to, I guess*, his first letter had said. I had cut that sentence, too) and put it in the packet for the letters to be dropped next port—where some other censor would check my work before shipping the letters on home and let myself out of my cubby.

My office was private, too, and cubby was a good description of it. Small, boxlike, and filled with papers, there was barely enough room for a chair and a desk. I worked in silence, reading other people's mail, and making decisions about it. The room was windowless and charmless and in my time on that ship, I never decorated it. I guess part of me wanted it to feel dirty and secret like the job I was doing.

When I left the office, as I did after I read Briscoe's letter, I had to hide everything on the desk, then lock the door and pocket the key. I always tested the knob, just to make sure I didn't make a mistake. It was more for my protection than the letters'. The boys knew they were being censored; they just didn't have to see how much.

I searched out the captain and found him in the officer's mess, getting ready for lunch.

"You're early, Kenyon," he said as he took a cup of coffee to a nearby table. He was a burly man with a perpetually red face. His short blond hair made the top of his skull perfectly flat, as if someone had cropped it with a machete.

"Yes, sir," I said. "I have something to discuss with you."

He grunted and gestured, looking very uncomfortable. The last time we'd had this type of discussion, I'd shown him four letters from Ensign Zuklor in which he mentioned committing suicide before we reached the front.

Zuklor was sent to the ship's doctor, and dry-docked in Hawaii, considered too unstable to handle work in the pressure cooker of a battleship.

I decided to plunge right into it. "Have you heard any talk about a ghost ship?"

The captain's smile was faint. "On every trip, someone mentions a ghost ship. You'll have to learn to live with the lore of the sea, Kenyon."

I almost defended myself, but held back. I learned long ago that the captain didn't like to be contradicted about anything.

"I've seen a specific ship mentioned in three letters now, sir," I said.

The captain raised his head and looked at me. His eyes were bloodshot and lined with fatigue. I wondered if he ever got more than four hours a night.

"If it's a real ship, someone's being derelict." His tone was ominous, and I had to struggled to maintain my composure. There was no love lost between us, and things had gotten worse since Zuklor.

"I don't think it's real, sir. One of the boys said it looked like a pirate ship, with masts and everything. Another wrote home, saying we were being dogged by Blackbeard's ship."

At that moment, the cook came out and set a plate before him. Roast pork sandwich complete with gravy. By this point, the men in the regular mess were eating chipped beef with everything. Only the officers got real meat any more.

My stomach growled. The cook looked at me as if I had invaded his kitchen. "You want him to have some?" he asked the captain.

"Won't hurt," the captain said, although he sounded a little reluctant. Apparently he had wanted a semi-private meal. In fact, until that moment, I hadn't thought about how often he came in early. He was usually just finishing when the rest of us got our meals.

The cook disappeared.

"You ever sailed these waters before, Kenyon?" he asked me.

"No, sir."

He grunted and sliced his sandwich. He had no qualms about eating before me. "There's always talk of something here. Doesn't surprise me that the men are seeing a ghost ship. There are just parts of the sea that have haunted places, echoes, whatever you want to call them. You get used to them."

"Briscoe also mentioned it in his letter home," I said. "He thinks the crew is going crazy."

The captain smiled faintly. "I'll have someone check on it," he said in a tone that told me he wouldn't.

"Sir, I felt strongly enough to come to you—"

"And I appreciate that, sailor. I told you I would take care of it." He ate a slice of pork, and then looked at me, as if measuring me. "You got anything else?"

"No, sir," I said.

He slid his fork in the gravy, sighed, and glanced around the mess. So far, we were the only people in it. "I gotta tell you, Kenyon, you're here on suffrage. The Navy insists in a war that we have a man like you, and I follow orders. But your job is to make sure that nothing leaks in those letters to the folks back home. Not to report every little problem to me."

"Sir, according to my training, I am supposed to report oddities to you."

"Oddities." He leaned forward. "I think men have a right to privacy, Lieutenant. The fact that you violate it every day as part of your job is something I have to live with. But mostly, I don't want to hear about it. The men need a place to let off steam, and they do it in their letters home. That's better than doing it on each other, or making this ship hell."

The cook stood in the door, my roast pork sandwich steaming in his hand. The captain beckoned him forward.

The cook scurried over, set my sandwich down, and vanished again—as if he wanted to stay as far from this conversation as he could.

My stomach growled. The food smelled heavenly. Hard to believe a man could work up an appetite reading other people's letters.

"Yes, sir," I said, picking up my fork.

"But you don't agree." He must have caught something in my tone. I didn't agree. And now he had opened the door.

"No, sir. Forgive me, sir, but if it weren't for me doing my job, Ensign Zuklor might be dead now."

"Half these boys might be dead in another month. Hell, in another week, if the Japs mined areas we don't know about." The captain sounded unconcerned, but the lines around his eyes deepened. He was letting me hear one of his constant worries.

"But Zuklor was unstable."

"You say." The captain sopped up the rest of the gravy with the last of his bread. "I wonder how many other men just don't write down their fears. Maybe we punished Zuklor for being honest, for confiding in someone who would listen. Maybe he was just letting off steam, and he would have been a good sailor after that. Have you thought of that, Kenyon?"

Actually, I hadn't.

"What's private should stay private," the captain said.

"And if Zuklor had killed himself while we were on the seas, unable to dock anywhere? What would that have done then? You just said sailors are superstitious. Would that have made this a doomed ship?"

The captain stared at me for a moment. His blue eyes were hard and cold, and I thought I saw hatred in them.

"People live and die on ships. Some of us spend our whole lives on them happily, and hope for a burial at sea."

His intensity disturbed me. I made myself eat some more of the sandwich. The pork was heavily salted and a bit old.

"So Zuklor's suicide wouldn't have caused a problem?"

"If he would have committed suicide," the captain said. "I think it was just talk."

"Yet you sent him to the ship's doctor."

"Who asked him if he wrote the letters, and made his recommendation based on that." The captain put his hands against the table and shoved his chair back. "This is a tense ship. Has been ever since we left Pearl."

"And you blame me."

The captain stood. "Don't you?"

I hadn't until that moment. "Sir, it's part of my training to report anything suspicious to you."

"Suspicious," he said. "I don't think sightings of ghost ships, or a man's personal doubts, are suspicious. Unless you got evidence of murder or collaboration with the enemy, I don't want to hear about it. Do you understand?"

It was my turn to stare. The training had been so clear—so blunt. The letters were a window into the ship, into the morale, and the ideals (or lack thereof) of the crew. Yes, I was supposed to guard against information leaving the ship, but I was also supposed to use the information I gathered for the good of the ship, and now the captain did not want to do that.

"Do you understand, Lieutenant?"

"I guess so, sir."

"No guessing, Kenyon. You're on my ship. Whatever those moles who trained you told you is their business. But here, you do as I say. If you have problems with that, I'll let you off at the next base, and my recommendations won't be charitable. Is that clear?"

"Yes, sir."

"From now on, your lunchtime in this mess is 1300 hours. If I see you here one moment sooner, you will be written up. Good day, Kenyon."

He was gone before I could answer him, slamming the door of the mess behind him. I made myself eat some more lunch. My hand shook as it brought the food to my mouth. I had been warned, when I entered intelligence, that we were hated among the old guard. I guess I hadn't realized how much until that moment.

No one joined me for the last half of my meal. No one even came in the mess. It was as if they all knew I would be there, and they all decided to avoid me.

I went back to my cubby, and continued to read in silence.

From Steig's letter to his wife: *Remember how we used to compare dreams, Irene? I had the strangest last night. A big old pirate ship, flying the skull and crossbones, stopped our ship, and demanded we pay tribute. I was on watch. I said, we're the United States. We don't pay tribute to no one. And the pirate, a grizzled guy like you see in the movies only dirtier, said, I don't mean honor, stupid. We need a toll, or you can't get through.*

Well, I says, I'm not authorized to make that decision. You gotta see the captain. Get him, the pirate said. But I woke up before I did.

From McNamee's letter to his best friend: *So I go looking for the captain, and of course, he's nowhere. I come back to the bow and I shout: we're a battleship. We don't carry money. But we could blast you outta the water. And the men on the pirate ship laugh . . .*

From Porter's letter to his mother: *For three nights, I search for the captain. I finally find him, and he says he'll take care of it. I hear him using the bull-horn, saying that because the schooner's not real, they can't collect tribute.*

Strangest thing was, Ma, the next day, I saw the captain and when his gaze met mine, it felt like he knew, like we had the same dream. That ain't possible, is it, Ma? You ever hear of anything like that in this day and age?

The letters were full of odd things: dreams, ghost ships, bright lights to sea. And fog. We seemed plagued by fog.

I was beginning to wonder if the letters were revenge for Zuklor. Someone, some wag from below, thought maybe they'd see if I'd break. Maybe the captain put them up to it so, that I'd make the early report, and I'd then be stuck with this knowledge, that the entire crew was having an experience that I wasn't, an experience that just wasn't possible.

I thought of challenging him again, but that would only upset him further. And I couldn't, under my orders, discuss the letters with anyone but another intelligence officer or my captain. I decided to save the bunch until I had someone to consult.

But that didn't stop me from being curious. I had a fairly lively imagination. It was one of the reasons I got this job in the first place; I could imagine all sorts of gloom and doom scenarios from a single sentence. I knew, intellectually, that this had to be a trick, but emotionally, I found myself wishing that the ghost ship existed.

I found evidence that it did in the most unlikely places. Men who didn't normally speak to each other were writing about similar dreams, similar experiences. I wanted to believe that they wouldn't talk to each other, that they wouldn't hate me so very much that they would combine their efforts. Yet I knew that was probably what was happening.

I had been warned during my training that my job would make me a pariah. I had thought I was a loner, thought I wouldn't mind. But I did mind.

I just hated to admit it to myself.

For the next two nights, I couldn't sleep. Finally, at 0100 hours on the second night, I got off my tiny little mattress, wiped the sweat from my face, slipped on my uniform, and went onto the deck.

The cold air woke me up further, but managed to clear the cobwebs from my mind. A fog had rolled in, as it had every night for the last week. A thin fog, almost like a ground fog—the kind you'd see over marshes and rivers on fall nights back home. But this wasn't fall, and we weren't anywhere near ground.

Young Ashburton was on watch. He saw me, saluted, and then turned away, as if I weren't worth his time. Odd. If the war hadn't happened, I would have thought him not worth mine. We came from such different backgrounds— him from the slums of Columbus, Ohio, me from one of the wealthier families in Connecticut. It was his letters that made me realize that he was a guy I could like. He was surprisingly articulate and well-read, with a great deal more ambition than I would ever have. He loved his high school sweetheart with a passion foreign to me, and it seemed, from my lofty, lonely perch, that Ashburton had learned more about living in his eighteen years than I had in my twenty-five.

So it cut when he turned away—and he probably didn't even know it. There was no way he could know as much about me as I did about him. No way at all.

The deck was slick with fog-soaked damp. I walked to the railing and stared down at the froth we were churning up. The moon was nearly full, sending its bright light onto the strange fog hovering over the water's surface. Usually fog trapped sound, but on this night, the sound seemed to dissipate. Instead of hearing the constant thrum of the engines, I could only feel it through the bottoms of my regulation shoes.

The water itself seemed unusually silent. Usually the splash caused by our movement was a constant, reassuring sound. I couldn't hear it either—at least not regularly. It was as if I could see and feel the world, but not hear it, almost as if I were in a dream.

Then Ashburton whimpered, like a dog startled out of a good night's sleep. I turned, but couldn't see him. My heart was pounding. My head told me that this was part of the trick—alarm Kenyon when he came on deck—but I had to check it out. I'd be derelict if I didn't.

I walked toward Ashburton's perch. He was huddled there, staring forward, and I knew he didn't see me at all. He wasn't even thinking of me. He was staring at the ocean as if he had never seen it before.

I stared, too, but I would be lying if I said I saw the ship. What I saw was white, like the fog, and it vaguely resembled a ship, the way that clouds sometimes resemble recognizable shapes. The air had gained even more of a chill, and I wrapped my arms around myself for warmth.

Part of me wanted to run belowdecks, but the rest of me was curious. I walked forward, wondering if my eyes were deceiving me, wondering if I saw what I wanted to see. My footsteps echoed on the deck. As I got closer, Ashburton whirled, startled. His wide eyes met mine and then he flushed, as if I had caught him doing something illegal.

"Everything all right?" I asked in my calmest voice.

He nodded, a short, rabbity movement that belied his answer.

"See anything?"

"No," he said, but somehow couldn't resist a look over his shoulder at the sea. The fog was still there, rising above the waves like a live thing. If I squinted, I thought I could see three masts and a hull, all white and opaque.

"Is that a ship?" I pointed at the masts.

"N-no," Ashburton said. "It's the fog."

I nodded, squinted, and couldn't really tell if he was right or not. It looked like fog. It looked like a ship. It looked like anything I wanted it to.

I was getting very cold. I shivered, and water droplets fell from my hair onto my face. They felt like ice.

Ashburton was covered with water drops, too. The fog had risen to the deck level and the wetness in the air was making us damp.

"Ever seen anything like that?" I asked.

"Fog is fog," Ashburton said.

I remained unconvinced. I stood there for a moment longer, hoping to see the Blackbeard of the letters, but I saw nothing. Even the so-called ship seemed to lose its form. I shivered once, then went below, got out of my wet things, and slipped back into bed.

But I didn't sleep.

Exhaustion can do strange things to a man. It makes him desperate if there's no underlying cause. Insomnia had never plagued me before, but it plagued me now. Two more nights passed without any real sleep. I did not go back to the deck. I didn't want to see that fog, or the specter of a ship that really wasn't there. Instead I spent the frustrating nights, tossing and turning in my bunk, trying to get other people's words out of my mind. Trying to think about anything but the mystery of the ship.

Finally, I took an afternoon and paced the deck, getting

as much exercise as I could so that sleep would be inevitable. I asked cook to give me some warm milk before bedtime, and he obliged, adding a dab of honey and lemon—a concoction my dead mother used to make when I was ill.

Either the milk or the exercise did the trick. I fell into my bed, and was asleep long before I had a chance to toss or turn. I didn't even dream. The cycle of worry, or whatever it was, had ended.

The next day, I felt refreshed. Ashburton's refusal to meet my gaze when we saw each other at 1200 didn't bother me, nor did the three more letters I read that discussed the ghost ship. Rumors were flying on our own ship that we would see action soon, although I thought them the talk of a restless crew. Attention seemed to be turning elsewhere.

I went to bed that night with no thought of walking the deck in the fog or of hot milk and insomnia. Instead, I closed my eyes, and fell into a sound sleep like I had done most of my life.

Only this time, I dreamed.

Fog slid under the door like a wraith, curling and rolling forward, its whiteness so bright that it illuminated the room. The fog beckoned me outward, like a lure. I got up, then walked forward, opening my door to see what had gone wrong.

Fog poured down the steps and into the narrow corridor. Ground fog, thin and rippling, the fog of my youth, the fog of bogs and swamps and rivers. The fog of land, not the fog of the sea.

I missed land. I hadn't admitted that to myself until then.

I followed the fog up the stairs and to the deck. The deck was empty, the engines silent for the first time since we'd left port. Fog enshrouded everything, making it look as if we were encased in ice.

Directly in our wake, however, was a pirate ship. It had three masts and a wooden hull. It looked old and well used. It didn't fly the Jolly Roger, though. It had no flag at all. I had no idea how I knew it belonged to the pirates. I simply knew that it did.

"So," a voice said behind me.

I whirled. A man, dark and grizzled, stood behind me, his feet lost in the fog. He wore three layers of clothing, most of it tattered, and in his left hand he held a pistol. Not a modern pistol, but a muzzle loader with a long barrel and a flint.

"Your people are refusing tribute." His eyes were black and they glittered in the strange light. "They do not believe we're a threat."

"You're not a threat," I said. "You're a dream."

His smile was thin. "Perhaps. But if we're not, every life on this ship is forfeit."

I glanced at his ship, with its cannons on the side, ragged men staring at me across the expanse of fog-covered sea. "If you're real, you have no hope against us. We could sink your ship in a matter of minutes."

He laughed, then nodded. "That's the first sensible remark I've heard."

"If you were real pirates," I said, emboldened, "you wouldn't give us so many chances."

He raised his chin slightly, as if I had challenged him. The water, from the humidity in the air, was beading on me, but not on him.

"If you are real," I said, "and you can somehow invade our dreams, you don't need to talk to us to plunder our ship."

"We no longer seek gold," he said. "We have no use for it."

"Then what do you want?"

"Tribute."

"Recognition? Is that why you visit our dreams?"

"No." He suddenly seemed impatient with me. "We charge a price to anyone who sails these waters. If you do not pay us tribute, you and your ship and your crewmates will not survive the year."

"And if we do pay?"

"You're protected from harm. Forever."

My gaze met his. "How can any man guarantee such a thing?"

"A man does not," he said. "But we both know I am no longer a man."

I woke up in my bed, with no recollection of walking back down the stairs. One moment I was on the deck, the next I was in bed.

I sat up. The dream had been very real, frighteningly real. If that was what the men had seen, then no wonder they were writing of it in their letters home. It had startled me, too.

I shivered. The room had a chill. I rubbed my hands on my arms and realized that my sleeves were wet. I touched my hair. It was wet, too.

I opened the door to my cabin. There was no fog in the hallway, and the engines thrummed as they always did.

It had been a dream, I thought. It had been a dream. It could have been nothing else.

From Redgen's letter to his best friend: *He said he was doomed to sail the seas for a thousand years, haunting the places where he had sunken other ships, stolen men, hid-*

den treasure. Penance, he said, was hard, because he and he alone had that sentence, and he could not handle his ship without help. He was a strange man. It didn't sound like a curse, at least not to him. Sounded like he wasn't willing to give up the sea, like death wasn't going to stop him. He wanted me to believe he could give us a gift in return, but pirates don't give gifts. Not even dead ones.

From Glassman's letter to a colleague: *So I'm wondering if my subconscious hasn't made him up. Part Black-beard—who never sailed in this area—and part Barbary pirate, part legend and part myth. I'm thinking perhaps that he's a lord of the sea. All seafaring cultures had sto-ries about creatures that wanted something valuable in ex-change for a magical gift. Would you look him up for me? I think these long days at sea are bringing back memories of stories I studied years ago, and I would like to know which one is haunting me now. . . .*

From Minter's letter to his sister: *I offered to help him, but I couldn't do nothing. I didn't know what he wanted. Kinda strange, now that I'm awake. I wonder if I was doing the right thing. But the men are so scared. The captain don't know that, how scared we all are, and if we could get through without a scratch, a miracle ship surviving years of war, then that'd be worth some raggedy dream pi-rate tribute, don't you think?*

Don't you think?

I stared at the words before I inked them out. Before I inked out the entire section. Men are always so supersti-tious. Worried about the past, worried about the future. Worried about figures that appear to us in dreams.

Mass dreams. Mass hysteria. An image we were all see-ing. Was it the suggestibility brought on by such close quarters? A half-remembered story started in the crew's mess? Or was it as simple as discomfort brought on by the fog?

I sighed and opened another page of Minter's letter, in which he discussed more mundane things, like the quality of the food, and a Christmas memory that seemed incomplete.

I found my mind wandering, playing over the words I'd read. What if everyone had approached the old pirate wrong? They all seemed willing to believe he was real. But what if he was just a dream—or, more accurately, a nightmare? And what if the only way to exorcise him from the mind was to give him what he wanted?

I set down Minter's letter and stared at the pile of letters, waiting to go out. I knew the crew's secret thoughts; they didn't know mine. If I told them what I was thinking, I'd have to speak the idea aloud. They got to write the ideas down, to trusted people, beloved people. These men would never have spoken about these things to each other—at least, not if they didn't know each other well.

And while I knew them all well, they didn't know me at all.

That night the fog seeped into my dreams, perhaps because I was expecting it, because my mind was ready for it. Because I had been thinking about it all day, and planning for it. I let myself sink into the dream and its logic quicker than I had before.

The fog on the deck was white and waist-deep. The air was moist, as it had been before, and so cold that I thought I'd never get warm. I carried my blanket with me this time, and wrapped it around me as if I were an old woman.

He didn't have his pistol. Instead, he stood, legs parted and disappearing into the sea of white. The fog looked al-

most solid, as if it were ice, and I could walk across it to the pirate ship beyond.

I glanced at the ship. Other letters had mentioned the skull and crossbones flag, but I didn't see it. The ship looked like one I had seen in Boston harbor when I was a boy; small and snug and somehow safe, despite the power of the sea.

"Beautiful, ain't she?" he asked. His voice was growly, with a bit of a British accent. I didn't remember it from before. Was it there because I expected it?

"I've never seen anything like her."

"Nor will you again." He clasped his hands behind his back. "So, are you ready to pay tribute?"

"If I do, no harm comes to us. Any of us?" I was thinking that even in the dream world, this was a bargain.

"No harm comes to any man on this vessel."

I stared at him a moment. I was thinking that even in the dream world, this was a bargain. There'd be no more nightmares, no more ghost ship, no more watchmen whimpering in the fog.

"What do you want?" I asked.

His smile was feral, and my heart started pounding hard. I wondered if it would wake me up.

"I need a crewman, a man with salt in his veins and the sea in his heart."

"Not larceny?" I asked.

He laughed. "That, too."

"Why? Shouldn't your men travel with you for eternity?"

"That's my sentence, not theirs. They live their natural life, and then they retire. And when they do, I need a replacement."

"Pirates retire?"

His smile again, wolfish, a bit too bright. "They're not pirates. They're just my crew."

"You feed them? Clothe them?"

"Laddie, you've eyes. They live in a place where they don't want for anything."

I stared at the ship, simple in its old-fashioned beauty. It looked like a palace made out of fog. *"One man?"*

"One man, with no wife to pine for him, no family to miss him, no friends to see him off." His eyes narrowed. *"Know a man like that?"*

My mind scanned through a thousand letters. Every letter I'd ever read, every face I'd ever seen. A man who lived for the sea. A man who had nothing to go home to.

A man who wanted a burial at sea.

"Just our captain," I said.

The pirate raised his eyebrows. I clearly hadn't said what he expected. *"You'd leave this ship in the hands of the first officer?"*

"He must be competent, or he wouldn't hold the position."

"That's one way of looking at it," the pirate said. *"Are you sure?"*

"As sure as I can be."

He nodded, then reached out a grimy hand. After a moment I took it. We shook, and I wondered what kind of honor this cursed thief thought he had.

"Tribute's paid," he said, and vanished.

I woke in my bed, cold, the sheets so wet I worried that I had a fever. I was shaking and shivering and wondering how dreams could be so very real.

I fell into a restless sleep, broken before 0600 by the sound of booted feet, running past my door. More feet on the deck above, and then voices, low and panicked. In my fogged state I wondered if the pirates had boarded after all, if they had taken the ship, and then someone pounded on my door, startling me.

The first officer stood there, back straight. Only his flushed cheeks showed that something was wrong. He came in without waiting for my permission, and closed the door behind him.

"Have you seen the captain in the last six hours?" he asked.

"No." I rubbed my eyes, trying to force myself into full wakefulness. "Is something wrong?"

"Did he put anything in his letters, something that might have—" his voice broke.

"Might have?"

"Shown his mental state?"

"I'm not permitted to discuss letters with anyone but an intelligence officer or the captain."

"Or the captain's representative," the first officer said.

I stood slowly, my mouth dry. The sheets fell away, but landed in a clouded heap. They were still clammy, and my boots shone with a wetness they hadn't had when I first went to bed.

"What's happened?"

"He's not on the ship."

"But that's impossible."

"He's gone. It appears he was dragged from his bed." The first officer ran a hand over his face. "Some of the crew are reporting dreams of pirates pulling him off the ship, screaming."

"To cover up their own actions?"

"You think this was a rebellion?"

"Do you?"

We stared at each other. And then, almost at the same time, looked away. He cleared his throat.

"Letters?" he asked again.

"Nothing," I said. "He never wrote to anyone. He had no one to write to."

The first officer looked at me, nodded, and left the cabin without another comment.

I sank back down onto the bed. No one could have known about my choice—my dream choice. I had been in my cabin all night. Alone.

I put my head in my hands and wondered what sort of creature I had bargained with the night before. Then I looked at my hand, the one I had used to shake his.

It was covered with dirt.

After we searched exhaustively for the captain, we were ordered to return to Hawaii. Another ship met us within a day, and its crew became our guards. The U.S. Navy believed we had mutinied and murdered our captain, but they never did find enough evidence to charge us.

We were all given stateside assignments, far from each other, in places where we could not influence the war effort, where we could serve out our terms without distinguishing ourselves in any way.

Safe from harm.

I bounced from post to post, reviewing the mail—only this time it had already been inked, so the reading was less interesting—with no one to talk to and nothing to do with my time except think.

And it wasn't until the last year of the war, that I finally understood the expression on the old pirate's face. He had been surprised because he had chosen me for his crew. I had no wife to pine for me, no family to miss me, no friends to see me off. The old pirate hadn't known my job, hadn't realized that I would know everything about everyone on the ship.

He had simply figured that I would volunteer.

And I hadn't.

I had volunteered another man's life, a man who hadn't liked me, a man I hadn't liked.

Perhaps I hadn't been so altruistic after all. Perhaps my imagination and my powerful mind had formed a denial so great that I hadn't been able to see my own actions, my own selfishness.

We had came to no harm. In fact, nearly sixty years later, we're still alive. All of us, every member of that crew. Everyone who had been on the ship that morning when I woke up.

After the captain vanished.

We're all healthy, vigorous, never been sick a day since we turned back.

Was sentencing one man to a living hell worth all that?

Sometimes I like to think so.

Sometimes I like to think I did no harm.

Guess my denial's as strong as ever. And my lack of will just as bad. I can't go back to that long stretch of nowhere on the Pacific. I tell myself I don't know where it was.

And I wish I could believe the lie.

MAGICAL MARITIME

Some have chosen oceans of imagination where ships and warriors meet magic and wizardry and where creatures of legend occasionally bear sailors to far-off destinations.

Whether it be airships or dragonships, magic potions or mighty statues, the magical maritime is not a place for cowards.

In the words of the ancient mariners, here there be dragons—and not all of them are friendly.

MIDSHIPWIZARD

BY JAMES M. WARD

A STORMY, demon-inspired day blew the mist-shrouded, salty sea air across the busy docks. No one paid it much of a mind. The war kept everyone hellishly busy.

"They're cursed ships. Everyone knows it."

"Demon things, I say, shouldn't even be in the king's navy."

"I've heard they eat their crew when becalmed, I have."

Two old salts leaned over dock crates looking at the king's dragon ship, *Sanguine*, moored in the misty distance. A chill went up Midshipwizard Halcyon Blithe's spine as he and his trunk maneuvered in and out of the crowd around the dock to get to the magnificent, half-living ship.

"It's going to take more than that to slip the wind from my sails," he muttered to himself, disgusted by the nay-sayers scoffing at the dragon ship. "I'm a man with prospects."

He had just turned fifteen the day before. Now dressed in a shiny new midshipwizard uniform, it was plain to see he was green as grass. It was also plain to everyone that he was a wizard as his heavy trunk floated along behind him. Even though there were hundreds of people moving on the dock, the cumbersome trunk never touched any of them as it followed its owner to the waiting launch.

"Ahoy the jolly boat! I'm Midshipwizard Blithe with papers to deliver to the captain of the *Sanguine!*"

"Ahoy yourself, young idiot!" came the answer from the launch. "You'll be delivering those papers to Midshipwizard Fallow, and you'll ask my permission to come aboard my jolly boat as I'm three ranks above you. I'm Midshipwizard Seventh-class Dart Surehand. As we row to the dragon, you will tell me how you magicked your trunk. That's a keen spell, that is!"

The short trip allowed the two youths to become fast friends. Dart spent most of his time describing Captain Olden and Ashe Fallow and passing on some wisdom about keeping on their good sides. The dragon ship drew near as they paddled out. The dragon's head dipped itself into the hay boat and crunched on a bite as big as a house. (Ocean dragons loved the taste of any dry-land vegetation.) The huge shell on its back had several deck sections bristling with magical blasting tubes. Enormous masts rose above these filled with crewmen in the rigging.

Hal stepped aboard his first commission on a small set of stairs cut into the dragon's armored shell. As he reached a middle deck, he was whistled aboard as an officer of the ship. He first saluted the king's flag and the whistler, then turned to salute and hand his papers to a huge man.

"Midshipwizard Tenth-class Halcyon Blithe requesting permission to come aboard, sir."

Hal looked at First-officer Dire Wily. There could be no mistaking him. Dart had warned that there was a hellishly powerful wizard on board as first officer. Hal could sense the waves of magic moving under Wily's skin.

"Young Blithe, welcome aboard," he said. "You will give your papers to Midshipwizard Fallow. He will be found on . . ."

ROAR!

The dragon let out a deafening, angry scream. Suddenly, drums were beating all around the ship, and men were running everywhere. Some were pointing away to starboard. With his mage-trained senses, Hal could feel two other dragon ships approaching fast through the mist.

First-officer Wily grabbed Hal's shoulder. "It's battle stations, boy! Get below and stay out of the way until it's all over!"

"Get below? Where . . ." But Wily was long gone down another almost invisible set of stairs. Surveying the deck, he saw there were only two dark entrances and several sets of stairs going up to other decks and down the way he had come. One cavity into the ship was jammed with men moving in and out, but the other was clear. Hal took the path of least resistance.

The second he stepped through the entrance, it closed on him. A large chunk of dragon shell completely blocked the way. Hal's first reaction was to blast the closed shell with magic, but he thought better of it.

"Light!" His trunk, still floating along behind him, glowed on his command. The corridor was made of bone and muscle, and it pulsed with the dragon's movements. Touching the side, he marveled at the warmth.

His sense of duty led him forward. The corridor branched into two small sections—one had men uncrating magical devices of some type. Maybe he could help here. He moved up to the officer.

"Sir, may I be of ass . . ."

"Out of the way, boy! Can't you see we are at battle stations? Find your post, idiot, and that's an order! Fire!" The tubes belched magical green goo that whistled through the air and out of sight. Crews raced to reload the tubes.

Hal ran the other way into the empty corridor and down to another large open door. Immediately he knew he was somewhere he shouldn't be. At the center of the large chamber hung a huge red and purple beating muscle. Giant strands of muscle led off from it in all directions through the floor and ceiling.

"The dragon's heart!" he muttered softly. He leaned in to get a closer look, but out of the corner of his eye he glimpsed someone leaving the heart chamber through another door. An officer, judging by his hat and battle cloak.

"Sir?" he called, but the officer was gone before he could answer.

BOOM! The dragon ship lurched, and Hal fell to the chamber floor. The enormous heart beat faster and louder, and from where he had fallen he could see a line of green goo at the bottom of the heart. Where it touched the heart, there came a sizzling sound and a whiff of burning meat. The goo was burning a hole in the dragon's heart!

BOOM! Again the ship rocked, and the rip in the muscle of the heart grew even wider. Hal saw the goo burn deeper with every beat of the heart.

This can't be good! This has to be stopped! he realized.

Throwing open the lid of his floating trunk, he searched for anything to stop the tearing. What could he use? He had to do something! Reaching into a secret compartment he pulled out his mother's gift to him. It was a vial of wishing potion she had gotten from the hill people. Using high magic like this was something he'd never tried before, but it was do or die, for him and for the dragon ship!

"Here goes," he whispered, splashing the contents of the vial all along the tear he summoned up the high magic and cast his will over the tear. A ten-foot waft of ice formed, completely sealing the smoking hole and freezing the spreading goo. Completely spent in the summoning, Hal collapsed unconscious to the floor.

*   *   *

Click!

Hal awoke. Heavy chains weighed him down.

"What the demon hell is this!"

A hand held him down in the bed.

"Midshipwizard Halcyon Blithe, it is my duty to inform you that you have committed an act of treason. You are to be judged by three officers of this ship to see if you should be hanged. The manacles I've placed on you are enchanted and won't allow you to use magic of any sort."

"Who are you, sir?" he gasped, remembering to be dignified.

"My name is Ashe Fallow, Midshipwizard First-class. Do you understand what I've told you?"

"Yes, sir. But I've done nothing wrong!"

Hal found himself weak in the knees. The manacles weighed him down, and their magic drained him somehow. All of his enchanted senses were blunted.

"Stiff upper lip, young man. You don't want the other officers to see you're scared. Walk in there proud and don't let them take anything away from your honor. Show them the metal of a good Lankster man."

Ashe helped him stand straight and he walked out the door and up the steps to a large chamber where the walls were of white dragon shell and light came in from the ceiling and sides.

Three officers stood at attention when he entered. The center officer was clearly Captain Tannen Olden, from Dart's description. He used a long dagger to ring a ship's bell on the table. He rang it three times and they all sat down, placing the dagger sideways on the table.

"I am Captain Olden. To my right is First-officer Wily, and on my left is Second-officer Gunnery Master Griffon. We are holding summary court on Midshipwizard Tenth-class Halcyon Blithe for violation of bann number 16, the use of high magic within a king's ship of the line. How do you plead, Mr. Blithe?"

"I don't understand what I did wrong. I don't know how to plead. Can someone explain things to me so that I don't say something wrong?"

"Bring him a chair, Mr. Fallow," said Wily. "I will explain things to him." Mr. Wily stood up and walked around the table. He waved his hands, and an image appeared in the air. It was an illusion of the heart chamber. There was a chunk of ice at the bottom of the heart where Hal had laid the potion.

"Mr. Blithe, you are charged with using high magic in the heart chamber. The use of high magic inside any king's ship is forbidden because of its powerful and unpredictable nature. This is bann number 16. All thirty-three banns are read every morning to the crew and officers of every king's ship. We fought a battle yesterday in which we destroyed one enemy dragon ship and drove off another. During this skirmish you felt the need to cast a powerful spell on the heart of our dragon ship. You need to tell us why you did it. If this court finds in your favor, you will live. If we find your reasons were not sufficient, you will hang an hour after that verdict is given. Do you understand?" Wily's huge form loomed over young Hal. The First-officer's black eyes bored into Hal's mind, numbing him. It was with great effort that the young midshipwizard threw off the effects of the officer's gaze.

"I now understand. May I tell my side?"

First-officer Wily sat down.

"Tell it, tell it! We are here to clear this up and get on with the war. Why in demon hell's name did you cast that infernal spell on the heart?" The captain was clearly agitated.

Hal, knowing his life was on the line, gave them every

detail from the time he got on the dragon ship to the time he cast his spell.

The captain roared at him. "Catalyst primer?" Hal didn't know what that meant. "Some hell-damned traitor put catalyst primer on my dragon's heart! I have to see this!"

All the officers got up and Hal started to as well. Mr. Fallow placed a hand on his shoulder and firmly held him in his chair. "Your betters can go. You have to stay here until they decide your case."

After the officers left, Ashe Fallow turned and faced young Hal. "I don't know the right or wrong of this case, but I will tell you how life is. Those three fine gentlemen will decide your fate. Before they announce if you will hang or not, they will tap that stupid bell three times with the ship's dagger. Then, if the dagger is placed blade forward, the verdict is death. If the blade is placed handle forward, you live. You will be given a chance to say something before the verdict. You and I are Lankster men, so I'm giving you this piece of free advice. If you are to die, don't go wailing about your sad life. Just take it like a man. If you are going to live, you make sure you tell them that you would do what you did even knowing about the banns because it was the right thing to do. You understand me, Halcyon Blithe of Lankster?"

Hal straightened his shoulders. His thoughts were of his home and family, of the people he would miss. "Perfectly Midshipwizard Fallow, perfectly. Thank you for the information."

Suddenly, the sound of boots could be heard in the corridor. The three officers came in and stood at attention behind their table. The captain rang the bell softly three times and placed the dagger hilt toward Hal.

"We have seen your impressive magic and noted the catalyst primer. Do you have anything to say before we pass sentence on you?"

"Captain, I did what I did to save the heart and the *Sanguine*. I thought the ship was in danger. I would do it again in the same situation, begging the captain's pardon."

"Well, be that as it may, this court finds you guilty of defying the king's bann number 16. After researching your statements, as the captain of the ship, I absolve you of your guilt as it clearly saved the life of the dragon. As punishment for your crime, you are sentenced to guarding the heart as your battle station for this tour of duty. This court is adjourned."

All smiles, First-officer Wily walked up to Hal. "Well done, young Blithe! After we investigated your magic, we could clearly see there was an act of sabotage and your action saved the ship. It's that type of thinking that makes fine officers. Keep up the good work."

Hal just stood there with a stupid grin on his face. He wasn't going to die. He'd even been told he'd done good work. The manacles fell to the floor.

"Don't be thinking you've done anything great, Mr. Blithe," Ashe chided. "You've a long way to go in this king's navy before you'll be treating with the likes of your officer betters. Now give me those papers you should have given me before we were blasted by dragon tubes and let's get you settled in proper."

"This is your standard boarding pike. In the hands of an expert it's the deadliest weapon on this ship. You, young gentleman, will learn how to use it and it just might save your life some day." Ashe scowled and scanned the midshipwizards present. "Mr. Blithe, come up here and take the instruction."

"Watch yourself, Hal, boy." Dart was all smiles. Until

Hal came aboard, Dart was the one to catch most of Ashe's ire.

Day ten of the voyage was much like all the other days. Hal had spent hours every day guarding the dragon's heart. No one ever came in or out of the chamber, so he didn't understand why it needed to be guarded. His magically formed ice had stayed there, and none of the ship's wizards could melt it. That gave Hal some satisfaction, but it kept his duty station mighty cold. The living dragon was great fun to explore, and Hal had learned to appreciate the soothing pulse of the living ship as he went to sleep every night. Ashe Fallow, on the other hand, was an entirely different matter. Despite being a fellow Lankster man, he was a beast.

"Hurry it along, Mr. Blithe! King and country won't wait for you to get up off your arse!"

Hal took the offered pike and instantly felt its magic. "There's an energy in this?"

"Yes, you young officer idiot. It should come as no surprise as we are on a magical living ship that some of its weapons have magical properties." Ashe was in a rare mood today. All of the midshipwizards were stripped down to work togs. Ashe was in a padded suit of armor covering him from head to toe. The armor didn't seem to slow him down much.

"The weapon you hold in your hand is ten feet long with a magical steel blade two feet long. One side of the blade is curved and razor sharp to deal with unarmored foes. The other side has a spike perfect for punching through armor. The magical energies in the blade are used mainly for defense, but a skilled spell caster can use them for offense as well. Now, Mr. Blithe, come at me with your pike and try to take my head off."

Hal couldn't believe what he heard. He just stood there amazed. "Won't I hurt you?"

"Idiot! Why do you think I have on all this padding? Have at it, man! Show some spine for a change!"

Hal swung the pike halfheartedly as Ashe.

THUNK!

His head slammed against the shell of the dragon ship's deck as Ashe's pike shaft tripped him up and sent him falling to the deck.

"Think, man! You aren't using a shovel. Lunge first to get the feel of your foe, then try all the stupid moves you want!"

Hal looked at the world through a haze of blinking stars and pain. He slowly got up.

"Mr. Fallow, would you mind if I took a turn at that?" First-officer Wily stepped up and took Hal's pike. The weapon appeared small in his massive hands.

"Gentlemen, Mr. Fallow here is the ship's expert with the boarding pike. But if you are quick enough and use the length of this fine weapon you can do him some damage. Let's have at it until first strike, Mr. Fallow."

"Begging your pardon sir, but you aren't armored, if it pleases you, sir."

"Really not a problem, Mr. Fallow." With a wave of his hand, a red glow covered his body. All of the midship-wizards were stunned. Defensive magic like the shield Mr. Wily had just put up usually took hours to conjure and lots of mystic words and gestures to perform. It was an impressive display of arcane skill.

"Well, then," Ashe suggested, "let's give it a go."

They both whirled like lightning. The young officers in attendance learned a great deal in the next few minutes. Tripping tricks, feints that were fake and strikes that were not, and all sorts of ways to twirl the heavy weapons were put on display. The combat made it very clear that both officers were masters of the weapon. In a blazingly fast move, First-officer Wily struck at the padded hand of Ashy and the battle was over.

All of the midshipwizards looked at each other, wondering why the two had stopped. Ashe saw their questioning looks and spoke up as Mr. Wily gave back the pike to Hal and walked to the outer circle of the deck with a smile on his face.

"His blow would have taken off my hand. It's difficult if not impossible to use the pike one-handed." Ashe was breathing hard and clearly angry at the defeat. "I believe that should be part of your training as well. Mr. Blithe, let us say you have had your left hand wounded in battle and can't use it. Try and figure out the magical defensive properties of the pike and stop me from ramming my weapon down your throat."

Hal knew he was in for it by the sound of Ashe's voice. The teacher ran and lunged. Hal could think of nothing but throwing all of his magical energies through the pike. A huge, yellow pulse of power flowed from the pike bathing Ashe in a blast that blew him off his feet and threw him twenty feet across the deck.

"Ack!" Ashe's armor was black, and there was a disjointed look on his face. As the others crowded around him, all he could say was a very soft, weak, "Ack."

"Dart, get the ship's doctor." First-officer Wily lifted Ashe's head. "Well, gentlemen, you have just gotten an early preview of the magically offensive properties of the boarding pike. I think the lessons are finished for the day. Don't worry about Mr. Fallow, he'll recover very quickly. Young Hal, well done, few wizards could force the power you did through that pike. It's clear Mr. Blithe is an officer to be reckoned with. You all should take note and learn from him."

Wily was all smiles, so Hal knew he wasn't in trouble. Things would probably go hard on him when Ashe got out of sickbay, though.

"Ack."

By the look and sound of the man, that wouldn't be for a few days.

Day twenty-four found the dragon ship off the Demon coasts looking for enemy ships. Dragon ships were often given single duty apart from the fleet. They were fast and deadly vessels easily capable of battling four or five normal enemy ships of the line. The living vessels didn't usually work well with other ships of their kind. Dominance clashes among dragon ships of the line were frequent and unpredictable when more than one gathered together for any reason.

The cloudy, windy day made the sea choppy. The dragon was nervous as well, constantly trumpeting its battle cry over the sea.

Hal heard the captain say, "Well, if our dragon yearns to do battle, we might as well oblige the lady. Mr. Wily, we will do battle station drills all day."

Hal knew what that meant, and he picked up his boarding pike and walked the stairs to the heart chamber even before the battle drums set their beat.

Hours later, a miserable Hal stood at attention at his post. Dart and his other fellow midshipwizards got to man the blast tubes or sail the ship in complicated battle maneuvers. They got all the fun tasks while he guarded a chunk of ice of his own making and a heart no one paid any attention to most of the time. He found himself wishing he'd never walked into this chamber. What good was it to be an officer in the king's navy if he never got the chance to look out onto the sea?

"So much for being a man of prospects."

"Feeling sorry for yourself, Mr. Blithe?"

Hal twirled to discover First-officer Wily at his side. The officer was in his battle cloak, and the red magical shield was activated around his body. The big man moved like a cat. Hal hadn't heard anything, and the officer was standing not two feet away.

"Aye, sir. I mean no, sir. Just standing my post as ordered."

"Well, I think you've done enough guarding of our ship's heart. Go down to the gunner's post and help man the tubes. Now there is a good post for an officer of your talents."

Hal couldn't believe his luck. He moved to go and then realized his mistake.

"Sorry, sir. You don't know how much I would love to do that. Bann number 1 states that no crewmember may leave his assigned post during battle stations unless the captain orders it or there is an emergency. I appreciate the offer, sir."

"It wasn't an offer, Midshipwizard Blithe, it was a direct order." Wily seemed to grow larger and magical energies visibly crackled around his body. "Move your arse out of here and report to the gunnery officer!"

"I can't, sir. You know that. What are you thinking?"

The doors to the chamber all slammed shut. First-officer Wily loomed over Hal. His eyes began to glow, harsher than they had at his trial. Hal gestured and placed a simple yellow protective force over his mind and body.

"I'm thinking, you fool, that this ship and its crew need to die! I must now destroy this heart!" Demon horns burst through the skin on Wily's forehead. Black, crackling death magic stretched out from his hands toward Hal.

"You're a shapechanger!" Horror filled Hal's mind, but his training saved his life. He used the defensive energies of the pike to block the deadly magic. Yellow sparks stopped the black death energies just short of touching Hal. They would have killed him instantly. Hal cast all the protective magic he knew on his body and mind. With this terrible creature changing in front of him, he had strong doubts they would be enough.

"We will just have to take that toy away from you."

Hands gnarled into talons and the demon shapechanger's bones crackled and popped as it grew to at least eight feet in height. Clothing tore and fell away as the man became an enormous monster of razor-sharp scales and four-taloned arms.

"Oh, yes, that's much better." Its voice was deep and menacing, its accent unknown to Hal. "You little humans are such boring creatures. And having two of most things, I've always wondered how you can stand it."

Hal faced a creature from his worst nightmares. It had a huge head with four eyes and four ears. There were fangs jutting out of its mouth in all directions. Every time it moved its neck or arms, it made noise like grinding bones.

Hal lunged and used all of his magical force to plant the spike in the heart of the monster, but the weapon bounced off the creature's red-shielded chest.

"You just aren't strong enough. Maybe if you would have lived another hundred years or so, you could have managed that cut. Give up, little mortal. Why make this more difficult than it has to be?"

Hal tried his yellow pulse. Knowing his life was on the line, he put all his magical effort into the act. A huge blast of sun-bright energy bathed the monster, but didn't move it an inch.

"Oh, a nasty attack that, and so bright, too. I think maybe

it's possible you've singed some of my hairs. Pity. We monsters love to look our best, don't you know. Well done, but I think you'll find your magic lacking against me."

With a chuckle, the Wily monster plucked the pike from Hal's hands and threw it to the side. One-handed, he picked up young Hal and lifted him high off the deck. Panic filled the midshipwizard. He tried to think of something, anything, he could do. The monster's grip on his throat was killing him by inches.

"You would have become quite a powerful wizard, human. It's a good thing I caught you before you could do some real damage to me and my kind. I sense you have such a powerful essence. But enough talk! It's past time to take your life and get on with destroying this ship!"

Gray draining magics flowed from the creature's talons to cover Hal's entire body. He tried to scream from the pain and cast protective magics, but caught as he was in the monster's clutches, no sound could come from his throat. The gray draining energies tore at his heart and mind.

Hal gurgled a scream and suddenly dropped to the floor. He was loose! A boarding pike erupted from the chest of the monster, spilling blue gore in all directions. Hal heard Ashe's voice as the creature hit the floor.

"There's more than one officer aboard this king's dragon ship who can move quietly and get through closed doors, sir! I think you will find a boarding pike in the hands of an expert can be the deadliest weapon on this ship!" The monster's eyes glazed over and it went limp. "Stupid, shapechanging monsters who would imitate their betters would do well to keep that in mind as I send them back to hell!"

The monster fell to its knees. To Hal's horror, the huge, gaping wound started closing and regeneration magics wove its flesh back together with a knitting-needle sound. Ripping the weapon out of the creature's chest, Ashe turned it and chopped off its head, casting his own emerald magics to penetrate the shapechanger's red magical shield.

"I think you will find, First-officer Wily, that it's difficult to regenerate a head, even for a shapechanger. Well, my boyo, I thought our traitor would try something while everyone was busy."

"You knew he was the traitor?" Hal rubbed his nearly crushed throat and caught fresh breath.

"Yes. I've been hanging around these parts and heard your little give and take with our Mr. Wily. While you aren't the smartest card in our deck, you did yourself well to last even those few seconds against this monster."

"Thanks, I think."

"I must apologize for the delay in making the killing stroke. If it would have known I was behind it, this battle would have gone much differently. This little action is another of life's lessons for you, Mr. Blithe. If you can't be the most powerful, it's best to have a few tricks up your sleeve. After our monster Wily bested me the other day, I did a little research on his crimson shield and how to get around it."

"I never thought of you as a bookworm," Hal confessed.

"Being prepared is the duty of any officer. It was just my lucky day that I could put my new knowledge to such good use."

Ashe Fallow took the pike and bathed the monster in more emerald magic. The thing melted on the chamber floor, turning into a hairless, featureless humanoid thing and then became nothing more than blue ooze.

"Nasty business, shapechangers. A smelly mess this. Now, normally I would make you clean this up, Mr. Blithe."

"Aye, Mr. Fallow."

"None of that now. We Lankster men must stick together. I'll send Mr. Surehand down. He could use a little scrubbing detail, don't you know."

"Excellent thought, sir. I'll continue manning my post."

"Well spoken. We'll make an officer of you yet. I'll report to the captain."

Mr. Fallow handed back the pike and left the cabin.

Hal found himself thinking guarding a dragon's heart wasn't such bad duty after all. He would, however, need to work on his defensive spells. Eight-foot tall, ravening monsters shouldn't be able to kill him that easily.

He was a Lankster man after all.

Dart came in holding his nose, asking, "Whew, what is that stink?"

Hal just smiled.

CATCH OF THE DAY

BY JEFF GRUBB

Therefore will we not fear, though the earth be re-
moved, and though the mountains be carried into the
midst of the sea.

—Psalms 46:2

OLD Eustes, perched up at the peak of mainsail, spotted Scholar August Gold first, and let out a sea-cry to
warn the rest of the *Antigiam*'s crew.

"The new bird has arrived!" he bellowed with leathery
lungs. "Tell the captain!"

"What sort of bird be he?" responded the ship's master, her round face turned skyward.

"Paycock, by the looks of 'im," shouted Eustes, not di-
minishing his volume in the least. "With a long tail as
well."

Indeed, the ship's master had to agree with the wizened
lookout as she saw the new arrival striding down the broad
granite stairs of Calendonia Harbor. This newcomer was a
flashy bird, all right, his buff coat still single in color and
unstained by the elements, and his trousers ironed with
creases that could cut cold butter. His face was smooth,
but narrow, partially concealed by pince-nez spectacles, and
the neatness of his outfit was spoiled by the casual disar-

ray of his hair, its short brown spikes pointing to every direction of the compass and a few new points as well.

In his wake the newcomer towed a veritable army of bearers, each carrying an overstuffed crate or trunk. Two bore spools of rope, and two more carried what looked like small anchors.

The ship's master ran her heavy fingers through her graying hair and sent one of the deckboys below for the captain. She hoped the arrival of this peacock, this passenger, would at last calm the captain's obvious feelings of ill ease. For the past three months since taking command, "Black Cat" Meridan had acted as if she expected the roof to fall in on her. Perhaps this would dispel those worries.

For his part, the peacock, August Gold, paused and inhaled the mist-laden harbor air. The *Antigiam* was berthed right where the harbormaster said it would be, past the two xebecs and just before the drydocks. The xebecs and the *Antigiam* rocked gently at their moorings, their hulls half-sunk into the heavy clouds that supported them.

Indeed, the day was perfect; there were only light striations of overclouds moving like a schoolteacher's scrawl over a deeper blue vault, steadily moving on a northern breeze. The real cloudscape, the stuff that man sailed upon, was a thick blanket surrounding the mountain peak that was Calendonia. It looked solid and heavy and thick enough to eat with a spoon.

He knew that if he continued down the mountainside, he would pass through and fall under the shadows of those clouds, into the dimly-lit world of foothills and valleys that rarely saw light.

That was the world below, the world of lightning-storms and bitter rains, the world where man used to live (if the old tales were true), where all manner of fantastic beasts once dwelled. Unicorns. Elves. And most of all, dragons.

Now, August Gold, newly minted researcher of the newly minted College of History and Mythology looked upon the ship that would carry him to that land.

The *Antigiam* was a small ship, almost a skimmer, and was dwarfed by the heavier, slowly rocking xebecs along the quay. It was narrow, and fitted with an outrigger, a secondary spar of floatwood lying along the ship's left side.

August pursed his lips for a moment. Not left. Port. The *Antigiam* had a port-mounted outrigger. Despite a second in atmospherics at University, August knew little of sailing itself, and most of what he did know came out of several small digests that were packed away with the rest of his library.

August, his retainers in a slow train behind him, paced up the gangplank. He was met at the top by a thick-bodied, gray-haired woman, wearing the torc of a freewoman. He gave a crisp University bow.

"August Gold, reporting to the *Antigiam*," he said, then added uncertainly, "permission to come aboard."

"Sandotter, Master of the *Antigiam*," said the woman, and August's hand drifted to his vest pocket. "You'll be wanting to give those papers to the captain. I'm only the master—I take the ship where the captain tells me. She's the true commander of this vessel."

August noted the slight stress on the word "she," a testing of the waters, a hard look to see if he would flinch. Some men reacted to the old-fashioned notion of freewomen badly, and there were those within the Commonwealth Chambers seeking to phase them out. It was a touchy political issue.

August, for his part, merely bowed slightly and said "My humble mistake. And our captain is . . ."

"That would be me," said a tall, imposing woman by August's right shoulder. He had not heard her approach. She had a well-formed face and deeply-set eyes, eyes that in another place and time could be considered "laughing." But not here, on the deck of her vessel. Here she was the commander, and her hair was a thick black mane that framed her strong features like smoke.

"Jemmapolis Meridan," she said, extending a hand. "Captain of the *Antigiam*. You must be Scholar Gold."

"Just Mr. Gold, if you please," said August.

The captain took the oilskin folder, breaking the blue-leaded seal with the offhanded ease of someone who had dealt with admiralty orders all her life.

She scowled at the orders for the long moment, and the entire ship seemed to fall silent. Indeed, the entire world seemed to wait.

Then she snapped, "Madam Sandotter!"

"Captain?"

"Are we ready to sail?"

"Awaiting your orders, ma'am."

"Cast away, then, and make a heading past the Deep Rocks, bearing south by southeast."

"South by . . ." the ship's master paused for a moment, "That's Church waters. You mean we're . . ."

"Yes," said Jemma Meridan, "We're bound for the Holy Sea."

"It's the most dangerous patch of ocean in this misbegotten world," said Captain Meridan, slapping the rolled orders in one hand. "Exactly why are we going there? These orders fail to elaborate."

They were in the forward quarters set aside for the scholar, a tight space even before Gold's arrival. Now it was loaded with the crates, barrels, two small anchors, two

huge rolls of rope (bringing rope and anchors onto a ship?
she thought; what was the scholar thinking?) and books
(far too many of these). Meridan was used to cramped
quarters, but this was tight even by naval standards.

Gold leaned back, and almost lost balance from his perch
on the back of a sea chest. Meridan stifled a chortle.

"It all breaks down to a question of history, a question
of the old tales," he said, readjusting his spectacles. "A
question of dragons."

Despite herself, Meridan grimaced. Scratch a scholar,
and find a nostalgic, one pining for the supposed golden
age when the world was not wrapped in eternal clouds,
cloaked save for a few mountain islands and plateaus. A
time of heroes, it was said, a time when mankind sailed
on water, not on the cloudscape canopy.

She confined herself to a brief, "Dragons are a myth,"
and looked at her green-ink instructions again, as if to seek
out some overlooked illumination. They remained mad-
deningly unclear.

"Myths have their basis in truth," said August, "and it
is the scholar's job to find that truth."

And the captain's job to haul you about while you search,
thought Meridan, but she only nodded and said, "And the
particular truth you seek is dragons."

"There are numerous legends of the great beasts," said
August. "Check your Horatio, check your Aubrey. Check
all of your great historians . . ."

"Poets," said Meridan.

"Poets as well," nodded August. "Visionaries of their
times. They speak of dragons that flew through the sky,
defying all science and magic, breathing fire and raining
destruction down from above."

"And you want to *find* these creatures?" said Meridan.

"If anything survived the deluge and devastation," said

August, "if anything survived the Times Before, it would be them. Huge creatures they were, resistant to storm and lightning alike. They fought over their territories like ancient barons, often to the death. Only the bravest and most fortunate survived them."

Now the scholar's face was animated, and his features positively glowing beneath his spectacles. Not only a nostalgic, thought Meridan, but a would-be poet as well.

"In deed," said Meridan, making it two words, the repeating. "And you want to find these?"

"Of course," said Gold. "My thesis depends on it."

"And all this . . ." Meridan pointed to the collection of chests.

"Some notebooks, some research texts," said August. "A lot of cable. About a mile's worth, hemp wound with steel strands for strength. Lanterns. Anchors, of course, with sharpened blades. And replacements, of course."

Meridan was impressed. She said, "And you think the dragons would be . . . ?"

"Before the Deluge, the area we are making for was a broad, rich plain, filled with herds of wild beasts. Perfect hunting grounds. If the dragons survived, they would be there."

"That 'broad, rich plain' is now under nearly a mile of cloud-cover," said Captain Meridan.

"Which is why we haven't found them so far," nodded August.

"It is also territory claimed by the Holy Church. They're quite prickly about Commonwealth Ships in general, and scholars in particular." And me most of all, she added to herself.

August Gold's face fell only a trifle. "I was informed that you knew your business, Captain," said the scholar. "When I made the request three months ago . . ."

"Three months ago?" said Meridan. "How long have you been planning this little expedition?"

"Why, this type of research, these resources, take years to work up through the hierarchy," said August. "Three months ago I finally received the full grant, and requested through the Admiralty board for a fast ship and a fearless captain. I was informed that Black Cat Meridan was the best choice. I'm sorry, have I offended?"

Jemma Meridan tried to erase the frown from her features. "No, of course not," she began to explain, but then young Smith appeared at the hatch, saying the harbormaster had signaled. "I'm needed on deck, Scholar . . . Mr. Gold. Please stow your gear, as best you can, and join me when you are available."

Calendonia was the last of the Commonwealth ports to the southeast, hard on the bookbanging thunderheads of the Holy Sea. From the small quarter-deck of the *Antigiam*, Meridan saw the harbor now drop away, the low mountains of the headland becoming a muddy purplish shadow only broken by the beam of the jetty's lighthouse.

The *Antigiam* cut a nice figure, reaching a point abaft the beam with only its mainsail unfurled, lanteen-rigged in the southern style. There was no need for the sternmast yet, nor the spankers, not until they had lost the landbreeze entirely. In the ship's wake, the clouds beneath churned in two lines—a wide one for the main hull, and a thin, pencil-like scrawl of the outrigger.

Three months, thought Jemma. That fit exactly with the commission from Lord Simon, unexpected and unhoped for. There were more than enough captains without ships dogging the halls of the Admiralty, and Jemma had earned both cheers and jealous stares when it was reported in the

Gazetteer. Few captains get a posting after losing a ship. And Jemma had lost two.

The nickname Black Cat did not come from her hair, but from her run of luck.

But here she was, back at the helm once more. This August Gold must have pull. In deed.

She had had three months of message-carrying and hunting phantom pirates. Of training the crew. When she had gotten her, the *Antigiam* had its share of malingers, impressed mountain men, and deck lawyers, but over time and with the incessant rhythm of the life on the clouds they had been whipped into a reasonable shape.

What they sorely lacked was gunnery. She had but two cannon, a squat flight-gun in the stern and a chaser in the bow. Still, with only three rounds of powder on board, it was a dumbshow drill, shorn of real shot, and she was unsure how the crew would perform under fire. Not that it would matter—if they ran into anything larger than a holy hymn-boat, they would have to run.

There was a flurry of japing laughter on the main deck, and Meridan snapped back to the real world. Mister Gold had apparently arrived on deck.

The scholar was costumed as a tortoise, carrying a curved board strapped to his back, and a similarly huge plank over his chest. Additional shards of wood were strapped to his forearms and thighs. His spectacles were covered with additional heavy lenses set into a broad leather band that encircled his head.

Old Eustes was nearly cataleptic in his delight at the sight of the scholar, and Knorri and Gunnar were busy slapping each other on the back in convulsives. Even Crossgreves, the sourpussed purser that counted every gram of gunpowder like it was gold, cracked a smile.

"What," said August Gold, looking as proper as man can be when dressed like a shelled reptile, "is so funny?"

"What is the meaning of this, Mr. Gold, disturbing my crew like this?" said Meridan.

August thumped the front of his chest, "Floatwood, Captain. The same as in the seam of your hulls. Finest grain, I was informed by the salesman."

August's statement of his wooden armor's provenance sent Eustes and the others into further paroxysms of laughter.

"The finer the grain, the better the floatation," continued August.

"Have you had the chance to test your . . ." Meridan tried not to crack a grin, "suit?"

"I was unpacking and thought there was no time like the present."

"Indeed," said the captain, adding sharply, "Mr. Gunnar, what is the sounding?"

At the sound of her demand, Gunnar stopped in mid-chortle, "Ten fathoms, by the pilot's chart."

"Then play out fifty feet of rope," said Meridan, "Mr. Knorri, please secure Mr. Gold's . . . outfit . . . securely."

The wide-shouldered Norlander worker quickly fit August with a firm harness, lashed at the back.

"What is all this?" asked August.

"An experiment," said the captain. "As any scholar would know. Mr. Gunnar, Mr. Knorri?"

"Aye, Captain?"

"Throw our guest overboard, please."

August Gold let out a squawk as each of the sailors grabbed him under the arms and pulled him to the port side. Without a pause or even a grunt on their part they heaved the shouting scholar over the side.

He hit the clouds and disappeared, leaving a hole like

a cannonball through the canopy and a lingering scream. The line played out behind.

"Slow that line!" snapped the captain, "I don't want to hang him! Easy now. There. Hold him at fifty." A slow count to ten, then, "Haul him back up."

The August Gold that returned to deck was red-faced and sputtering, chewing off curses. As soon as Gunnar untied the harness, the scholar was ripping off his wooden armor, flinging pieces of it overboard. When they landed on the cloud they disappeared, falling through.

The angry scholar turned toward the captain, and for the first time Meridan saw the fury contained within the slender man. It lasted only an instant, but it was there, a very unscholarly passion.

Quickly August composed his features and said, "You knew."

"I suspected," said the captain. "Often the gaudier the armor, the less protection it offers."

"I should have guessed," said August. "Often the flashiest relic of the past is really some huckster's trick. It never occurred to me that someone would lie about floatwood."

"It's better to find out now, as opposed to later," said Meridan. "Mr. Crossgreves?"

"Aye?" said the purser.

"Fit Mr. Gold with a proper belt of floatwood. I'd say two spans should do it. Enough to keep him aloft." The purser knitted his brows together at the thought of opening something else of his precious stores, but nodded.

"And Mr. Gold?" the captain added toward the scholar's back.

"Yes?" said August, and the captain caught another flicker of lightning beneath that brow.

"I would like to invite you to dinner tonight," said the captain. "Unless you have other plans?"

"No other plans," said August Gold. "I will be there."

Wine soothes many ills, reflected August Gold, and washes away much embarrassment.

Captain Jemma Meridan served a fine table, and it had only benefited from its recent stay in port. A half-boar, laid out on wild rice seasoned with currants and apples dominated the small table. In addition, Crossgreves had laid in some very fine bottles of an Eastern Bloodwine, and didn't even seem perturbed as the captain opened the third one of the evening.

The quarters were tight, but no more than at a scholar's dorm. And indeed, August's stomach responded quite easily to the rocking motion of the clouds beneath the ship's hull. In the tiny gunroom were Gold, Crossgreves, Mr. Baker the master's mate, and Sandotter, as well as Young Smith, doing the serving.

And the captain, of course, her broad shoulders rising above her compatriots'. The *Antigiam* was a small ship, but even so, as captain it was her duty to lead the conversation.

"Eat up," she encouraged, "for it will be rice pudding and jerky for the next week, and after that we'll be down to normal fare—bangers and mash."

"And weevil-biscuit and water if we stay out too long," noted Crossgreves, and August had little doubt that the purser knew to the minute when that instant would be.

The topics wavered with the wine. Meridan would tolerate no talk of national politics at the table, but there was enough with stories from port, of prizes taken against the Ruq, and the various sizes of Churchships. Meridan commented on the apparent superiority of the *Antigiam*'s rigging, though its own strength put horrible stress on the ship's frame. Burrows, the ship's carpenter, was continually complaining.

"Antigiam," said August. "That was a hero's name, of course."

"It is named after another ship," said the captain. "The first was the discoverer of Thunderer's Cove and set aflame at the Battle of the Dunne."

"Aye, but before that," said August. "Before the Deluge."

Meridan shook her head, but August pressed on. "Antigiam was a hero, back in those days; in a suit of glittering armor he battled against the hordes of darkness. He alone defended the Khelson Pass against the unliving forces of an ancient necromancer, and when they found his body after four days of battle, it was surrounded by a mound of bones twenty feet high."

"You said 'found his body,'" said Sandotter. "So I take it he didn't survive the experience."

"He did not," said Mister Gold. "But his legend lived on, such that the first *Antigiam* was named after him."

"Fable," said Meridan. "Epic poetry."

"Lost fact," countered August. "I take it you do not believe in the Lost Times?"

"If you challenge me to deny that man once lived beneath these clouds, I will defer to your greater knowledge. But if you ask me if I am a nostalgic, longing for the past, the answer, I'm afraid, is no."

"I confess surprise," said August. "I always thought of captains as romantics at heart."

"We captains are pragmatics," said Meridan. "You have to be, to survive away from the safe shores of the peaks. You cannot long for the past, I'm afraid, so I leave it to the poets."

"And historians," said August evenly. "So tell me, Captain, what do *you* think happened to the world? How it got like this?"

"It doesn't matter much, does it?" said the captain. "The world is as it is, and we just have to live in it."

"I always heard," said Baker, "that there was a crystal heart at the center of the world, and someone broke it and released a cloud that wrapped around the globe."

"Nay, you're daft," said Crossgreves. "They had too much hocjo. Too much magic. That caused the world to cloud over."

"You're both wrong," added Sandotter. "It just started raining one day and forgot to stop. It's just simple natural processes."

The captain, pouring herself another mug of wine, asked, "So, Mr. Gold, how *did* the world come to be wrapped in clouds?"

"No one knows," said August Gold. "But *I* think someone killed a god."

There was silence for a moment around the table, then everyone broke out at once. All except Meridan.

"Really," said Sandotter with a giggle.

"Now *that's* daft," said Crossgreves. "Begging your pardon, Scholar."

"It would explain why the Churchmen act like they have a wasp up their kirtles," said Baker, "if somebody killed God."

"Not God," corrected August. "*A* god. There were many such powerful beings once, the old tales said. Only some being of that magnitude could cause it to start raining and *keep* raining for a hundred years, wrapping the world in a blanket of clouds such that the only survivors had to hike up to the mountaintops and start again. And only killing such a being could release such power."

Crossgreves snorted, but Baker and Sandotter nodded.

"Have you proof of your gods?" asked Meridan.

"No. I don't even have proof of my dragons yet," said August.

"I've been meaning to ask, Mister Gold," said Meridan. "Tell me, how *do* you intend to prove the existence of your fabled dragons?"

"Why, Captain, I thought you had figured it out, looking at my equipment," said August Gold calmly. "I intend to go fishing for them."

"Bait," said August, holding up a blackened vial stoppered in wax. Meridan saw something gelatinous ooze within the glass walls.

They were in the hold of the ship, around the deadman's hatch. On a traditional boat a hole in the bottom would be suicide, but beneath the *Antigiam*'s hull were only thick clouds. The deadman's hatch was traditionally used to consign the bodies from the ship into the cloud beneath.

The three of them, Meridan, Gold, and Baker, now clustered around the open deadman's hatch. Beneath them there were only the reddish clouds. August had set up a great spool of his wired rope alongside the hatch, with a second spool next to it.

They were three weeks into the voyage, well into the bangers and mash stage, and would not have to "hit the biscuit" for another two weeks. Twice they had to run before a storm, and three times spotted sails on the horizon and fled before discovery. Now, however, a thick mist rose in the morning, providing more than enough cover the *Antigiam* to drift, its sails furled, for August Gold's experiment.

"Enough for two tries," said August. "I tried to get a sample from another museum, but the curator was . . . well, let's say that we had words, and I queered my chances."

"And in that glass is . . . ?" said Meridan.

"Dragon's Blood," said August, "or at least what we think is Dragon's Blood. It may be another hoax, like the floatwood armor." He reddened for a moment, then pressed on, "But the provenance is good."

"Don't Dragon's Blood prove there were dragons?" said Baker.

"Doesn't," corrected August, "and it proves there *were* dragons, but not that there *are* dragons."

"And this will prove it how?" asked the captain.

"The Old Tales, the 'Fables,' say that dragons were very territorial creatures," said August, "such that the smell of another dragon in their territory would bring them out for combat."

"Sounds like the Churchmen," said Baker with a grin.

"But this blood is ancient," noted Meridan. "Surely even a reptile won't be brought up by cold blood."

"Which is why I created this," said August Gold, pulling out a lanternlike device. "This censer will vaporize the blood into a fine mist, which should be carried by the undercloud currents. If there's a dragon here in the Holy Sea, we'll find it."

"A large if," said the captain.

"A large dragon," countered the scholar.

After another twenty minutes of fiddling, August poured a small bit of the fluid into the lantern's porous mantle, and set it aflame. The mantle guttered for a moment, then sprang to life, and a rich, sanguine odor permeated the hold.

Meridan's eyes watered, and Baker held his nose, but to August it seemed he was sniffing a fine wine. He shut the door of the censer, clipped the lantern to the sharpened flukes of one of his great anchors, and dropped the entire collection through the hatch. Baker stood at the spool, the crank in hand.

"Carefully lower it now," said August, fishing out a note-book and pen, "and call out the measurements as they pass."

Long moments passed, broken only by Baker's regular chanting as the wire-wound rope unspooled. A hundred feet to clear the cloud canopy. Then two hundred. Then three hundred. Six hundred. At nine hundred the scholar said, "Hold."

Meridan looked at them, the scholar hunched over the deadman's hatch, the master's mate gripping the crank. A long moment passed. The musky fumes had cleared out of the hold now, though Meridan had no doubts that they were steaming away far below them.

Five minutes passed. At last Meridan said, "In deed. I don't think your dragon's at home."

That's when the ship's line went taut, and the entire hull shook.

"Snag?" said Meridan.

"Depth by the pilot's chart?" said August.

"Nearly a mile," said the captain. No, she realized, it wasn't a snag.

Then whatever it was at the far end of the line pulled, and Baker was flung forward into a bulkhead from the sudden jerk on the spool.

"The crank!" shouted Meridan. "Grab the crank!"

But it was already too late. The creature at the far end of the line dove like a trout taking the bait, unspooling the line behind it. The crank whipped around now, almost a blur, a heavy club to threatening to break the fingers of anyone who attempted to grab it. The wire-wound rope began to smoke from the friction of its unplaying.

Captain Meridan realized what would happen when they reached the end of the rope. She ran to the deck hatch and bellowed upward. "Make sail! Spread the cloth!"

"How much, Captain?" came the reply.

"All of it!" shouted the captain. "Every sheet and spanker!"

Overhead they could hear the clatter of feet running to unfurl every inch of sail. The captain went forward in the hold. Through the bones of the ship she could feel it straining already as it gathered the wind within its sails and surged forward.

For his part, August could only watch the rope unspool, the line nothing more than a blur. Surely whatever it was at the other end would abandon the bait with the heavy line behind it. Surely . . .

But no, the last of the line, firmly secured to the heart of the spool itself, unleashed, and pulled tight.

The entire ship gave a heavy shudder, the wind above pulling one way, the creature on the line the other. Even August could feel it now, the tension carried through the rope and into the ship itself.

Then, above, more shouting. The ship was not making any progress. Indeed, it was starting to slip backward through the clouds, leaving its wake ahead of it.

Worse yet, the stern was starting to dip deeper into the clouds themselves.

August Gold was frozen until the captain returned, an ax in hand, and took it to the rope. The rope, strengthened by the wire wrapped around it, refused to part despite her best efforts.

Above, more shouts. Something about the mainmast.

Meridan wheeled to August and snapped, "Tell them to drop the sails. Just drop the rigging!"

August stared at her goggle-eyed.

"The tension is too much. The mainmast is splintering!" snarled the captain. "Drop the rigging or we'll lose it!"

August staggered off to the deck hatch and bellowed up the captain's order. There was more scuffling of feet, followed by a great thunderous crash as the main boom landed on the deck above them.

When August turned back he saw that the captain had abandoned attacking the rope and was taking out the spool's mounting instead. The heavy chips of wood flew in all directions as the spool splintered, but still it refused to part from its mounting.

August stumbled back to the deadman's hatch. They were almost through the cloud cover now, and the reddish darkness of the land spread beneath them. It was illuminated by lightning storms far below. Despite himself, August gripped the belt of floatwood that he had been fitted with, and hoped that this one worked.

The line itself drifted like a silver line, drawn with a ruler, straight astern. And there, at the limits of his vision, was something hooked to its end.

Something indistinct in this twilight realm, but incredibly large.

Finally there was the shriek of wood giving way and the shattered spool uprooted itself from the deck. The smashed disks of the spool flickered briefly, and then they were gone.

The *Antigiam* surged upward like a cork, and August was knocked from his feet again. There were shouts of panic from above, and the ship rocked precariously to the starboard, its outrigger raised high in the open air. Then another sway as it stabilized.

Meridan pressed past him. August checked on Baker, to find the young man knocked out, his breathing ragged, then staggered upwards to follow the captain.

When he got to the deck, the captain was already talking to Burrows the carpenter, a young lady who said everything in a loud, Scolven accent. He clearly caught: "Nearly *splin*tered as it wah-ess. Can't tay-eck full sail."

The captain cursed, and August said, "Mr. Baker's been knocked out. It might be a concussion."

Meridan turned toward him, her face filled with thunder. "We have no doctor. Can you address it?"

August's jaw flopped open a moment, then he said, "I have some basic physiology."

"Do what you can," said the captain. "I'm going to take us back to port."

"Port?" said August, startled, "We can't go back now. We're on the verge of discovering something amazing!"

"We have discovered something that can drag this ship to the bottom of the cloudscape," said Meridan. "You can go back to the ministry and get a larger ship. This one is done."

"I still have Dragon's Blood," started August, "and another spool. I brought replacements. We can't return as long as there are options available."

Meridan turned to say something, but the words came from far aloft. "Sail ho!"

Immediately the captain craned her neck upward, the scholar forgotten. "Position?"

East by northeast, said the watch, and Meridan was up the ladder for the quarter-deck. As she passed, she snapped at August, "Scholar, I think we're suddenly out of options."

The rising mist had served to conceal the *Antigiam*, but had concealed their pursuer as well. Now as the fog burned off, it was large enough on the horizon to see clearly without a lens. Meridan brought it under her glass and cursed loudly.

"Church?" asked August.

"A Holy Tomebook of a ship," said the captain, "Not a Bible, one of the big ones, but big enough. And it has the wind gauge on us."

"Meaning?"

"When we turn, it can turn to follow us more easily. Madam Sandotter!"

"Ma'am!"

"Haul that sail off the deck and heave to!"

"Captain, that last stunt nearly splintered the mast," said Crossgreves, Burrows in tow. "If we rig it up full, it could splinter clear through."

"Then spread cloth halfway," said Meridan, "and get the sternmast and spanker rigged. We're going to need all the speed we can muster."

August said, "We have guns."

Meridan shook her head, "We have two small chasers that can't be brought to bear at the same time. A crew that hasn't fired live ammunition since we commissioned. A Tomebook-class ship has at least a dozen guns to a side, likely."

Around them the ship's master was shouting at the crewmen, as every bit of sail that could safely be spread was issued. Even so, the mainmast creaked dangerously in the wind.

On the horizon, the Churchship grew larger. August could see it had three masts, and stacks of embroidered sail.

"If they catch us . . ." started August, then stopped, and started again. "The Church does not care for scholars."

"It does not care for much of anyone," said Captain Meridan in a clipped tone. "Look at the forward mast. It flies a Brothers' pennant, you see. This ship has a single-sex crew. Those are always nasty fighters, and they particularly don't care for mixed crews."

"So they'll catch us and . . ."

"Kill us. The Church is very imaginative when making martyrs. Do you have a knife?"

August blinked, "Surely you don't think we should kill ourselves rather than . . ."

Meridan waved him silent, "You'll need a knife once you go overboard. The trick is to whittle away a bit of your floatwood spans at a time until you can settle to the ground. Then it's a long walk back, but it's better than the Church."

August looked at Meridan, and from her gray pallor it was as if she *was* discussing suicide. And indeed, for a captain to discuss losing her ship, it was.

August looked around. Surely the crew must have realized the hopelessness of the situation. Yet they were all at their posts, nursing as much speed out of the *Antigiam* as they could, pressing her until the mainmast made its squawking complaints, then easing off quickly.

And the sails on the horizon loomed larger. There was a puff of smoke from one of the guns, and a few moments later, the sound of rolling thunder crossed the cloud tops. The crew did not seem to notice it.

"Finding range," said Meridan. "That means no powerful priest on board. But still they'll find and splinter us. Prepare to abandon ship!" Her pallor was now that of a ghost.

"Captain, no!" said August, suddenly.

"I know you don't want to lose your books," said Meridan. "But it's them or our lives."

"No, I mean we can escape if we work up a distraction."

"Distraction? In this cloudscape? Can you whistle up a Commonwealth Man-o-war, or a Dwarven Siege-Barge?"

"I can whistle up something," said August Gold, "if you can sail."

*   *   *

To the captain of the Churchship, the Commonwealth vessel made a sudden, fatal mistake. The Commonwealth captain should have spread full sail and trusted to the winds to let the lighter ship escape. Instead, the intruder kept its main sail half-banked, allowing the larger ship to close further. Then, in panic, it jerked to port, trying to sail across the bow of the Tomebook.

Had the Commonwealth ship had any real guns, the Churchship could have countered by turning itself. But the Tomebook was sufficiently powerful to maintain its course, cross the "T" behind the *Antigiam,* and unload a hellish broadside against it. At that range the long 24s would reduce the *Antigiam* to splinters.

On the quarter-deck, Jemma Meridan shouted as three crewmen manhandled the stern chaser into a rough firing position. The angle was still horrible, but it was enough to unload one ball before the Churchship crossed behind them. Time enough to keep the Church's full attention on the *Antigiam.*

In the hold, at the deadman's hatch, Carpenter Burrows had rigged up the other spool of wire rope. This time, however, it was fastened to the deck with a single beam, and the woodworker gripped it with both hands. Baker held a dark-stained rag against his bloodied head as he watched August lash several splints of floatwood to the second lanternlike censer's sides. With sure, deft motions, the scholar then filled the lantern with the last of the Dragon's Blood.

"Will it work?" managed the master's mate.

"It will have to," said August through thin, bloodless lips. "Otherwise it will be a long walk home."

The scholar lit the mantle of the lantern, and blew on it so it would catch. Baker shuddered as the warm musky scent permeated the hold once again. Without another word he dropped the floatwood-bound lantern out of the hatch. Supported by the floatwood, the lantern bounced along the bottom of the ship, and then was clear, dragged behind them, along the tops of the clouds.

"It's away," said August, softly.

"*It's awee-ay*," bellowed Burrows, and Baker clutched the rag tighter to his throbbing head.

"It's away," said Meridan. "Let's keep their attention. Fire at will, Mr. Knorri."

The hulking crewman stuck his tongue out of the corner of his mouth as he touched the burning taper to the slow match fuse. There was a flare, and the gun jumped. The angle was not good enough yet, and the clouds fifty feet in front of the Churchship's bow rose in a rough plume.

They could hear the cheers of the Churchship—they knew the *Antigiam* would not get another shot from the flight-gun before they had it under its own broadside. A hymn broke out on board the enemy ship, an anthem of smiting the godless ranging over the choppy cloudtops.

Meridan could see the Churchship clearly. It was called the *St. Guthrie*, and was fitted out in the rich trappings of a Tomebook with many sanctioned kills. Pennants draped from its spinnaker to show all of its actions and captures. The gun crews were huddled on the port side with their slow matches, waiting for the command.

And Meridan saw the *Guthrie*'s commander standing on the sterncastle, his tall helmet glittering in the sun, his robes flowing backward. The helmet gave a small dip, a bit of salute to a fellow captain, and the rich sleeve raised to give the broadside order.

And then the sun went out. More accurately, a shadow fell upon both the *Antigiam* and the *St. Guthrie*, as something rose on the far side of the Churchship.

It was huge, boiling out of the clouds like a nascent island, covered with barbed shields that Meridan realized were no more than scales. Its eyes were half the size of the *Antigiam* itself, and beamed with their own yellow radiance. Its maw was larger than the Tomebook.

And that maw was open, its jaws lined with innumerable teeth the color of stained ivory, as long as jollyboat oars and curved inward. Catfishlike tendrils jutted from the jaws. Then Meridan realized these were not whiskers, but rather rope, bound with metal wire, fixed with August's hooks.

Those aboard the *St. Guthrie* had time to react, to shout out, and for the quick-minded and truly devout, to pray before those gaping maws beat down upon the Churchboat. The mainmast snapped at once under the assault as it dived upon the ship, dragging it under with a single, graceful move.

Meridan, Knorri, and Sandotter stared as the huge island-fish dived now, taking the church vessel with it. Its scales flashed in the sun like the shields of a long-lost legion, showering the area with prismatic sparks.

Meridan found her voice and shouted, "Cut away!"

"Cut away!" shouted August, now halfway up the deck-hatch.

"*Cutting awaa-ey!*" sang Burrows, pulling the timber support away from the spinning spool. The entire assembly pitched forward, and like the first spool, was gone.

August Gold made it to the deck only in time to see the last of a scaled tail, an appendage the size of a scholar's tower, flick upward, and submerge beneath the cloud. The clouds roiled for a moment, and then were still.

"What happened?" said August. "What did you see?"

Meridan turned to the scholar and blinked, her eyes still wide as platters. "I saw our salvation, and a very good reason to get out of here. Sandotter!"

"Yes, ma'am!"

"Full sails as we can manage for home! And get Burrows to look for a decent splint for the mainmast! I don't want to be here when our friend comes looking for dessert!"

The great beast seemed content with its sacrifice, and did not resurface. By the end of the day, they were two hundred miles closer to home, and scheduled to reach it before reaching the weevil-biscuit stage.

Crossgreves had acquiesced to breaking out the last of the Bloodwine vintage on board, and August, Burrows (replacing the ailing Baker), Sandotter, and the purser were once more in the gun room. The captain was strangely silent, but August made up for it with his complaints.

"I cannot believe that I missed it!" fumed August, his irritation fading only slightly with every glass.

"You have the descriptions of most of those on deck," said Sandotter, philosophically.

"Yes, descriptions that grow with each telling," said the scholar. "Big as a house. As two houses. As the Commonwealth House. And eyes that were beacons. No, huge slabs of amber. No, liquid fire. Pah!" He waved an empty mug at Young Smith, who brought the ewer.

"And you saw a bit of it yourself," noted Crossgreves.

"Only the tail!" said August. "Only the last bit of the tail." He let out a long, protracted sigh. "At least I've proved that 'here be dragons,' eh?"

"Not necessarily," said Captain Jemma Meridan softly.

Eyebrows around the table raised, and August said, "Surely, Captain, you cannot deny your own eyes! Something rose to the bait we cast out behind the Churchship and took it to the bottom of the clouds! You don't deny that!"

"I don't deny it. Oh, I'm no denier of reality," said Meridan, "but I just express doubt that what we saw was one of your old-fashioned *dragons*."

Sandotter swirled the dregs in her mug and said, "What else could it be?"

"I'm just saying it's not necessarily a dragon," said the captain. "What if it is something else? Something that perhaps *ate* all of the dragons after the Deluge."

August Gold blinked. "A dracovore? No, it couldn't . . . but yes, there's no proof that it isn't." The scholar managed a weak smile, "I guess we'll have to go back again and look for firm proof, after all."

The captain chuckled and said, "I have no desire to meet again anything that could *eat* a dragon. And now we've given it a taste of cloudships as well. No, I think we should avoid the Holy Sea for a while to come, and let the Holy Church deal with this particular devilfish. In deed."

THE COLOSSUS OF MAHRASS

BY MEL ODOM

1

"WHAT the hell are you looking at?"
Jaelik Tarlsson—captain of *Rapier's Thrust*, which flew the black flag in Roostaan waters that guaranteed a hangman's noose for any man of age caught aboard her—grinned drunkenly at the young giant in Roostaan Deathwatch sergeant's leathers.

"Now there's a pretty question, laddie," Jaelik said smoothly. "You see, if I knew the answer to that, I wouldn't have to be looking so long, now would I?"

The young sergeant blinked owlishly. Nearly seven feet tall and broad across the shoulders, he sat hunched over one of the slipshod wooden tables at the back of the Blistered Mermaid tavern. His huge fists rested on either side of a wooden platter piled high with gnawed rib bones. Burgundy sauces and grease stained the broad, brutish face and uniform blouse. Dark, stringy hair trailed to his shoulders. His scabbarded sword lay across the table, close at hand, and showed plenty of wear and tear.

"You never seen a man eat before?" the sergeant asked belligerently.

The nearby crowd grew silent, and the effect spread throughout the tavern. It didn't take long for the whole place to go silent because the drinking establishment wasn't big. The tavern perched on the sagging pilings that hung out into the dock, a cancerous sore that protruded out into the harbor. Red lanterns marked its roof so ships' helms could see it clearly in the dark, and men needing a cheap drink or bill of fare could find it whether tired or already working on a drunk.

The Blistered Mermaid was one of several ale houses along the seedy docks of Roosta, and the port city was home to some of the vilest fighting men to ever stand a ship berth or guard post. As the forerunner of the League of Alpatian Sea Nations—merely a fancy name for the organized freebooters that had rallied to Turkoth Blackheart's crimson flag—Roosta held order through a combination of martial law, blackmail, and bribery.

The city, and others of the League like it, had become a haven for raiders and pirates who preyed on the weakened nations around them. The hard-fought war against the invading barbarian hordes from the north had consumed years, men, and materials.

Unfortunately, the threat from the North was the only things that had bound the seafaring nations in centuries (that, and the trade they managed with the great nations to the east and the west).

Far Exterre, of the glittering onion-domed towers, beautiful doe-eyed women who masked their faces by custom, and powerful arcane magics that—some said—could raise the dead, didn't care who managed the Alpatian Sea as long as their goods got through on time. Likewise with Lythaan, the great sea power that held all the Western Ocean in thrall with their vast warships and first-rate navies and armies.

The tiny nations and city-states lodged in the harsh mountainous terrain that framed the crescent body of the Alpatian Sea were too deeply rooted for either Exterre or Lythaan to attempt to conquer. Both powerful nations would have had to sacrifice far more than they were willing to give up, and with the mountains and the barbarians to the North, there was nowhere for the Alpatian countrymen to go.

"Oh, I've seen *men* eat before," Jaelik stated pointedly, "I was just interested in watching you."

The sergeant spat out a chunk of chewed gristle that bounced from the stained tabletop. The Blistered Mermaid wasn't known for its cuisine. He looked like he was trying to make sense of what Jaelik said, or perhaps it was only indigestion.

"Mayhap," Alff whispered at the captain's elbow, "ye could see to properly antagonizing one o' them a little closer to our own size."

Jaelik grinned and whispered to his companion. "Where would be the fun in that?" He was a couple inches shy of six feet, with a frame made broad by years of handling oars and sail. He'd first crewed aboard flatboats hauling goods from one ship to another in port cities, then on cargo ships. Now he was captain of his own vessel as a privateer under the Letters of Marque granted him by Vellak, from whence he hailed. Vellak was one of the few port cities Turkoth hadn't managed to gain control of. At least, not yet. Vellak's policy of free trade cut deeply into Turkoth's coffers.

Jaelik wore his blond hair cut short on the sides but braided in the back, and went clean-shaven. A few years short of thirty, his skin was browned from seasons spent at sea and facing harsh weather. Scars marked him, from rope burns to sword cuts. He remained short of handsome, too, carrying a face that too many could easily forget, which served him well as a privateer captain.

He wore a dyed blue silk shirt with belled sleeves, white leather pants, and black, cracked leather knee boots rolled over generously. An unadorned rapier hung from a broad black belt brocaded in gilt and fancy stitchery. The belt was there as part of his disguise as one of the many ne'er-do-well merchant princes that trolled the waters around Roosta these days, but the sword was one he was familiar with.

"Aye, an' as I were to recall," Alff grumbled, "we're not here to be after having fun. We're here 'cause a that thrice-damned ha'nt that them blamed sea Gypsies cursed you with. Cegrud the One-Legged take 'em all."

"You know better than to speak ill of the dead," Jaelik cautioned.

Alff shrugged and shook his head. He was a beefy man with a shock of red hair, a fierce curling mustache, and was nearly twice his captain's age. He crewed aboard *Rapier's Thrust* as quartermaster, and he was the man Jaelik had learned to favor having cover his back.

"Aye," Alff replied, "an' I figger they done and gone too far when they up an' make an honest man's life an unjoyous hell. Me, I'd rather be chasing after a godspeaker what could banish ha'nts than what we're after doing." He squinted up one blue eye at Jaelik. "An' begging the cap'n's pardon, but ye still ain't sure ye ain't just gone a little daft."

Jaelik shot the man a look.

"Hey, an' I said a *little*," Alff replied, spreading his hands in supplication. "I've knowed ye to take a couple hard shots to the gourd in the past, an' mayhap a binge or two in one of them Krillican drinking dens. Either one of them can leave damage what can return an' addle a man now and again."

"She is not some hallucination triggered by an old injury or exotic drink," Jaelik stated. Only he could see the woman aboard *Rapier's Thrust*. "The Gypsies knew about her."

Alff scratched his whisker-stubbled chin. "Aye, I been

thinking on that somewhat, too. Mayhap they just kinda put that thought in yer noggin an' let ye summon up yer own demons."

"She's a beautiful woman," Jaelik protested.

"Aye, an' what other kinds of demons would a rogue like ye be summoning up, Cap'n?" Alff grinned. "Ye remember them twins in Xzanl? The ones that wanted to boil yer—"

"What the hell are you two talking about?" the sergeant bellowed angrily. He leaned toward their table, and the Roostaan soldiers leaned in with him expectantly.

Roostaan soldiers, Jaelik knew, weren't touted as being generous or gentle. However, they also didn't kill people they believed to be merchant princes, who might be ransomed back to some well-to-do trading house.

Jaelik grinned again and jerked a thumb at Alff. "My friend here said he believes you have an interesting face. All pointed like it is, he thought it should be rendered on the prow of a fighting ship."

Alff sighed deeply and whispered, "Cap'n, ye could have left me out of this altogether. That is one brutish man, and I don't take a beatin' near as well as I used to."

"Now me," Jaelik went on, pouring a little more mulled wine from the pitcher he'd purchased, "I was thinking that a face like that could never be placed on anywhere other than the south end of anything northbound."

Face reddening, the sergeant reached for the sword and slid it free of the scabbard. "Now that," he roared, "I don't like at all."

"Oh, I don't hold you accountable for that," Jaelik said good-naturedly. "I blame your mother. Looking at you, there's no telling what she bedded down with. That's not your responsibility at all."

With a cry of rage, the sergeant surged up from the

table. He brandished the sword, and the pale light from the oil lanterns gleamed dully in the pocked finish.

"My apologies," Jaelik said unctuously. "Obviously I've struck a nerve. I wasn't aware that you know the lady."

"Get him, Portnoy!" one of the other Deathwatch guards urged. "Split him like a rotten melon!"

2

The sword cleaved the air and smacked into the table, shattering the wooden pitcher of mulled wine and jarring the cups to the floor. Two of the slats making the tabletop splintered.

Alff calmly backed away and walked over to the long bar in the corner.

Jaelik stood as Portnoy bellowed in rage, obviously past the point of control. "You're leaving me to fight him?" the privateer captain asked.

"Aye," Alff growled. "An' it's yer fight. Ye picked it." He slammed a fist on the bar and ordered ale. "I'll tell folks ye died well." He gave a big wink to the incredulous people around him, blew the froth off the ale, and drank down half of the contents.

The Blistered Mermaid tavern crowd cleared a fighting area in time that showed frequent past history with such events. Deathwatch guardsmen as well as dockhandlers shoved tables and chairs clear of the central area, stacking them efficiently.

"I'm gonna cut you!" Portnoy screamed. "I'm gonna cut you so bad you're gonna wish you was dead!" He circled cautiously, showing rudimentary training, but favoring his greater size and strength.

Jaelik circled with him, grinning. Portnoy swung at him, a long, clumsy blow but still possessing enough raw strength

to shear through an oak cask if it had hit. Jaelik batted it
aside, then casually reached in and pinked his opponent's
shoulder.

Portnoy glanced at the wound in disbelief, leaving himself open.

Quick an a blood-incensed shark, Jaelik stepped in and
struck again. The rapier blade razored across the big man's
Deathwatch blouse, cutting through the grim skull face that
was Turkoth Blackheart's standard. When the privateer captain stepped back, the burgundy-sauce–stained proud blouse
hung in tatters. The flesh beneath was left unmarked.

"He's a swordsman," one of the crowd observed.

Feet together, grasping an imaginary cloak, Jaelik
pressed the rapier hilt against his forehead and gave a for-
mal bow to the crowd. His smile, however, mocked them.

While he'd been in the docks of Vellak, he'd learned
more than how to build a strong back. He'd had access to
teachers from a number of ports, and he'd sought out what
they could teach him. After he'd learned to read, his curiosity only increased. Swordplay had been a favorite endeavor, and he had a lot of natural ability.

"Get him, Portnoy!" one of the serving wenches shouted.
"Show that foppish bastard what-for!"

The crowd quickly turned bloodthirsty, screaming threats
and vicious encouragement. Their suggestions would have
shamed a butcher.

"Ye know," Alff hollered from the bar, "ye didn't have
to go and turn this into something personal."

Circling again, knowing the young giant was gathering
his faltering courage, Jaelik knew he might have made a
mistake. It was one thing to challenge a hometown favorite
to a bar fight, but it was another to make a fool of the man.

Portnoy telegraphed his swing again, cutting cross-body.
Jaelik ducked clumsily, as if the wine he'd consumed

had dampened his reflexes. He stumbled to one side, thinking he could let Portnoy have the upper hand for a moment, and fell against a table. He breathed hard for effect, gasping like a mullet too long out of water.

The young giant, however, pressed his advantage at once, bringing the blade down in an overhead swing.

Barely able to restrain the immediate response to step in and gut the Deathwatch sergeant while avoiding the blade, Jaelik hooked up a chair with one hand and brought it into line with the sword blow. The heavy steel crashed through the wood, but it was deflected to one side. The sword buried in the table only inches from Jaelik's head.

"By Cegrud's cold, staring left eye, I thought he had ye then," Alff called out from the bar. "Couldn't believe ye letting a lummox like that takin' ye so easy like. Woulda looked bad on yer gravestone, it woulda."

Several of the crowd turned on Alff at once, hurling imprecations at the red-haired quartermaster. Alff reviled them with oaths that would have seared barnacles from a ship sunk a thousand years ago. Some of them Jaelik had never heard before.

Portnoy yanked on the sword, drawing it from the wood with a shrill creak. A grim smile played on his sauce-stained lips when he thought Jaelik was in an uncompromising position.

Jaelik couldn't use his rapier, but that didn't stop him from balling up his empty fist and putting his shoulder behind a vicious roundhouse. Even big as Portnoy was, the young giant was rocked back on his heels and sent stumbling backward.

Blood spurted from Portnoy's nose. The Deathwatch guardsman snuffled and wiped it with the back of his hand.

After giving the bigger man only a moment's respite, Jaelik threw himself forward, turning his rapier down and stepping in with a forearm shiver across his opponent's ribs, following it with a shoulder. Portnoy's breath exploded from his bloodied lips in a warm, wet spray across Jaelik's back. Digging his feet in, the privateer captain shoved upward, thinking he was going to bust a gut with the effort required to move the big guardsman, but refusing to give in just the same.

Incredibly, Portnoy's feet came free of the rolling tavern floor. The big guardsman didn't go far, but ended up on a table behind him. The table's support struts cracked like the winter ice floes before a steel reinforced keel in the Wintry Sea north of Dassoic. Portnoy collapsed on top of the ruined table, clattering around the wooden platters and pewter ale mugs.

Jaelik lashed out with a boot, snapping the big man's head back with a smacking thump against the floor. He yelled in pain, surprising since most men would have been too dazed to give voice at all.

"Get him!" someone yelled.

The privateer captain spun, watching with a careless half smile on his lips as the rest of the Deathwatch guardsmen galvanized into action. Swords, cutlasses, daggers, and axes bristled, but inexperienced ruffians already deep in their cups wielded them. At another time, Jaelik felt certain he could have broken free of them and vanished in the shadows of the night draping the city.

Without warning, the ghost appeared at the periphery of his vision, standing somehow in the midst of the guardsmen launching themselves at him. She was perhaps a handful of years younger than he was. Her dark hair framed an angular face that possessed a gossamer smoothness. A light lavender gown flowed over generous curves that would have caught the privateer's attention even if he hadn't known she was a ghost. Her emerald green eyes bored into his reproachfully.

"I'm not leaving," Jaelik growled at her irritably. In the last twenty-three days, she hadn't spoken one word, just followed him constantly. Even his sleep had fallen victim to her silent presence.

Her mouth worked, and though he couldn't hear her, he could read her lips. *Don't die!*

The grin on Jaelik's lips spread, remembering all the sleepless nights he'd spent aboard *Rapier's Thrust*. There'd been no mercy. "Demanding wench, aren't you?" Then he was covered over in the initial tide of guardsmen that bore down on him.

Instinctively, Jaelik used his attackers' very numbers against them, twisting his opponents' arms and legs into the paths of their comrades. Almost instantly, the concerted attack became confused. Sober men would have spaced themselves out better, and more complete training than simply overrunning a ship by sheer numbers would have provided better experience for close-in fighting.

Jaelik worked hardest to keep from harming any of his attackers. If he drew blood, he doubted even his ne'er-do-well merchant prince cover would save him. He backhanded a man across the face, grabbed an arm with his other hand and twisted, drawing the man into two other men and dropping them all in a flailing tangle of arms and legs. He cracked another man on the skull with the rapier pommel, knocking him cold.

The deep, roaring bellow behind him told him Alff had joined the fray with a true connoisseur's enthusiasm. Grunts and groans echoed at once. Alff in a fight was always noisy.

Jaelik hoped his friend remembered they weren't there to win. The ghost stood off in the distance, watching. The privateer captain relished the worried look on her translucent features.

"Move 'way!" Portnoy roared. "Move 'way! I'll have his guts for tripe!" The giant guardsman bulled his way into the midst of the action, his great blade raised high, smashing against one of the oil lanterns hanging from the ceiling and setting it spinning. Twisting shadows raced across the walls.

Several of the men moved aside, leaving Portnoy a clear path. Rage masked the big man's broad face.

Moving back, giving the appearance of frightened stumbling, Jaelik knocked the pouch from his belt. The pouch hit the tavern floor with a leaden thump and spilled gold and silver coins in all directions.

For an instant, all the uncoiling violence came to an abrupt halt as greedy eyes tracked the coin spillage rolling across the warped wooden planks. Then avarice won out, and most of the guardsmen and tavern clientele scrambled for the coins.

Jaelik couldn't believe it; his attackers had forgotten about him. He looked over his shoulder at Alff, who shrugged, a puzzled look on his craggy face. The privateer captain muttered an oath.

At another time, the coin loss—less than a hundred newly minted Turk Imperials—would have been an excellent opportunity to escape. However, in this instance, escape wasn't the objective.

Snarling profanity, Jaelik kicked the man nearest him. "Stay away from those coins! They're mine, by Cegrud's diseased entrails, and none of you mangy curs will have them!" He continued battling the tavern patrons and guardsmen, finally forcing them to turn their attention to him.

He fought them bravely, but kept his blows largely ineffectual, landing enough of them only hard enough to incense his attackers. In the end, it was Portnoy that surged up with a huge fist and caught Jaelik on the chin.

Actually somewhat dazed by the thunderous blow even though he'd slipped most of it, the privateer captain flew from the floor and landed heavily on his back. He feigned unconsciousness, trusting the ill lighting not to betray that he peered through slitted eyes.

Portnoy raised his massive blade in both hands as he towered over his vanquished foe.

Quietly, Jaelik slipped free the dagger from his right boot, knowing he could deflect Portnoy's blow enough to roll out of the way unharmed if he had to.

"Hold, Portnoy!" one of the other guardsmen cried out. "Don't kill him!"

"Why not?" Portnoy stood with shaking arms, poised to strike.

Jaelik's stomach tightened and turned sour. The ghost was still visible at the crowd's edge, worry in the dark emerald eyes. *Damn the winds that brought me to the shore of this dilemma,* he thought.

The guardsman gripped the bigger man's arm. "Because Turkoth will have that great, thick head from your shoulders and on a pike by morning if he found out you killed a man that could be ransomed back so handsomely to his kith and kin."

"He hurt me!" Portnoy roared, touching his bleeding face.

"You're always making complaints, Portnoy," another guard called out while hunting frantically for more dropped coins. "Kill him, and Turkoth will kill you. Bet you complain about that, too."

Portnoy screamed vehemently, but he lowered the sword, shaking with restrained fury.

Jaelik was just letting out a slow breath of relief when

the big guardsman drew back his boot and kicked him full in the face. He struggled to hang onto his senses in spite of the sudden rush of agony, but they slid as if off a table's edge into a waiting pool of blackness that carried him away.

3

Jaelik woke in a shadow-drenched dungeon cell with a throbbing head and a dead woman's kiss on his lips. He blinked as the ghost drew away from him, wondering if she only been worried about him or was working some new arcane magic on him. The slight smell of roses seemed to twist through the malodorous salty and sour stench that clung to the dungeon.

"I knew you were alive," she said, smiling hesitantly. Though slight, her voice carried to his ears above the half-hearted cursing and moaning that echoed throughout the cavernous dungeon.

Rumor had it that Roosta had some of the biggest dungeon areas in all of the port city empires, and it was nearly filled with malcontents that had spoken out against Turkoth. Those who'd taken up arms against the new Roostaan ruler were killed out of hand.

"Aye," Jaelik growled low in his throat as the pain cascaded between his temples. "Though I've yet to be convinced that is a good thing."

"By Cegrud's shriveled and diseased tallywhacker," Alff cursed somewhere nearby, "this has got to be the worst mess he's ever gotten us into. After seeing this, I'm willing to wager it'll take him a compass and both hands to find his—"

"There is not much time," the ghost implored. "You must get moving."

"Aye, girl. I've gotten that impression from you since

the first." Cautiously, feeling as though his throbbing head might roll from his shoulders, Jaelik sat up on the bed chained to the wall. A thin straw pallet, soured from dampness, covered wrought-iron bars coarse enough to cut flesh.

"Ye're awake," Alff snarled disgustedly, showing his captain a cyclopean stare. His left eye was swollen shut, and there was an impressive lump on his left jawbone.

"Unhappily." Every movement Jaelik made created a new hurt in another spot. "How long was I out?"

"After they stopped Portnoy from gutting ye on the tavern floor, then carried us into this wallow of despair?" Alff shrugged. "Fifteen, twenty minutes. How're yer ribs?"

Jaelik shifted, feeling the nauseating pain shuddering through his midsection. He cursed, then apologized to the ghost, who turned her face from him disdainfully. Maybe she was embarrassed, but the privateer captain couldn't be sure. He looked down, drawn by the unaccustomed heaviness at his ankles. Chain links clanked on the stone floor between his feet. "Leg irons?"

"I guess they didn't want to take any chances with such a ruffian as ye."

Jaelik ignored the sarcasm and hefted the chain. The links felt heavy and strong, slick with whale oil to keep them from rusting. "My ribs?"

"Portnoy," Alff confirmed. "After he smashed yer kabob for ye. He was still kicking when his mates pulled him off of ye. How about that ha'nt? Is she about still?" The quartermaster squinted his good eye and stared into the shadows filling the cell.

Jaelik nodded and instantly regretted it. "Aye. Only now's she's talking."

Alff sighed heavily. "By Cegrud's big broken right toe, but it's getting worse."

A grin fitted itself to Jaelik's face when he saw the young woman's obvious irritation with the quartermaster.

"It was bad enough when she was keeping ye up nights," Alff stated. "Even worse when she took over yer hand and made ye write them notes to yerself, commanding ye to get to Roosta's dungeons, but now she's talking to ye?" He cracked his knuckles. "There's naught but ill to be had of this."

"You could have stayed aboard ship," Jaelik pointed out. He examined the tattered remains of his belled sleeves. The men who'd robbed him hadn't missed the coins he'd had sewn into the material there. He touched the short, hard shapes inside the drawstring of his breeches and smiled. They'd *almost* searched him thoroughly.

Alff made a discourteous noise with his lips. "And what's she got to say for herself?"

"I don't know. I've been listening to you complain instead of asking her questions."

"Oh, sure," Alff said disparagingly, "an' now I'm the one who's to blame for this debacle." He stared through the thick bars at the front of the cell.

The view, Jaelik had to admit, wasn't a promising one. The row of cells was set a little higher than the central hallway that wound through the dungeon, allowing them to be more easily sluiced out. Though from the stench pervading the dungeon, Jaelik doubted that any of the cells were cleaned unless someone died in them. Probably not even then, he decided.

Torches lined the stone walls, soot staining them above the flames. Garbage lined the hallway, showing the high-water mark resulting from the infrequent cleaning by running water through the area. Mold clung to the stones and mortar, leaving cracks and crevices between the limestone chunks that showed no sign of upkeep. The walls seemed bowed by the weight of the military garrison above it.

After another deep breath, the pain in Jaelik's head seemed less likely to threaten explosion. He stood on shaking knees, grateful that the weakness quickly fled. The last few weeks of sleeplessness contributed to the overall fatigue he'd been feeling, but the beating hadn't helped.

He grazed at the ghost, remembering the nights she'd stood at the foot of his bed in his cabin and stared at him. She'd stayed with him all over *Rapier's Thrust*, and in the four ports they'd put in to during that time. Despite her beauty and the curiosity that filled him, he knew her to be grim and relentless.

"We're here," Jaelik said softly, struggling to keep the irritation out of his voice. "Now what?"

"You're locked up," she protested.

Jaelik grinned. "You did say I had to enter the dungeon."

She made fists of her hands and pressed them down at her sides. Anger gleamed in the emerald eyes. "Not like this. You're no good to me locked up."

"Aye, lass, and that's the crux of it, is it?" Jaelik leaned against the stone wall and crossed his arms over his chest. The motion caused his ribs to hurt intolerably, but he didn't move his arms. Stance and posture were the cornerstones of command. "Of what good am I to you?"

"That's not all of it." Tears filled her eyes as she gazed around the dim prospects offered by the dungeon.

Off in the distance, a man started screaming. "Vanyan! Vanyan!"

Another voice, gentler, spoke up. "Go easy there, lad. He's gone from you now. He's made his last escape from this fearful pit."

The words and their connotation weighed heavily on the

young woman. "I didn't mean for you to die here," she
said to Jaelik.

"Then what did you intend?" Jaelik asked. "A woman
haunting a man's thoughts like that isn't natural. Except
for love or lust." Despite the shadows, he thought her face
turned dark in embarrassment. "Up all hours of the night,
never a private moment to myself in weeks. Didn't you realize that I might not be exactly straight thinking by the
time we got here? You drove me hard, woman. How could
you believe I'd keep my sanity?"

"I needed you to get down into the dungeon," she replied.
"Not get locked up."

"And I've found it much easier to break out of a dungeon than to break into one," Jaelik answered. "Getting in
can be easily accomplished."

Farther down the row of cells, a man sobbed broken-
heartedly, calling out softly to his dead friend.

Jaelik noticed the momentary flicker of pain that filled
Alff's good eye. Both of them had been in similar situa-
tions during their time together and before.

The woman turned toward him, showing uncertainty for
the first time since she'd appeared. "You planned this?"

Jaelik grinned at her and raised an eyebrow. "You
thought I got sloppily drunk and attacked a mountain of a
Deathwatch guardsman by accident?"

Obviously resenting the carefree manner he exhibited,
the young woman drew herself up and turned cold. Jaelik could actually feel the temperature drop in the cell
around him.

Alff rubbed himself vigorously. "Ooch, and where did
that breeze come from?"

"She's mad at me," Jaelik answered, his skin prickling.
Ghosts, he knew, had limited involvement with the physi-
cal world, but their manifestations could alter temperatures.

And there were reports of ghosts that had physically harmed and killed the living. "She thought I'd gotten drunk and been thrown in the dungeon before I could carry out her wishes."

"You were not," the young woman stated haughtily, "someone I would have willingly chosen to carry out this mission."

"Mission, is it?" Jaelik asked. "For whom?"

"For the Roostaan cause," she replied. "Turkoth Blackheart cannot be allowed to remain in power here."

Jaelik shrugged. "That doesn't make any difference to me."

"You war against him."

"I take Turkoth's ships whenever I am able," the privateer captain corrected. "And I divvy up his cargo between the Vellakyn crown and my crew. That pursuit provides a prosperous lifestyle. Were Turkoth to be taken from power, I'd lose my livelihood."

"Do you dismiss the suffering of these people so casually?" she demanded.

"I am no hero," Jaelik replied.

"*That* I'm very well aware of."

The reply stung Jaelik's pride even though he'd been prepared for it. "Perhaps you would have been better served by one of the sea Gypsies that passed you on to me."

"They are not fighters," the young woman told him. "And after what I've seen tonight, I'm having my doubts about you."

"Yet you see no harm in haunting me, keeping me from my bed and my rest—"

"And those harlots in Marryl," she added vehemently.

Jaelik chuckled, amazed at the breadth of the young woman's emotions. Were those really the green lights of jealousy in her eyes? "You tried to keep me from them.

As I recall, you were shamed into leaving the bedchambers."

The dark flush returned to her translucent features. "You're crude, Captain Tarlsson."

"Aye, but there were no complaints from the ladies." He grinned wolfishly.

"I have made a mistake."

Jaelik waved idly toward the rows of cells in the dungeon. "Perhaps. Of course, there are all these other would-be Roostaan heroes to choose from now that I have you here. I could simply pass you along, should you prove willing."

Without warning, the young woman crossed the distance separating them. She stabbed him with her forefinger, driving it sharply against his chest, able to touch him for the first time. The contact surprised Jaelik because it was so unexpected. "Don't mock them," she warned. "Or me. They've given their lives to fighting Turkoth."

Shamed himself, Jaelik dropped his head. "Aye. You're right."

The woman spun from him, wrapping her arms about herself. "There is more at stake here than you know."

"Then tell me."

His sincere tone, delivered so effortlessly in the heat of the moment, caught her off-balance. Despite her best efforts to keep it in place, the anger sloughed from her face.

"Turkoth has found some arcane talismans of immense power in Roosta," she said softly. "Things that would be better off forever lost. Things that he came here seeking."

"What things?" Jaelik asked. She hesitated before answering, but in the end the privateer captain knew she had no choice.

"One of them," she answered, "is the Crown of the Storms, crafted by Slamintyr Lattyrl."

"The elven mage?" Jaelik was surprised in spite of his best efforts to be prepared. Slamintyr Lattyrl's name invoked the essence of magic simply by utterance alone. The elven wizard had descended from the lofty Falconspurs Mountains to the Roostaan frontier nearly thirteen hundred years ago, helping shape and defend the port city. No one knew what had happened to his clan, but rumors had spread of terrible wars among the elves, spurred on by the near-mortal wounds the wizened elf had carried.

"Yes," the girl replied.

"But the mage has been dead a thousand years and more."

"And he left a legacy of treasures behind him."

"I thought all of his creations were safely kept by the Wizard's League." The League was a self-empowered group of learned men educated in arcane ways who assumed control of a number of powerful weapons and spells they deemed unallowable to the general populace of all nations.

The woman shook her head. "He never wanted anyone to have all of his things. He was much too proud. He knew the human mages were jealous of the power he wielded, and he knew they would lock away his creations until they understood them. So he created others, some very powerful, and he left hints for a few of his trusted followers. However, Turkoth learned of some of them. And in learning of them, he was led to others. Many have died in his search."

"And you among them?" Jaelik asked, trying not to think how callous his question sounded.

"No. I died long before this time."

"Who are you?"

"I am Ryla," the young woman said. "I was the daughter of Slamintyr Lattyrl."

4

Daughter?

The announcement slammed into Jaelik's brain like a sudden scurvy-induced fever. "Slamintyr Lattyrl never had a daughter."

Reproach filled Ryla's face. "Are you a scholar as well as a historian?"

"No," Jaelik answered. "But every seaman worth his salt knows of Slamintyr Lattyrl. There are hundreds of stories regarding ships bearing personal things of his that put out to sea and disappeared. When the ocean occasionally gives up a ship that it has taken and held for a long time, there are always hopes that it was one of those."

"My father never trusted anything to the sea," Ryla replied. "His magic was of the earth, of stone and soil. The sea leeched at those things."

"But you're not an elf." Jaelik studied her further, thinking perhaps her ears were a little pointed.

"I'm half-elven. My mother was human."

Jaelik shook his head. "The elves don't mate with humans. They prefer to remain among their own kind."

"Normally, yes. But these were not normal times. My father grew lonely, and my mother wanted a child. Despite his own selfish view of life, he allowed that to happen. But no one was ever to know."

"I'm the only one?"

Ryla shook her head. "There are others who suspect."

Jaelik took a moment to think. It was hard to do with his head throbbing the way it was. "Why didn't you seek them out?"

"I couldn't. Those men wouldn't have Roosta's best interests at heart. Wizards, especially human ones, have a tendency to put their own interests first, last, and always. In the beginning—"

"When was the beginning?" Jaelik asked, looking at the girl and guessing that she couldn't have been over twenty.

"More than a thousand years ago." Ryla paused only a moment, as if the cold certainty of speaking those words was surprising. "In the beginning, I was able to look after my father's things after he died."

"What happened to your mother?"

"The Kriffith Plague," Ryla answered. "I was nine when it swept through Roosta and took one person out of three. My elven blood seemed to make me impervious to the sickness."

The last outbreak of the Kriffith Plague had taken place more than two hundred years ago, but men still spoke of it only with fear. "Then what—?"

"Before my father died," Ryla continued, her gaze growing distant, "he magically bound me to his work, declaring that I, followed by my issue, would protect it from those who would take it. After he died, one of the human mages in Roosta broke into my father's tower. I tried to protect the items my father had entrusted to me, but I was cut down." Unconsciously, she touched her neck as if checking the wholeness of her flesh.

The calm, emotionless way the young woman relayed the tale left Jaelik cold. Over his years, he'd seen many bodies of innocents who'd died hard deaths.

"Bound as I was to the magical talismans, without issue to pass the responsibility on to, I became bound to this mortal world even after death."

"You should have haunted him," Jaelik stated. "I'll wager he would have returned the things he'd stolen,"

"I did haunt him," Ryla said. "He banished me, trapped my essence in a bracelet that I was freed from only three hundred years ago. In that time, I have managed to track down and destroy some of the items my father created. Only a few weeks ago, I learned that Turkoth had come into possession of the Crown of the Storms." She paused, looking at Jaelik. "He must be stopped."

Jaelik shook his head. "Even were I the hero you hoped for, I've only got one ship at my disposal. And I'm no hero."

Ryla stepped close to the privateer captain.

Remembering how sharp and painful the ghost's forefinger had been, as well as horror stories of everything ghosts could do to someone if they managed to draw blood, Jaelik drew back until the cell's bars pressed into his back.

"You're no hero," she agreed, "but I can guarantee that you'll be the most miserable man you've ever known if you don't help me."

Jaelik locked eyes with her. He'd gone along with her this far because doing without sleep had become a near-impossible thing. Of course, there were a few nights when he'd had enough liquor to pass out comfortably, dead to the world himself for a handful of hours at a time. Drinking to excess, however, was not something he'd do every night by choice.

"I'll even learn to put up with the women you buy," Ryla threatened. "I won't be so easy to embarrass from the next bedchamber you choose to frolic in."

Her tone told Jaelik that she meant to carry out her threat. "What did you hope to gain by having me steal into the dungeons?"

"There is a tunnel here," Ryla told him. "The passageway was long ago forgotten by the handful of people who know about it, and it leads to a device that has been hidden for all these years that have passed since my father's death."

"What kind of device?"

"You don't need to concern yourself with that."

Deliberately, Jaelik sat on the edge of the bed. The stench of the sour straw surrounded him. "Then I shan't concern myself at all."

Ryla faced him imperiously. "What are you doing?"

Jaelik laced his fingers behind his head and leaned back against the slime-covered stone wall. He crossed one ankle over the other, the leg irons barely permitting that small movement. "Nothing."

"Get up."

"No."

"You can't refuse me." Her eyes flashed.

"I have refused you," Jaelik said.

"And what are ye after doing now?" Alff asked. "Arguin' with the ha'nt?"

"I prefer to think of it as negotiating."

The quartermaster scowled, the lumpy distortions caused by his injuries drawing the grimace into an even grimmer rictus. "Waste of time, arguin' with the ha'nt. She's got nothing ye want."

"Actually, it turns out she's the daughter of Slamintyr Lattyrl."

Alff hacked and spat, crossing the cell to join Jaelik on the bed. "The dead daughter of one of the most powerful wizards in the Alpatian Sea nations? It figgers. When yer luck sours, it has a habit of turning plumb rank. I've had occasion to see it before."

Ignoring the quartermaster's sarcasm, Jaelik quickly informed his friend of the gist of the conversation.

"So," Alff said when he finished, "do ye propose that we fester and rot in this cursed cell?"

Jaelik shrugged, struggling to keep the smile from his

face. "She may grow bored and go off to haunt someone else."

"Aye." Alff peered intently, as if he could see the ghost as well. "An' we'd be well rid of her."

"Although," Jaelik went on, "now that I get a better look at her, I find myself thinking she's a rather comely-looking wench." He pushed himself from the bed in a sudden eruption of movement, crossing the cell with apparent ease despite the aches and pains that rattled around inside him.

Ryla stood her ground. Maybe she thought that he would only pass through her, but whatever power or circumstance had allowed her to touch him only moments before now allowed him to touch her.

Jaelik had a brief impression of soft feminine flesh against his chest and the scent of crushed rose petals. Instinctively, his hand cupped and stroked the curved hip before him, feeling warm flesh beneath the thin lavender gown.

Uttering a gasp of outraged surprise, Ryla stepped back from his clumsy embrace. She slapped his face hard enough to turn his head.

Temples thundering with pain, Jaelik paused and shouted, "Damnation, woman! Would you have me beaten senseless?"

"If it would stop you."

Jaelik glared at her.

"Siddown, ya loon!" a gruff voice ordered from the nearby cell. "Ya been talking to thin air for damn near long enough, by Cegrud's thrice-curdled phlegm."

Alff casually reached through the bars, grabbed the offending speaker by the hair, and yanked his head into the bars. The other prisoner cried out in pain and dropped to the floor.

"What are you doing?" Ryla asked, gazing at the fallen prisoner.

Squinting through pain-cracked eyes, the privateer captain said, "Now you've gotten her mad at you."

"For what?" Alff asked. "Ringing that scurvy sot's bell?"

"She didn't like that," Jaelik said, keeping the mirth from his voice.

"No," Ryla ascertained, "I didn't. That man gave up his independence fighting Turkoth's—"

"Tell her to look at that man's left wrist," Alff grumbled. "That blue-and-gold tattooed spider there will tell you he's a Danaper thief. They mark all their kind in such a manner as that."

Even in the darkness and from the distance, Jaelik noted the offensive tattoo of a black widow spider poised to strike. Alff had always possessed quick, keen eyes.

"Probably put here as a spy," Alff guessed. "Or mayhap, just chose the wrong purse to lift."

The privateer captain glanced back at the ghost.

Ryla fell silent.

Jaelik glanced at her. "Tell me about the device."

She held his gaze and matched it.

"Feigned stubbornness may be fetching in a bedchamber," the privateer captain warned, "but it's damned unattractive now. If you want help from me, then tell me what's at stake. It's my neck and Alff's you're risking here."

Her eyes flashed emerald fire. "Have you heard of the Colossus of Mahrass?"

"Aye."

Stories about the Colossus constantly threaded through the tales told about Slamintyr Lattyrl. The elven wizard had come down from the Falconspurs and taken up residence in Roosta, but had chosen to defend Mahrass from the invading Exterrean pirates less than two score years later. Mahrass had been a neighboring port city, little more than a fishing village, but the remedies used there by the local herbalists had interested Slamintyr Lattyrl.

"It's said that Slamintyr Lattyrl retreated to the foothills of the Falconspurs and raised the Colossus from iron-veined stone," Jaelik said. "Some also say he sacrificed three un-born children in its making." The thought made the priva-teer captain uneasy.

"That's not true," Ryla said. "My father never killed an innocent."

"But he killed plenty of others," Jaelik responded.

She didn't bother to argue. "The magic my father used left him drained for weeks, but Mahrass had its defender."

According to the stories, the Colossus had been almost twenty times as tall as a man, a juggernaut that neither blade nor arrow nor flaming catapult load could harm. It had waded out into the arriving pirates and decimated their forces long before they reached the shores. For years, the Colossus had remained as Mahrass' guardian. During that time, Slamintyr Lattyrl had learned the secrets of the herbal-ists, and Mahrass had joined with Roosta.

"The device that lies in that tunnel controls the Colos-sus," Ryla continued.

Jaelik narrowed his eyes in perplexity. "The Colossus disappeared after your father died. Some believe that it re-turned to the Falconspurs and to the earth that spawned it."

"No," Ryla said quietly. "The Colossus lies out in the harbor. If we can recover the device, we can rouse the Colossus and use it to destroy Turkoth's military fleet."

"What's this business about the Colossus?" Alff de-manded.

Jaelik quickly explained, speaking in low tones that didn't carry past their cell.

Alff crossed his arms over his barrel chest and shook

his shaggy head. "Impossible. Even with the Colossus. Turkoth has thirty warships a-lyin' out there in them waters, an' if he's got them wizard's widgets the ha'nt is talking about, it's gonna be even more impossible."

Jaelik didn't bother discussing the varying degrees of impossibilities, instantly agreeing. He faced the woman once more, getting ready to let her know his feelings.

"Before you turn me down," Ryla declared, "let me tell you this. Turkoth plans to sail come the dawning red of morning, and his first target is Vellak, your homeland."

5

A cold chill seized Jaelik as he faced the ghost. "Vellak can stand against Turkoth's forces. That's why they haven't attacked so far." Images of the walled city where he'd been born and lived most of his life when he wasn't at sea filled the privateer captain's mind.

So many still lived among the staggered docks along the harshly broken shorelines of Vellak: his parents, three brothers and two sisters, nieces and nephews, old Noddy, who'd first taught him ropes and knots and cursing, Tarrys, the candle-maker's daughter, who'd first shown him the secrets of love; a hundred others and more.

"Vellak's walls can stand against enemy ships," Ryla said, "but they can't stand against my father's magic. The Crown of the Storms can call forth storms—winds, rains, and lightning—that will reduce that Vellak to ruins."

"The ha'nt's threatening Vellak?" Alff asked.

"No," Jaelik answered. "She says Turkoth plans to sail for Vellak in the morning."

Alff's good eye narrowed. "An' him having them wizard's widgets?"

"Aye."

"You believe her?"

Jaelik studied the ghost before him. "Aye."

"Then, beggin' the cap'n's pardon," the quartermaster stated, "I think them negotiations are done."

Jaelik nodded. "Agreed." He unfastened the drawstring of his breeches.

"What are you doing?" Ryla asked, taken aback.

"Getting us out of here." Jaelik worked the drawstring loose, then shoved forward the two small lockpicks secreted in the cord till they popped out in his palm.

He retied his breeches, then set to work on his leg irons. Under his expert skill the locks gave and the shackles dropped to the stone floor. Thankfully, the gloom pervading the dungeon prevented any of the other prisoners from seeing them.

After freeing Alff, Jaelik turned his attention to the cell door, managing the lock with the same ease. He fisted the door and swung it cautiously, listening to the grate of metal on metal.

"Which way is the tunnel you're talking about?" he asked the ghost.

"Deeper into the dungeon," Ryla answered.

Jaelik glanced back toward the dungeon's entrance. A long, winding stairway led back to the ground level inside the keep. Glancing in the other direction, following the long line of cells to his right, the passageway sloped steeply into the bowels under the building. Rumor had it that the dungeon coiled like an eel, plunging deeply beneath sea level, and that parts of the dungeon were now submerged.

It wasn't a happy thought.

He turned to the ghost. "You're sure the tunnel's deeper in the dungeon?"

"Yes."

Alff grimaced. "The deeper we go, Cap'n, the longer the fight we got to get back topside."

"Aye," Jaelik gritted. He pushed the cell door open, instantly drawing the attention of the nearby prisoners.

Scarecrow men, half-starved, malnourished, and all but broken, stumbled to the fronts of the cells and stared at Jaelik with rheumy eyes. "Free us," a bearded man called out hoarsely. "If you fight against Turkoth Blackheart and his accursed Deathwatch, we'll join you."

"Got the makin's of an army here," Alff whispered.

Hardening his heart, Jaelik reached for a nearby torch in a corroded wall sconce. "We don't need an army." He lifted the torch, spilling the light down the dungeon passageway, listening to the hoarse susurration of voices that fled with the shadows.

"You can't leave them here," Ryla objected.

"And what do you propose?" Jaelik demanded. "If we release them and they head to the keep, they'll be a walking announcement that someone has escaped these foul pits. And they're too weak to put up much of a fight. They'll be killed out of hand."

"Better to die a free man than the way before us now," the prisoner said.

"Free them," Ryla instructed.

"No." Jaelik faced her, watching how the bright torchlight shone through her, letting him see the empty cell behind her they'd only just quit. "I won't be party to their suicide."

"But you would be party to their murders?" Ryla asked.

"They can be freed later."

"There may be no later for them. Free them."

Jaelik thrust the torch at her, causing her to instinctively step back. "Which is more important? Them or your father's geas?"

"Or Vellak, in your case."

Just as the privateer captain started to vent his frustration in colorful curses, Alff slammed a big hand into his chest and pushed him back against the wall.

"Someone's a-comin'," the quartermaster hissed, glancing back toward the stairs.

Jaelik peered toward the far end of the dungeon, listening to the scuff of boot leather and jingle of chainmail descending into the chamber.

"We'd never make it," Alff stated calmly.

"I know." Quickly, Jaelik thrust the torch back into the wall sconce, then followed Alff into the dungeon's shadows a little farther down the passageway. They stood mostly hidden behind one of the support pillars built into the wall on the other side of the cells.

Every nerve in Jaelik's body screamed for him to run. He held himself steady through iron will, taking small sips of air so he'd be ready. He watched the steps as four men stepped into view.

Three of them wore the black leather of the Deathwatch, but the fourth dressed in white-and-crimson robes. A beaten copper skullcap gleamed dully above the old man's features. A long white beard trailed down his chest and he walked with his hands tucked into the opposite sleeves.

"Damned wizard," Alff whispered.

Jaelik gave a slow nod, his mind racing. He noticed Ryla stepping into hiding on the other side of the passageway. It was said that wizards sometime summoned ghosts as their familiars, binding them into unholy service. Maybe ghosts weren't invisible to wizards the way they were to most people.

"Where are these men, lieutenant?" the wizard asked, gazing coldly into the cells they passed.

One of the Deathwatch guards hurried forward, coming

to a stop in front of the cell Jaelik and Alff had vacated. He stared for a moment, then pulled the unlocked door open.

"Now!" Jaelik said, throwing himself at the Deathwatch guard. Alff moved like a shadow, following him step for step as they crossed the intervening distance.

The Deathwatch lieutenant spun and tried to free the sword at his side.

Jaelik moved without hesitation or remorse. The fight in the tavern had been fought with the intent of killing no one, but they had no choice here. Whatever had brought the wizard down to their cell, he was certain it was for nothing but ill.

The privateer captain slammed the guard against the cell bars with his body weight, trapping the man's hand against his side. The guard struggled, shoving his free hand into Jaelik's face, gouging for his eyes. Jaelik fisted the dagger on the man's right hip, yanked it free as he headbutted the man and almost passed out from the impact, then buried the short blade in his opponent's throat.

Alff bowled over the other two guards, taking them down with his weight. The quartermaster stayed on top of them, hammering them with great, meaty thwacks of his bunched fists. A man's nose broke, sounding like a snapped twig.

Feeling the dying man's warm blood course over his hand and arm, Jaelik quickly spun him toward the wizard. Torchlight splintered from the skullcap as the old man drew his hands from his sleeves. His fingers twisted together in an arcane symbol as he spoke.

Violet lightning arced from the wizard's hands and peeled the flesh from the Deathwatch lieutenant's chest. The scent of boiled blood filled the dungeon.

White-hot heat scorched Jaelik's chest. He shoved the

dead man from him, gazing down fearfully, knowing he was going to see a gaping hole where his own heart used to be. Reddened, blistered flesh—scarcely the breadth of his palm—showed through the burned tatters of his shirt. Flecks of orange coals still smoldered in the material.

The wizard worked his fingers again, calling out to his gods as he summoned another spell.

Jaelik knew that most wizards carried enchanted items, objects that would hold a small portion of the power they drew from the weaves that linked them to their chosen sanctuaries. Very few were powerful enough to carry more than a few spells with them.

Ignoring the pain of his burned chest, the privateer captain pushed the dead guard to the side, releasing his hold on the knife and drawing the sword from the corpse's scabbard.

Ryla stepped through the cell bars, and from the way the wizard's gaze shifted to her, Jaelik knew the man saw her.

"Die, spellwyrm!" the ghost bade fiercely.

Steel hissed as the sharp blade came free and Jaelik saw fear dawn in the wizard's gold eyes as his attention turned back to his human opponent. The privateer captain struck mercilessly, cutting through the wizard's outthrust hands and lopping off fingers.

"No!" the wizard howled as Jaelik reached for him.

"Yes!" Jaelik snarled, grabbing the man's shoulder and yanking him forward, driving the sword under the wizard's ribs and into his heart. The privateer captain watched the wizard's gold eyes, half-filled with fear that he hadn't slain him. Some wizards didn't keep their hearts in their bodies.

The wizard's gold eyes flared with hate, then dimmed as death claimed him. He shivered on the blade and went limp.

Jaelik let the body fall, glanced at Alff, and saw the

quartermaster break one of his opponents' necks while kneeling on his back, hands cupped beneath the man's chin. The other Deathwatch guard lay still. Jaelik stepped on the wizard's body, half expecting the corpse to turn into a clutch of snakes that would strike in vengeance, and yanked the blade free.

"The keys!" the bearded warrior in the cell cried out. "If you have any decency at all, give us the keys! Once those guards and the wizard are discovered here dead they will have no mercy on us!"

Alff pushed himself up, shoving one of the bodies aside and revealing a short-hafted, double-bitted battle-ax. "That man has the truth of it, Cap'n. Ye leave 'em here now, ye might as well cut their throats yerself." The quartermaster ran a thumb along the keen blades and smiled appreciatively.

"You must free them," Ryla added.

Cursing his own ill luck, Jaelik searched the dead guard at his feet and found the keys on a massive iron ring spotted with orange rust. He crossed to the warrior in the cell. "Who are you?"

"Farryn Caerk, once of the Roostaan true army." Despite emaciation and sickness, the man managed to hold himself with pride. "As are many who are in these cells."

"If I free you, Farryn Caerk," Jaelik said, "then you must follow me from this place."

The warrior gripped the cell bars, desperation flaming in his feverish gaze. "You are not of Roosta. I know this from the way you talk."

"No. I hail from Vellak." Jaelik forced himself to ignore the burning on his chest. "Will you do as I command?"

"I will not simply take my freedom. I have a wife and children, the gods willing, who may yet still live in this city."

Other men echoed Farryn Caerk's sentiments.

"Then, damn you," Jaelik said fiercely, "live to fight another day. I offer you the only chance you may have to strike back against Turkoth." Provided the ghost was right, he reminded himself.

The warrior met the privateer captain's gaze. "I will take it. But there is no other way from this place save those stairs those men only now descended."

"There is another way," Jaelik said, and hoped that it was true. He thrust the big iron key into the lock and twisted. The harsh ratcheting testified as to how long it had been since the door had been opened.

"Cap'n." Alff held up another key ring, shaking it so that it rang for a moment.

"Do it." Jaelik watched Ryla as she approached the dead wizard.

The ghost's fingers passed through the robes and brought forth a pop-eyed toad carved from reddish soapstone. She brought the toad level with her gaze on her open palm. Then she pursed her lips and blew. Incredibly, the toad crumbled into dust that burned lambent green for a moment before disappearing. In seconds, nothing remained of the toad.

Ryla turned to him, noticing his interest. "It was my father's. Now it is gone."

While Alff went down to the next cell and set free the man there, surrendering the key ring, Jaelik took the torch from the wall sconce. He spotted the rapier carried by one of the men the quartermaster had downed. After he claimed the rapier for himself, he passed the sword to Farryn Caerk, who moved it to get the heft of it, showing past experience.

Holding the torch high, knowing time was against them, Jaelik strode down the twisting dungeon. Shadows bent and twisted on the walls around him, and the sudden emotion-laden whispers that followed him sounded too loud to escape the notice of the dungeon guards that had to be posted above.

Ryla drew even with him, her own footfalls totally silent.

"How far?" Jaelik demanded, failing again and again to stare through the darkness ahead.

"Only a little way now," Ryla replied.

6

Dark water filled the end of the dungeon ahead. The brackish stink of saltwater that had gone foul from being trapped underground for so long filled the passageway. Still, the tiny eddies Jaelik saw coursing through the pool in places testified that the water still knew the pulse of the Alpatian Sea.

The privateer captain raised his torch and cursed anew, listening to the drum of feet as Alff and the prisoners came to a stop behind him. The passageway roof dipped down only a few short feet above, turning at an angle to plunge into the unwelcoming water. No forward progress remained possible.

He turned to Ryla. "Did you plan on this?" he demanded harshly.

"I'd heard some of the dungeon had filled with water," the ghost responded. Her eyes glowed in the darkness as she surveyed the pool.

"We can't go through here," Jaelik said.

"I can see that, Cap'n," Alff spoke up. Knowing no one save his captain could see and hear the ghost, the quartermaster had taken it upon himself to carry Jaelik's seemingly one-sided conversation.

Ryla glanced at the tunnel roof. "The dungeon ends here,

but a wall collapsed shortly after my father's death. Another passageway lies on the other side of that wall, and no one except my father and myself knew about it. The room goes underwater here, but it's now open to the passageway on the other side. I used to visit these areas when I was a girl. My father worked on many dangerous things here."

Jaelik shook his head. "I'm not going into that water. Somewhere, somehow, it runs back to the Alpatian Sea. There's no telling how far it runs underwater. All of those chambers could be under the sea now. And there could be an undertow that can pull a man into a sumphole where he can only drown."

"No," Ryla insisted. "The passageway dips down here, but it rises on the other side. I'm sure of it."

"How far?"

"Wait here." Without another word, Ryla stepped into the water, seemingly unaffected by the near freezing temperature it exuded.

Despite the fact that the woman was already dead, Jaelik's concern for her safety washed over him. He made himself be still, watching as she dropped rapidly from sight, not even leaving a disturbance in the water to mark her passage.

"Cap'n?" Alff asked.

Over a dozen torches were reflected in the black water. "We're waiting," Jaelik said.

"Aye, sir."

The escaped prisoners shifted and whispered nervously among themselves.

While he watched for the ghost's return, Jaelik's mind wandered, trying to guess how long it would be before one of the Deathwatch guards discovered the prisoners had fled their cells.

Only a few moments later, Ryla returned. Her eyes appeared first, glowing white underwater. The sea fled from her, leaving her dry even as she again stepped onto the stone floor, but Jaelik felt the increased chill rolling from her. Her lips held a lambent blue cast.

"The passageway rises again on the other side and leads to the hidden chambers," she announced. "No more than twenty feet away. You can swim it easily."

"Is the device we seek still there?" Jaelik asked.

"No one could have gotten to it."

"Cap'n," Alff spoke up sharply, "there's only one way to answer them questions ye're asking yerself."

Jaelik cursed the dark water, wondering if there was something in the chambers that the ghost feared.

"If you turn back," Ryla stated calmly, "you'll have to fight Turkoth's warriors."

The privateer captain knew it was true. If it had only been Alff and him, he'd been certain they could have escaped the city before dawn. *Rapier's Thrust* would have met them at the prearranged rendezvous.

But there was no way all of the prisoners would escape notice as well. And if any got caught, Jaelik knew they would all get caught.

"We'll swim under," Jaelik said. "Protect the torches. We'll need them on the other side." He doused the torch he carried by wrapping it in the thick oilcloth Alff passed to him. He thrust it through his swordbelt.

"We don't know what's waiting in those waters," one of the men protested.

"Aye, an' yer right," Alff bellowed gruffly, "but ye fer damn sure know them Deathwatch guards are waitin' on ye back there. Put out them torches and protect them. We're gonna need them on the other side."

The dissenters quieted but didn't desist. The gloom, held

at bay by the torches, quickly closed in as the flames extinguished.

Before the last of the light fled the chamber, Jaelik waded out into the water. The drop-off put the brackish liquid up to his waist within only two short steps. He took a final deep breath and dove into the pool.

Underwater, he felt the slight eddy of current circulating sluggishly through the pool. He stroked through the darkness, occasionally trailing a hand above him to touch the low ceiling and keep his sense of direction. He found the end of the room easily, then located the narrow break in the wall Ryla had told him about. The sixth time he swam up to find the stone ceiling, his hand broke through into an air pocket.

The passageway rose steeply on the other side.

Foul air filled the chamber, causing Jaelik to breathe shallowly till he adjusted to the strong odor of mold. Only the wet slap of his boots echoed in the chamber. He couldn't see his hand in front of his face, but he spotted the ghost rising from the water behind him easily.

Jaelik stepped away from the water's edge, one hand out in front of him and the other sliding his rapier free. He pushed the blade before him, using it to make sure the way ahead was clear. Carefully, he made his way through debris on the stone floor that he couldn't see.

Alff came up somewhere behind him, gasping hoarsely and cursing.

Kneeling, the privateer captain laid the rapier hilt on his foot so he could find it by feel. Then he pulled the torch out and used the flint he'd taken from one of the Death-watch guards to relight it.

Smoke poured from the torch, coiling uneasily against the stone passageway above. The smoke pooled against the ceiling. If there were any drafts, they were too slight to move the smoke, and didn't speak much for the other exit Ryla promised.

He raised the torch as more men surfaced in the pool. Alff bellowed orders at them, getting other torches lit, shaping the men up automatically into a defensive unit.

Jaelik surveyed the passageway. Decaying mortar and stones lay on the dust-covered floor. A section of the wall on the left had crumbled, spilling mortar and rock across the floor. Dozens of spiders crawled through the hammock webs hanging ahead. The passageway curved to the right, quickly disappearing from sight.

Ryla moved through the webs without hesitation. Torchlight glimmered from the frozen sections left by her passing and from the chill she carried. Spiders retreated from the nearby webs as if they were aflame.

"Come," she said. "No one is here. No one has been here in a long time." She walked up the incline and down the passageway.

"Alff." Jaelik parted the webs before him with the rapier. He set fire to some of the webs with the torch, watching them curl and burn as they retreated. He melted a path through the webs, carrying the rapier tightly in his fist. His breath sounded loud in his ears.

The passageway continued to curve, and even rise and descend. Black-and-green stone doors marked with pointed sigils occupied the left and right walls.

Ryla studied each of the doors intently, pausing now and again to brush at the thick layer of dust that covered them, baring the sigils for better inspection. Spiders continued to clamber in the hammock webs around them. Little space was left open between the webs.

"What is this place?" Farryn Caerk asked in a hushed voice.

"The way out," Jaelik replied, hoping it was true. The torch's acrid smoke burned the back of his throat and turned his voice hoarse.

"It's one of my father's inner sanctums," Ryla said, abandoning the latest door she'd examined more closely. "One of the few that was never found." She continued, and Jaelik fell into step behind her.

Men cursed and prayed as they followed him. Some lamented that they were only going to their doom in some forgotten wizard's pit. Slamintyr Lattyrl was never far from any Roostaan's mind. And had they known the old wizard's dead daughter led them, the privateer captain felt certain they would have been even more unnerved.

Often, sections of the hammock webs above the men caught fire from the torches they carried. The silken strands flared quickly and raced briefly before going out, but the eerie flames given off further twisted the shadows gathered around them.

Around the next bend, the passageway split into two. Broken debris covered all but the bottom few steps of the stairs in the hallway on the right. Ryla passed the hallway by without a second glance, continuing along the main passage.

A horrified scream ripped through the passageway.

Jaelik turned instantly, thinking one of the scuttling spiders had finally chosen a victim.

"Damn thief!" a tall man muttered, backing away quickly. "Should know better than to try to get past a wizard's door."

Beyond the warrior, a short, thin man starved down to skin over bone dropped soundlessly at the foot of a door. When the man rolled over onto his back, his eyes rolled back white and a yellow-green pallor showed up even in the torchlight.

Alff strode forward and hunkered down near the body. He used a nearby rock to turn the man's head, then pressed it against his throat without response. "He's dead, Cap'n. Poison, by the looks of it."

"From the spiders?" a man asked, gazing upward fearfully.

"No," the tall man said. "He tried the door, barely laid a hand on it, and fell."

"The doors are protected." Ryla stepped beside Jaelik, her features cold and impassive.

"No one's to touch the doors," Jaelik ordered. "Not if they want to get out of here alive."

No one argued the point.

"Here."

Jaelik glanced at the door Ryla stood before. Twenty minutes had passed since the man's death. The spiderwebs had remained constant, as did their designers. In that time he'd grown weary of walking and would have been lost amid all the constant turnings and switchbacks had there not been only one passageway. Silently, he cursed ghosts in general and Ryla in particular.

"Is it safe?" he whispered, not wanting to show any hesitation in front of the men he led.

"It was under the protection of Slamintyr Lattyrl," the ghost snapped. "Nothing is safe."

"Can you open it?"

"I hope to."

"You hope to?" Jaelik's anger almost escaped his control. To be forced here, after many sleepless nights, leading a ragtag, half-starved miniature army that couldn't really be counted on to defend itself, and to know that his country would probably be under attack by morning was too much.

"I've never tried to get past my father's protective seals." Ryla cautiously approached the door. Fear shone in her face.

As he watched her, Jaelik's heart softened somewhat. "If you don't think you can do it, don't try."

"I have to. Turkoth has the Crown of the Storms."

"Maybe there is another way to take that from him. At the very least, once we're free of this loathsome pit, my crew and I can sail for Vellak. Perhaps a proper defense can be set up."

She turned her luminous eyes on him. "You've not seen the power of the Crown. Whatever navy Vellak could put into the water as a defensive line would only be reduced to kindling in heartbeats. The Colossus is the only way." She turned to the door again, stretching out a hand.

A low, keening moan filled the passageway. It grew louder the closer the ghost came to the door. It was the sound of the final breath ripped from a dying predator.

"Ryla," Jaelik called softly, stepping forward, reaching for her, dropping the torch into the dust at their feet.

She ignored him and chanted, placing her palm flat against the door.

Swirling red-violet light flared from the sigil drawn on the door as her palm came into contact with it. The light brightened, bringing tears to Jaelik's eyes with its harsh intensity. The privateer captain felt as though he were moving through a cargo hold swelled near to bursting with soaked rice as he reached for the ghost.

He touched her, a faint sensation of corpse-cold flesh, then she staggered back against him, dodging the huge triangular head that lunged free of the door. The mouth gaped, filled with rows of needle-sharp fangs.

7

Automatically, Jaelik struck at the mystical creature, swinging his rapier down, but the blade slipped through the creature without touching it.

The privateer captain halted the rapier only inches from his leg. He stepped back amid the shouts of Alff and the men, knowing they could see the creature as surely as he could. He held Ryla, one arm around her waist, struggling to pull her to safety.

"No," the ghost argued. "You can't defeat it without me." She closed her hand around his swordarm.

Jaelik felt heat surge through his limb, almost too hot to keep from crying out.

"Now!" she cried. "Strike!"

The eellike monster continued spewing from the sigil on the door, revealing over ten feet of wriggling, leathery scales covering a body bigger around than Jaelik's thigh. Slitted eyes burned with brass fires as they blinked and focused on the privateer captain. It lunged again, the terrifying mouth open.

Up against at least two of the men behind him, Jaelik swung, knowing he'd never get another chance. The blade cleaved the triangular skull deeply, spouting blood and showing broken bone. He held the open mouth from them through sheer strength, feeling that at any moment he was going to break.

The eel-demon writhed free of the door and wrapped around them tightly. But before it could squeeze the breath from them, it died, bursting into a cloud of glowing green crystals. The spiders clinging in the webs above spun the green crystals into their gossamer strand.

Only the sounds of the spider's legs weaving sounded in the passageway.

"It's gone," Ryla said. "The spiders will reconstruct it in time, but for now we can pass."

"I thought you could get past your father's defenses," Jaelik said.

"We did." The ghost pushed herself from his embrace carefully. She didn't look at him as she crossed again to the door.

"And if there's something else?" Jaelik asked.

"We won't know that till we find it." She pushed the door open, revealing only a darkened room.

Jaelik stooped and picked up the torch. Cautiously, letting the torch lead the way with the rapier close behind, he strode into the cavernous room.

Shelves lined the walls to the left and right. Books—bound in leather, stained glass, and precious materials, studded with gems and marked in arcane languages—occupied the shelves in company with vases, statues, and other objects. A large desk that looked like it had been cut whole from a massive tree trunk, polished so the age rings gleamed in the finish, sat against the far wall. Huge timbers ran across the ceiling and supported a wheel-shaped candelabrum.

For a moment, Ryla stood frozen in the center of the room. She stared at the desk.

Jaelik stood behind her and didn't press. With the other men crowding the doorway behind him, their torches held high and constantly moving, bitter, harsh shadows played on the far wall behind the desk. He watched them fearfully, thinking they might tear themselves free of the wall and attack.

"Cap'n," Alff called.

"A moment," Jaelik responded. He watched the ghost, suddenly aware of how heavy a thousand years and more of mourning could be. Still, he had carried through with what she had blackmailed him into through her presence. His responsibility was to his crew now, lying at anchor deep within enemy waters. "Ryla."

His voice startled her, but she kept her back to him.

Keeping his voice soft, Jaelik said, "We don't know how much time there is before morning. We should be going."

"Don't let anyone touch the books," she warned as she stepped toward the shelves. "Nor anything else in this room. It will all be protected. Perhaps even more strongly than the doors. This was one of my father's lore rooms, where he created items and spells. Walk carefully between the designs on the floor as well."

Jaelik gazed down, lifting the torch high so that he could better see the designs she spoke of. At least a dozen different areas were marked off. Glyphs and sigils appeared burned or carved into the stone floor. The designs had been filled in with precious metals and colorful crystals.

"The designs are doorways to other worlds," Ryla said. "Savage places for the most part, where my father gathered energies or treasures that he needed in his work. At least one of those places holds demons whose lives he purchased or stole." She reached for a small figure on one of the upper shelves, then gasped in frustration as her fingers slid through the figure. "I can't get it."

Avoiding the nearest designs on the floor, Jaelik joined her at the shelf. The granite figurine showed a broad-chested figure with sapphire eyes inset into a face that could only be called vaguely human. The mouth was a slash, barely visible in the round face. The privateer captain reached for the figurine.

"No!"

The sharpness in the ghost's tone froze Jaelik.

"Touch it and you die," Ryla told him.

"Then how are we to get it?" Jaelik asked in exasperation.

"Together." Ryla extended her hand, sinking her ghostly form into his flesh.

Instead of the extreme heat this time, Jaelik felt the aching bite of winter deaden his arm. His hand started to move of its own accord, but he held it in place.

"Let me have your arm," Ryla said.

"No. I can do this."

"Your pride is insufferable."

"My pride," Jaelik replied, "is what brought me this far." He tried to move his arm and couldn't for just an instant. Then Ryla relinquished control. He plucked the figurine from the shelf. "You're sure this is what controls the Colossus?"

"If I wasn't, we wouldn't be taking it."

"What am I supposed to do with it?" Jaelik asked.

"Wrap it in a cloth and store it for now. Do not touch it save with this hand while I protect you."

Cautiously, Jaelik did as she bade, ripping the tail from his ruined shirt and covering the figurine in layers. The motions were awkward with her partially controlling his arm. At her direction, he tucked the figurine into the pouch at his belt.

"Cap'n," Alff called. "We've got company coming."

Jaelik didn't bother asking who as he raced across to the door. He peered back down the passageway and spotted the torchlight coming closer around the last turn. Evidently, the dead dungeon guards had been discovered and pursuit had been quickly organized. Following the tracks through the dust leading up to the pool of standing water obviously hadn't proven difficult. Figuring out that the pool had an exit hidden in it hadn't been a great leap of logic either.

The recently escaped prisoners milled around under the swaths of spiderwebs. They didn't have enough weapons among them to make a decent stand, and they knew it. Jaelik knew they'd be cut down like swine led to a slaughterhouse.

The privateer captain swore and turned back around to Ryla. "I need that exit you promised. *Now!*"

The ghost fled to the back of the room and stepped into the corner to the left of the desk. "Here," she entreated. "There is a secret passageway."

"Where does it lead?" Jaelik demanded.

Ryla pressed against a section of the wall but nothing happened. "Outside. Perhaps a quarter mile from the city, along the cliffs to the east." She doubled her fist and pounded the wall. "I can't open it."

Joining her at the wall, listening to the rise of the approaching voices, Jaelik examined the surface. If this new passageway took them to the eastern cliffs, they'd be nearer the rendezvous point he'd set up with his crew. "Where?"

Ryla put a finger against the wall. "Here."

Even though he held the torch close, Jaelik couldn't discern anything different about the wall section. Still, he placed his hand over it and shoved hard.

8

Something grated within the stone, and a section of the wall no bigger than Jaelik's palm recessed the width of his thumb. Immediately, the V-shaped corner section started to revolve, carrying shelves around with it. The torch illuminated the narrow stone steps that wound up in the open space beyond.

"Alff," the privateer captain growled. "This way."

Quietly, the quartermaster herded the men toward the

hidden passageway. Most were reluctant to go, but the arrival of the Deathwatch troops gave them little choice.

"There they are!" someone shouted out in the hallway. The sound of slapping feet echoed in the room.

Alff quickly got the men moving. Amid the bumping and jostling that went on, a man stepped deeply into one of the designs. Black, liquid fog rolled up from the design on the floor, swirling quickly around the man and snatching him deep into the floor. The man's screams for help died the same instant the fog disappeared. A fetid blast of heat filled the room from whatever world had opened up.

Jaelik caught the door's edge and pulled it closed just as a throwing knife cut the air over his head. He wished he had some way to block the door.

"It will hold against them for a time," Ryla told him. "Even if there is a wizard among them, it will take considerable magical force to open that door. And if they've learned anything about the doors in this place, they'll be reluctant to touch it."

Knowing the ghost was right, Jaelik followed the men through the hidden door, shoving Alff ahead. They pounded up the stone stairs quickly. Thankfully, there weren't any spiders. As he stepped through the doorway, he noticed that Ryla hadn't moved, her eyes roving over the room.

For a moment, Jaelik could see the child she'd been. She shuddered when one of the Deathwatch guards started pounding on the door. The pounding broke off suddenly, interrupted by a scream of mortal agony. The scream ended in a broken, choked silence that was ripped apart by the sound of men cursing and calling on gods.

"Come on." Jaelik held out his hand.

After only a brief hesitation, Ryla took his hand in hers, covering his fingers in cool strength. She joined him on the first stair, then turned and pointed to another wall section. Jaelik pressed it, and the revolving section turned neatly back into place.

Holding his torch above them, he led the way up the stairs.

A quarter mile farther on, Jaelik guessed, the passageway led to another secret door that—once operated—opened into a small cave that fronted the Alpatian Sea. The surf's roar and the briny odor felt like coming home after all the hours spent in the dungeon area.

The escaped prisoners all wanted to return to the city to check on their family and friends. Jaelik argued with them while they climbed the hill above the cave, telling them that the Deathwatch guards surely knew who they were and would be looking for them. So far, none of the guards tailing them appeared to have found the escape route.

They followed a game trail up the hillside, all their torches now doused. From their present position, Roosta could be easily seen to the north. The harbor held nearly four dozen warships, all neatly berthed in rows. Occasionally the sound of rigging slapping against masts came to Jaelik; water carried sound much better than land. Lanterns created pockets of light aboard the ships as did the buildings along the docks and houses further up the hills behind them.

From the top of the hill, Jaelik also saw the white foam surging between the jaws of craggy rocks sticking up from the shallow sea floor in front of the caves. He glanced up at the stars, read the constellations, and made certain of his position.

"We don't intend to be kept from our homes," Farryn Caerk told Jaelik when they paused for a moment.

The privateer captain was conscious of all the eyes on him. Steeling himself, knowing the current battle could be lost in the next few minutes, he said, "They aren't your homes. They belong to Turkoth Blackheart and his Death-watch for now. If you walk back in there tonight, you'll just offer up easy blood to be spilled."

"We'll take a few heads of our own," one warrior promised.

"And you'll make no difference that way," Jaelik countered harshly. "If that's your plan, I might just as well have left you in that dungeon to die."

"Then what about you?" another warrior challenged. "Do you have a navy at your beck and call?"

"I have a ship," Jaelik answered.

Another man laughed bitterly. "A lone privateer, and you're gonna stand up against the armada Turkoth has at anchor in the harbor?"

Jaelik tried to find the words to give the men heart and to pull them to his side. If none of them were found before morning, there still existed an element of surprise. The Deathwatch guards might assume they'd fled through one of the designs on the floor, or all perished there. But there were no words he could give them.

"He is not alone."

Even though he heard the words, Jaelik didn't know the others did until their heads swiveled in Ryla's direction.

The ghost glowed like a soft white flame against the darkness as she stepped among the men.

Several of the warriors stepped back, their hands to their weapons. Others brought up religious symbols and prayed in quiet voices.

"Know me," the ghost said defiantly. "I am the daughter of Slamintyr Lattyrl, who once called Roosta home and offered its citizens his protection from the ancestors of the barbarian hordes."

"The elf wizard had no daughter," a broad warrior accused.

Ryla turned to the man. Quick as a striking snake, her hand flashed out. Her fingernails sliced tiny furrows on the warrior's cheek. She caught droplets of blood in her hand as the man dodged back. Curling her hand tight over the captured blood, she spoke arcane words. Purple lightning flashed in her hand and the big warrior dropped to his hands and knees on the rocky hill.

The other warriors stepped back further, warding themselves against evil and demons.

"Do not," Ryla ordered coldly, "ever seek to deny me my heritage or I will burst your heart."

The warrior tried to speak but couldn't. His face soon paled and his limbs trembled from the agony he was in.

After another moment, Ryla opened her hand, now blood-free. The warrior dropped to the ground, panting like he'd run a long way. The ghost stood among them, her eyes burning. "Any man who chooses not to follow Captain Tarlsson, I will bury in these cliffs this night."

The warriors shifted hesitantly, but when Farryn Caerk spoke, Jaelik knew he spoke for them all. "It will be as you wish, lady."

Ryla turned to Jaelik. "Take them, Captain Tarlsson. I will join you shortly."

"Alff," Jaelik called.

"Aye, Cap'n."

"Two by two," Jaelik said. "Quick as you can."

"Aye." The quartermaster bellowed orders, getting the men into loose ranks and heading them across the cliffs at a good pace.

Ryla stood her ground, her arms crossed, haughty and confident.

Only after seeing her for long days and nights, Jaelik

knew not all was well with the ghost. Pain and fatigue touched her eyes and features, though he doubted any would see those things in her except someone who'd been around her for a length of time. He waited till the last of the men was far enough away so they could speak privately. "Are you all right?"

"Why shouldn't I be?" she demanded, but the imperious note in her voice sounded hollow and brittle. She dimmed a little, and he guessed that he was the only one who could see her again.

"You've never shown yourself to anyone but me before."

"I had to. You would never have convinced them to go with you." Her voice sounded weaker, distant. Her image wavered from view for a moment, and when she reappeared, she was more translucent than ever. She took a step and almost fell.

Jaelik stepped toward her, trying to take her hand. But the contact wasn't solid, only a passage of freezing cold that left him drained and swooning.

"No!" She stumbled away from him. "Leave me alone! If you touch me now, it could kill you!"

Jaelik pulled his hand back, heart racing and head throbbing. His hand felt numb, like he'd held it for a time in freezing water. All undead things were vampiric in nature, feasting off of pain or memory or the flesh and blood of living things. She dimmed from view longer this time before returning.

"Ryla," he whispered.

She smiled at him bitterly. "After all these days, I think you'd look forward to getting rid of me."

"No."

His answer somehow discomforted her further. She

turned her face from his, crossing her arms over her breasts again. "Go. Not much time remains before morning."

But Jaelik couldn't make himself leave. "And you?"

"I'll be there by morning."

"And if you're not?"

"Then you should run for your life, Jaelik Tarlsson." Ryla turned and was gone, leaving the privateer captain standing alone high in the cliffs overlooking the city that Turkoth Blackheart held in thrall.

9

"Cap'n."

Before Jaelik came fully awake, his hand gripped the rapier's hilt, sliding it partially from the scabbard. Nightmares had dogged his sleep, rife with foul demons that had chased him and continually took Ryla from him. He blinked and focused on Alff's craggy face, feeling the quartermaster's callused hand gently staying his sword wrist.

"It be near to mornin'," Alff said. The bruises and bumps from last night's encounter had lost some of their swelling, but ghastly tints of purple and green had set in.

Jaelik shoved the rapier back home, then rolled from the hammock in his quarters. He glanced around, hoping to find the ghost somewhere in the room. His quarters were clean and efficient, packed with books he'd traded for or bought and rolled maps that he'd purchased, copied, or drawn himself. A small desk to his right held his personal log.

From the way *Rapier's Thrust* bobbed on the water, he knew they were still at anchor. He poured water from a pitcher into a bowl, then splashed his face with it. By the time they'd reached the ship last night, only a couple of hours remained before dawn. He hadn't thought to sleep, only to wait on the ghost.

But she had never come.

"Turkoth's fleet?" Jaelik asked as he led the way out of his quarters and up the short steps to the stern castle.

"Still at anchor," Alff replied.

The crew stood ready at their stations but the privateer captain knew they were all fearful. None of them had been happy about being so deep in Roostaan waters, nor in knowing that a ghost was leading their captain.

Jaelik had informed the crew of the night's events succinctly after reaching the ship. There had been little argument, for all of them knew that once their ship's master had made up his mind about a course of action no one could change his mind.

Thick, rolling gray fog blanketed the ship, making viewing anything more than a seventy or eighty feet an uncertain thing. It looked ghostly pale in the predawn darkness. Even the eastern skies were hidden from view.

"When did this damned fog set in?" Jaelik asked as he came to a stop at the plotting table near the great wheel.

"Near an hour ago, Cap'n," the helmsman replied.

Jaelik glanced up at the crow's nest. "What kind of visibility do we have from the rigging?"

"No better than this."

"You've got our position marked well?"

"Aye, Cap'n." The helmsman tapped a finger on the map on the plotting table. Glass protected the map. A wooden case held grease pencils, compass, and ruler.

"If you don't," Jaelik said, "we'll likely rip the bottom out of her on the rocks when we get underway." He crossed to the stern railing and peered out.

The cliffs soared almost straight up a hundred feet and

more to starboard, and only open green sea lay to port. Roosta lay ahead of them nearly a mile away around the curve of the shoreline.

"Mayhap the fog will burn off with the coming dawn," Alff said.

Jaelik shook his head. "Not this. It's thick as pea soup." He gazed down over the deck, knowing his crew would expect a decision and orders from him within minutes. The thick mist in the fog dampened the fresh clothing he'd put on after returning to the ship.

"What about the ha'nt?" Alff asked in a low voice.

"She's not here." The figurine rode in the privateer captain's belt pouch. He hadn't dared even look at it, but its weight was somewhat reassuring.

"Where do ye think—?"

"I don't know," Jaelik said hoarsely. "She used much of herself to stand up for us last night. Perhaps it was too much."

"A thousand years," Alff said. "I shouldn't give up on her quite so quick was I ye."

Jaelik peered up into the gathering fog. He could see the dim outline of the rising sun now, set like a pale, cold gem just coming above the horizon.

"Afore it burns off," Alff pointed out, "the fog will give us cover whether we run or sail into the harbor, but we can't linger in either case. We can make for Turkoth's fleet, or we can make for Vellak and hope to hold against an invasion. Which is it gonna be?"

Cold breath touched the back of Jaelik's neck and, knowing what it had to be, the privateer captain couldn't keep the grin from his face as he turned. Ryla stood beside the plotting table.

The ghost's lavender gown billowed in the breeze. Her green eyes met his.

"You made it," Jaelik said. From the way Alff glanced about, he knew she was only visible to him again.

"There should never have been any doubt," she told him. "Although I admit to some surprise of my own to find you here."

"If I should have left," Jaelik said, "I would have returned as soon as I could to determine your fate."

"Really?" Her eyes searched his face.

"Aye." An uncomfortable silence passed between them, punctuated by the lonesome cries of foraging gulls and the rigging popping against the masts and yardarms.

"My fate," she said quietly, looking away from him, "is already sealed, Captain Tarlsson. But I appreciate your thought. However, we have precious little time to us."

"What of the Colossus?"

"Do you trust me?"

"As much as I am able."

"Then trust me now. Get this ship underway. We have much to do."

Jaelik gave Alff the command to get the ship bound for Roosta. Swiftly, the crew pulled the great sheets into place as the anchor was raised. In minutes, *Rapier's Thrust* was fully trimmed, the sails belling out like the bellies of fat birds from all three masts. Jaelik gave orders to keep the ship close to the coastline and to let him know the minute the fog started to burn off.

Then he went below with the ghost.

"The Colossus owes its existence to magic ancient even by elven standards," Ryla said. She sat on the floor across from Jaelik and slipped her ghostly hands inside of his flesh and blood ones.

Jaelik felt the cold stinging of the possession, but he didn't fight against it. He watched as the ghost used their joined flesh to open the pouch and remove the cloth-wrapped figurine.

"In those days," she continued, "my father's people believed there were only four kinds of magic. The elves, being truly blessed by their gods, were given understanding of the earth and wind. The dwarves inherited the understanding of fire. And the sea? Only humans and their great sailing vessels come close to understanding the sea, able to cross the waters but unable to wrest the secret magics the oceans hide."

Together, they stood the figurine on the ship's deck. Jaelik didn't expect it to stand, thinking the figurine would tumble and possibly shatter as *Rapier's Thrust* cleaved through the water. But the little statue stood.

Her hands still joined with his, Ryla lighted seven candles around the figurine as she sang words Jaelik couldn't understand. She added powders from a pouch at her waist and the candle flames each changed, taking on the hues of the rainbow. Jaelik's skin prickled and tightened the way it would with a fast-approaching storm.

"As the elves sought to understand more of the magic they'd been given," Ryla said, "they also gave up spells as powerful as the Colossus. The more diversified their magic became, the less able they were to work magic from the Beginning Time. Only my father and a few others like him were able to wield both the Old and the New Magic."

The multicolored smoke whirled inside the cabin. Jaelik tried to breathe shallowly, but even slight breaths caused him to feel light-headed. His fatigue and pain washed away, but his body felt leaden.

"It was this diffusion of power that led to the downfall of so many elven cities. My father's people have forever been a jealous people."

For a moment, Jaelik thought the figurine had moved

on the ship's deck, and he guessed that it had been his imagination, addled by the magicked smoke. Even the crack of sailcloth and Alff's bawled orders to ship's crew sounded distant. His eyes closed, but he still felt Ryla's arms in his.

"Go to it," Ryla encouraged softly. "Wake the Colossus of Mahrass."

A waking slumber claimed Jaelik.

Jaelik swam deep beneath the ocean's surface, so far down that the water had turned from green to deepest blue. In the darkness he could only see a few yards ahead of him. For a moment he felt fear fill his belly, thinking that he was lost, thinking that he would drown. He looked upward, seeking the surface.

"No," Ryla told him from somewhere far away. "Seek the Colossus and don't be worried. You can breathe these waters."

Unable to hold his breath any longer, Jaelik gasped for his breath, believing water would fill his lungs. But it didn't. Incredibly, he was able to breathe normally despite the water and the depth. But he didn't know where he was supposed to go.

"Think of the Colossus," Ryla said. "You must find it and wake it."

Jaelik remembered the figurine, drawing its image in his mind. Immediately, he felt an urging rise within him, pulling him to the left. He swam strongly, knifing through the water at a speed that had to rival a dolphin's. The urging grew stronger, then pulled him further down.

He swam above a pink coral reef, startling schools of fish that darted in all directions. He was among them before they could get clear. Their scaly bodies brushed against his cheek and arms.

The urging became a hammering crescendo inside Jaelik. A moment later he spotted the wrecked cargo ship lying over on its starboard side. The ship was just over sixty feet long with a gaping hole in its hull. The forward mast had been snapped off.

Jaelik guessed that pirates had taken the vessel and sunk her decades ago from the barnacle build-up and reefs around her. He swam lower, still drawn by the urging that filled him.

"There!" Ryla said.

He pushed himself along the shipwreck, noting the skeletons picked clean and scattered over the surrounding area. Pots and clay shards looked black against the blue sand. Wooden chests lay half-buried, broken open, and shattered. Glass bottles and jars winked in the faint light.

"Where?" he asked, frustrated that he wasn't able to see what she saw.

"Beneath you."

Then he did see, and he realized that he'd missed it because it was so large. Even after all the stories he'd heard about the Colossus of Mahrass, he hadn't been prepared for how big it actually was.

10

The Colossus lay face-down across the ocean floor, its misshapen round head turned to the right. Its face was all but buried in the sand and the coral reef. It was more than twice the length of the cargo ship that draped across its massive hips that had looked like rock mounds. The mouth was a slash that held a school of bright red-and-yellow fish as long as Jaelik's arm. The eye was a hollow pit that housed seaweed and a pink squid that splayed out its tentacles.

"You must wake it," Ryla advised.

"How?"

"Swim to it," the ghost stated quietly. "I will guide you."

Dwarfed by the huge granite giant, Jaelik dropped feet-first into the deep sand beside the Colossus' head. Instinctively, he followed Ryla's lead, tracing sigils that blazed with faerie fire across the stone giant's forehead. He spoke, but it wasn't in a language that he understood, and the syllables echoed in the sea around him.

When he finished, he stepped back. He waited, thinking he'd done something wrong, that Ryla's guidance somehow hadn't been enough or had been wrong, or that the Colossus had been without life for too long.

Then the arcane creature shivered. The huge fingers clawed into the silt and debris of the ocean floor. Fish darted away in all directions, responding to the change in pressure caused by the Colossus' waking. The wrecked cargo ship broke into halves, then fell completely apart as the giant pushed itself up. The squid propelled itself from the eye of the Colossus, tentacles bunching together behind it as its head arrowed away.

The ocean moved around Jaelik, causing a riptide that sucked him up toward the Colossus. He tried to swim, then finally gave up and twisted so he could push his boots against the creature and spring outward. He continued rising till he floated in front of the huge, round face.

Intelligence glowed softly in the empty eye sockets. "I come," it declared in a thundering voice. Without hesitation, the Colossus turned and started walking, taking great strides across the ocean floor.

"Return," Ryla bade him.

Jaelik peered after the granite giant. "Does it know where to go?"

"Yes."

The privateer captain lost the Colossus in the darkness then, and he lost himself as well.

Jaelik opened his eyes and watched as the ghost took her arms from his. They were still seated near the candles, which burned without the colored flames now, but the figurine of the Colossus was gone. Feeling returned to his wrists and hands.

"It's done," Ryla announced weakly.

Jaelik pushed himself to his feet, then offered the ghost his hand. She took it and allowed herself to be helped up.

"When will the Colossus be here?" he asked.

"Soon," she answered. "If the gods favor us, it will be soon enough."

"Cap'n." Alff shoved his head inside the doorway. "The fog's lifting a bit, and we're gonna be within sight of the Roostaan harbor in minutes. I thought ye might want to be on deck."

Jaelik went, his hand tight on the rapier hilt.

The rising sun had burned through the fog to a degree, leaving it heavy and thick across the sea swells but thinning it out only an arm's reach or so above the mainmast.

Jaelik stood on the fighting deck built on the ship's prow, holding tight to a ratline. With a full wind in her sails, *Rapier's Thrust* cut through the emerald Alpatian Sea. His head still felt slightly fuzzy from the magic Ryla had worked.

He peered through the fog, searching for the Roostaan shoreline. He couldn't see it, but he could see the tallest of the Falconspurs thrusting up in the distance and knew that Roosta was nestled among the foothills not very far ahead.

None of the ship's mates spoke, all of them aware of

how voices carried across the sea. "Cut our speed," he whispered to Alff.

The quartermaster picked up one of the colored flags they used when they were running silent and waved it in the area. Immediately, the ship's crew worked to trim the sails. Others readied the four catapults carried in the stern and the six great crossbows lined on either side of *Rapier's Thrust*. Two dozen archers stood ready, shafts already nocked to strings.

Jaelik felt the ship slow in the water and felt more nervous. With the wind at their heels, sailing into the harbor had been no problem at all, but getting back out would be. Had he kept the speed up, tacking back into the wind would have been faster if they'd needed to reverse directions because they could have used the forward momentum.

Still, Turkoth Blackheart's soldiers were not seaborn as were the privateer crew. Turkoth had to depend on the few sailors and captains that had joined with him. *Rapier's Thrust* easily had the more experienced crew.

But the barbarian leader had the Crown of the Storms, and that still held unknown power and menace.

Jaelik gazed back in their wake, at the white streamers that cut across the leaden green sea. There was no sign of the Colossus.

"It will be here," Ryla whispered at his side.

The privateer captain said nothing. They'd come too far to turn and run now.

Voices echoed out of the fog, followed immediately by the sounds of ships' rigging as the barbarian crews fought to catch the wind and tack out of the harbor. Jaelik knew they were on either side of him now as well as in front. *Rapier's Thrust* glided through the water, poised expectantly to earn her name again.

The fog swirled, continuing to roll across the water, then

dim shapes began to appear. The sails of the other ships took on the appearance of lighter triangles against the grayed background. Startled shouts came from the other ships as the crews spotted the unfamiliar craft among them.

One of those craft was headed straight for them.

Gripping the ratline tightly, Jaelik shouted, "Hard to starboard!"

His crew responded instantly, shifting the sails as the helmsman altered their course. *Rapier's Thrust* heeled over, cutting down into the water as the wind seized her more firmly. The ship surged away from the approaching Roostaan vessel.

"By Cegrud's crooked elbow," Alff stated, "it's gonna be close."

"We're not going to get completely clear," Jaelik announced. He took a deep breath and bellowed. "Hold on! Stand by to repel boarders!"

In the next heartbeat, *Rapier's Thrust* butted up against the opposing ship. Both craft shuddered from the impact and timbers groaned in protest. Miraculously, both held together.

Jaelik rocked violently, felt the coarse fiber of the ratline bite into his palm, and he kept his feet with difficulty. Some of his men spilled across the ship's deck, but they saved themselves or were aided by other crew.

Unprepared as it was, the Roostaan craft lost nearly a dozen men overboard. Most of them fell into the harbor, but three of them fell to *Rapier's Thrust*'s deck. Crew dispatched them quickly, then rolled their lifeless bodies back into the water.

Hoarse shouts followed *Rapier's Thrust* as it cleared the opposing ship. She righted viciously, pushed by the wind she held captive in her sails. A weak volley of arrows spanned the distance between the ships, most of them getting caught in the sails.

"Archers!" Jaelik cried. "Feather that dammed crew and let them know they're facing fighting men!"

The archers loosed their shafts with deadly effect, piercing several of the crew on the Roostaan ship. At least three arrows struck the helmsman and dropped him to the deck. Out of control and off course, the ship drove prow-first into another ship. Timbers cracked and triggered hoarse, fear-filled shouts. The vessel struck amidships started going down quickly as the hole in its side allowed the sea in, but it also held the other craft captive, dragging it down as well.

The fog thinned as *Rapier's Thrust* neared the shore. Jaelik gazed at the ranked ships, now seen as shadows against the heavy gray air, seeking the Roostaan flagship. Turkoth Blackheart, the privateer captain was sure, would be with it. The barbarian leader wasn't afraid of battle, and the man liked his enemies to see him coming.

Drumbeats banged hollowly, echoing over the harbor.

"They're getting organized," Alff said gruffly. He turned the long-handled battle-ax in his callused hands. "Talking to each other by drumbeats."

"I know," Jaelik said. "Find that damned flagship for me." He turned and yelled up at the crow's nest. "Seramyn, use those eyes you were blessed with."

The young man in the crow's nest shaded his eyes, peering intently.

Jaelik watched tensely as the Roostaan ships they'd passed came around. Sails swung about as the vessels set up a blockade.

"If ye give the order now," Alff growled, "mayhap we can still see ourselves free of this mess. Ain't no way we're a-gonna take on this whole fleet."

Jaelik stared out at the ships and considered it. *Rapier's Thrust* had a better than even chance of getting free of the harbor with her experienced crew.

"Don't," Ryla pleaded softly.

The privateer captain glared at the woman, remembering how she'd plagued his every waking hour over the past few weeks, how she'd robbed him of sleep and other pleasures. But he also remembered the young woman that she'd been; the one who'd lost a hard and distant father that she'd loved in spite of his ways, and the one who'd been so untimely bereft of life.

"Hold the heading," Jaelik said to Alff. "You've always been a gambling man."

"Aye," the quartermaster replied. "But usually during them times, I could count on one of us to keep a clear head."

Jaelik returned his attention to the harbor. The drums hammered incessantly, and the ships ahead shifted slowly to intercept courses, their prows finding the speed to crash against the white-topped waves. Most of the vessels were too late to stop them, but they guaranteed that there would be no escape.

"The Colossus is my father's magic," Ryla said. "Very old magic. It will not fail."

But there was no guarantee that it would get there in time, either, Jaelik knew.

"Cap'n!" Seramyn hollered from the crow's nest. "The flagship!"

Jaelik followed the line of the younger man's pointing arm, spotting the Roostaan flagship in the clearing fog almost immediately. The ship was a great dreadnaught of power and defense, fully a third again larger than *Rapier's Thrust*. The Roostaan vessel's masts held few sails at full strength, obviously dropping speed as the drums continued to thunder around the harbor.

Taking his spyglass from his waist, Jaelik extended the brass tubes and brought the ship into focus. He swept the craft from prow to stern and found Turkoth Blackheart standing at the stern castle railing.

Turkoth stood broad at the shoulder and lean-hipped like a gaunt wolf. His shaggy black hair trailed below his shoulders, tangled in the wind now. A carefully trimmed beard and fierce mustache blurred the cruel lines of his scarred face. He wore a black shirt emblazoned with a silver bear's head in full-throated roar and dark leather breeches tucked into tight horseman's boots. Two curved swords hung at his hips.

"Make for the flagship," Jaelik ordered. *Rapier's Thrust* swayed beneath him as the helmsman brought the rudder into line with the new course.

Turkoth spoke briefly to the drummer beside him. Immediately, a new series of beats chorused out over the harbor. Men yelled at each other and four Roostaan craft changed course, coming at the Vellak fighting ship.

"Abram," Jaelik called out, dashing to the stern railing and looking down at the contingent of giant crossbowmen. He pointed at the Roostaan ship headed straight at them from less then seventy yards out. "Bust that ship up."

"Aye, Cap'n." Abram gave his orders in a hoarse, raucous voice. Immediately the deck-mounted crossbowmen took their positions. The basso throb of the huge lines sounded heartbeats apart as the gunnery commander called them out.

The huge, iron-tipped projectiles flew across the distance. Two of them struck the forward and center mast, but only the forward mast shattered. Rigging and sail came down in fluttering havoc, draping the midships and causing instant confusion. A third bolt caught a man standing at the port railing, nailed him to the man behind, and scattered crew in all directions before thudding home against one of the deck crossbows. Another struck the ship high on the port side, but the other two crashed through the hull beneath the waterline, ripping great holes.

"Reload, you great lummoxes!" Abram roared, pulling on one of the crossbow strings himself.

The stricken Roostaan craft veered off slightly and Jaelik shouted the course correction. Still, *Rapier's Thrust* butted up against the opposing craft, rising high out of the sea for a moment before splashing back down. The privateer captain saw some of the Roostaan archers fight free of the falling sail, take up positions, and draw back. Instinctively, Jaelik shouted out a warning and reached for Ryla. His hand was halfway through the ghost before he remembered what she was. Only a few arrows struck the fighting deck.

Archers from *Rapier's Thrust* opened fire immediately, feathering the crew unmercifully and driving them back. Then the Vellak ship was past, gliding back down into the water. Still, a half-dozen craft in front of the vessel maneuvered to block the way to the flagship.

Jaelik gazed hotly at Turkoth Blackheart. Even though he'd never met the barbarian leader, the privateer captain hated the man. The stories that were told about Turkoth's cruelties were legendary.

"By Cegrud's blind eye," Alff growled at Jaelik's side, "we're definitely in for a fight now, we are."

"Are you sure you don't want to call this a suicide run?" Jaelik asked bitterly. Still, he looked down on his crew with pride. Even in the face of certain death, they held their stations, though he wasn't fool enough to believe it was bravery that kept them there. They served the needs of the ship because *Rapier's Thrust* was the only chance they had.

"This," Alff said, clapping his captain on the back, "is gonna make one hell of a tale to be told. Whether by us or them that hear of it."

Jaelik kept *Rapier's Thrust* on course for the Roostaan warship, but he knew they wouldn't make it. If there had been a chance to board Turkoth's ship, chances were even slimmer that they could fight their way to the barbarian leader and hold the man captive.

Three Roostaan ships tacked in front of *Rapier's Thrust*, putting themselves between the Vellak ship and their leader.

"Ram them!" Jaelik cried, counting on the reinforced prow to hold them safe. He grabbed the ratlines and braced himself, watching the distance melt quickly.

11

The impact was ferocious, sending a shudder through *Rapier's Thrust*. Jaelik held on tightly, watching helplessly as two of his crew lost their grips and tumbled overboard. *Rapier's Thrust* rode up high against the starboard ship. Only Ryla remained unmoved.

Deathwatch guardsmen and Roostaan sailors surged forward. Grappling lines flew around the prow railings as the two ships bucked together.

Jaelik released the ratline and led the charge to repel the boarders. Alff stayed at his side, using both ends of the battle-ax to reap destruction. Jaelik turned one sword aside, then flicked a quick thrust that opened a Deathwatch guardsman's throat. The ships surged together again, separating for a moment, and the privateer captain skewered another man through the heart.

"Cut the lines!" Jaelik ordered. "Abram, ready the pitch-loads!"

"Aye, Cap'n!" Abram shouted commands, getting his artillery teams moving. The pitchloads in the catapults were quickly fired.

Jaelik cut and thrust, parried and blocked. Sweat mixed with condensation from the heavy fog covered him, made his clothing stick to his body. Blood, his own and from the men he fought as well as from others around him, made matters worse.

A Deathwatch guardsman attacked Ryla, watching incredulously as his blade slipped through her. The ghost responded immediately, driving her hand through his chest. When Ryla drew her hand back, the guardsman's chest broke open, spewing blood and broken bone.

"Fire at will, Abram!" Jaelik shouted.

Immediately, flaming pitch released from catapults filled the air. Unable to get the nearest ships, the catapult operators settled for any target within reach. The burning pitch sailed through the air and landed on vessels, spreading across sails, masts, decks, and crew.

Terror-filled screams pierced the incessant drumming. Flames climbed the ships, clung to the running crew that hadn't been killed outright when they'd been set afire. The pitch that missed the Roostaan ships splashed into the harbor and floated like lumps of coal.

Fiercely, Jaelik led his men against their aggressors. Even as they beat those men back, however, additional ships closed in. The privateer captain knew his crew was about to be overwhelmed.

Without warning, the ship in front of *Rapier's Thrust* rose from the harbor, held by two massive granite hands. The Colossus of Mahrass stood under the warship, holding it high above its round head. The great mouth opened, and an inarticulate cry of rage thundered.

Men spilled from the lifted ship as the Colossus turned and slammed the vessel down into the closest Roostaan ship. Timbers shattered with ear-splitting shrieks and the broken craft sank almost immediately. Despite the depth of the harbor, the waterline only struck the Colossus above the midriff.

The magical automaton moved much faster than Jaelik would have believed possible on the muddy sea bottom. Curling its hands into fists, the Colossus hammered the Roostaan ships. Men died instantly under those great blows. Decks, masts, and rigging splintered, and decks caved as if they'd been made of paper.

Eight ships confronting *Rapier's Thrust* sank in mere heartbeats. The harbor filled with drowning men, twisted sailcloth, and broken remnants of ships.

"By Cegrud and all his ills," Alff breathed as he drew his battle-ax from the skull of his latest foe. "Even after all them stories, I'd never have imagined the like."

Jaelik gazed across the harbor, staring in wonder himself as the Colossus waded steadily into battle. Giant crossbow shafts only shattered against the granite hide.

A huge arm swept out again as the giant roared anew. Masts ripped from the ship, and the blow ended up buried deep in the ship's fore as it finished, caving through the deck and splintering the figurehead of a naked woman from the prow. In less than a minute, *Rapier's Thrust* had almost become an island in a sea of debris.

Flaming pitch arced through the foggy air and slammed into the Colossus. The impact never even staggered the granite giant. The pitch smeared as it dripped down the Colossus's torso, leaving uncertain fingers of fire in its wake.

"Repel boarders!" Jaelik ordered. Now that the Vellak warship was the only serviceable craft around for a good distance, the survivors of the Colossus' onslaught swam for it. *Rapier's Thrust* had also become the target for the other surviving Roostaan ships. "Get us underway!"

He and Alff bailed from the fighting deck, lending hands where they could to the crew as the sails were run up again. *Rapier's Thrust* surged forward again, deeper into harbor waters.

Turkoth Blackheart hadn't been idle. He'd ordered his crew into motion, trying desperately to tack back out to sea. The Colossus turned toward them, focusing its full attention on the ship.

The barbarian leader stood on the aftcastle and removed an object from the pouch at his side. Carefully, Turkoth placed it upon his head, then held his hands up at his sides.

"The Crown of Storms," Ryla said as she joined Jaelik at the railing.

The sky overhead darkened, but it wasn't the fog this time. Lightning flashed in the sudden gathering cloud masses.

"He has learned the secrets of it," the ghost stated. "I didn't think he would do that."

"It won't matter, will it?" Jaelik asked. "The Colossus can surely stand against storms."

"Not these storms," Ryla answered. "They're as magical as the Colossus."

A lightning bolt lanced from the cloud mass and struck the approaching Colossus. Thunder pealed so loudly that for a brief time Jaelik was struck deaf. The bolt knocked the Colossus from its feet, sending it below the sea.

Turkoth immediately turned his attention to *Rapier's Thrust*. He screamed something that Jaelik couldn't un-

derstand. Another lightning bolt sizzled across the intervening distance and set the mainsail on fire.

"Get that out!" Alff commanded.

The crew swiftly dropped the mainsail and threw buck-
ets of water over it to extinguish the flames.

Turkoth missed with his next attempt, striking the water
near *Rapier's Thrust* and sending a wave over the bow. Before the barbarian leader could try again, the Colossus rose
from the sea, one hand outstretched toward the warship.
Steam from superheated rock rose into the fog. Even at
that distance, Jaelik saw the fierce and jagged cracks that
showed in the Colossus.

Turkoth blasted the granite behemoth again, knocking it
down once more. This time chunks of rocks the size of
boulders tore free of the Colossus before it vanished.

Glancing at the harbor, Jaelik saw the Roostaan ships
turning back around, coming to the aid of their leader with
the wind at their backs.

"Get those sails up, you dogs!" the privateer captain
commanded as he sprang to the fighting deck. "Into the
teeth of that bastard! I'll not go down without a fight, and
hell take any of you that keep me from it!"

Rapier's Thrust came around, gathering speed swiftly,
taking advantage of the wind at her back.

Turkoth used the arcane item again, blistering the deck
amidships and setting three crewmen on fire. Even before
their burned and withered bodies dropped to the deck, the
Colossus rose again.

This time the granite giant held a broken ship in its
hands. It threw the shattered hulk at the flagship, narrowly
missing and causing a huge wave that washed over the
decks, washing away several of the crew at the same time.

Turkoth faced the approaching Colossus again. Instead
of lightning, a waterspout whipped up from the sea, mar-

shaled by the winds spinning above it. The waterspout towered over the Colossus' great height, then it enveloped the magical creature.

The winds buffeted the Colossus, tearing at the granite hide with fangs. Scars formed on the giant's body where the whipping wind and water eroded it. The Colossus howled in frustration and perhaps pain, Jaelik wasn't sure. The thing staggered and flailed at its invisible opponent as more of its granite flesh was ripped away.

A spray of pebbles and rock shorn from the Colossus ripped through *Rapier's Thrust*'s sails and rigging. One of the crew lost an arm, falling in bloody spasms, and another man was dead before he hit the dock. The only good thing was that the flying rock was just as deadly against the Roostaan vessels, including the flagship.

"The Colossus can't stand against that," Ryla said.

"Nor could Vellak if Turkoth is given the chance to go there," Jaelik stated above the howling wind. He yelled orders to the crew, putting them on a collision course with the Roostaan flagship.

Continually battered by the magical winds, the Colossus still struggled to reach the flagship. The waterspout shoved at the creature, trying to push it under the sea.

Jaelik called fiercely to his crew as they sailed through the twisting winds that created the waterspout, preparing a boarding crew. Three Roostaan ships made a halfhearted attempt to follow them, but the captains were definitely not in favor of getting close to the carnage that wrapped the flailing Colossus.

Hurled by the wind at her back, *Rapier's Thrust* echoed her name as she cut through the sea. Wooden pilings left by the destroyed ships smashed against her prow, punctuating the howling winds with sharp cracks. The Colossus staggered and dropped into the water up to its chin, obviously on its knees as it slapped at the wind.

Jaelik clung grimly to the ratline, knowing he and his crew scarcely had a chance to keep control of their own fates. "Get us alongside that ship!" He glanced at Alff who kept a stern look on his bruised face. "Maybe we can get lucky with an archer."

Alff nodded. "Mayhap."

Rapier's Thrust glided through the harbor, riding out the rough water.

Turkoth turned his attention to the approaching craft. He gestured and the waterspout left the Colossus, dancing wildly across the white-foamed waters toward the warship. Alff cursed steadily as the howling winds quickly overtook them. Rigging snapped and tore free as *Rapier's Thrust* heeled over, first to one side, then to the other.

Despite the stinging blindness brought on by the saltwater spray thick in the wind, Jaelik saw the Colossus push itself up again. The creature seized the aft section of a shipwreck and hurled it at the Roostaan flagship. The waterspout suddenly left *Rapier's Thrust* and caught the flying shipwreck, hurling it back at the Colossus. The ship section shattered against the granite giant, knocking the creature off balance.

"Archers," Jaelik commanded as his ship came up against Turkoth's, "loose!"

12

Arrows feathered the warship's decks, driving the crew to cover. Most of them were barbarians, unused to the sea anyway and definitely not happy with it now. Still, none of the shafts touched Turkoth.

Without a word, Ryla flew from *Rapier's Thrust* to the

Roostaan warship. None of the Deathwatch guardsmen saw her, but Turkoth's head came around at once. The ghost didn't hesitate, moving smoothly despite the storm-tossed seas and whipping winds.

A grin painted Turkoth's face as he watched the ghost's approach. The diamond encrusted gold crown he wore flashed with inner lights.

"Damn," Jaelik breathed.

"What?" Alff asked.

"Turkoth sees her." The privateer captain called for the archers again and another volley of shafts raked the flagship. Glancing over his shoulder, he saw that the other Roostaan vessels grew steadily braver. "Get us alongside! Turkoth won't summon the waterspout too close to his own ship!" He hoped.

The Colossus disappeared beneath the raging waves, more eroded than it had been. The waterspout spun, then came for *Rapier's Thrust* again.

On board the flagship, Ryla flew to Turkoth, one arm extended, ready to strike and kill the man. The barbarian leader seized her wrist unexpectedly, dragging the ghost to her knees in sudden pain. He said something to her, but Jaelik couldn't hear because the howling wind ripped the words away. However, there was no mistaking the agony on Ryla's face.

Rapier's Thrust butted up against the Roostaan flagship hard enough to knock both crews from their feet, sending some of them into the harbor water. The Colossus rose again in the distance, turning its attention to a pair of ships bearing down on the Vellakian vessel. The granite giant brought its hands together across the sea surface, spurring up a massive tidal wave that swept across the decks of both craft. Timbers broke and men washed over the sides.

"To me!" Jaelik cried, brandishing his rapier and dashing for the enemy ship. The grappling crews on the fighting deck tied onto the flagship quickly, hauling out planks that spanned the fluctuating distance as the ships continued to bump each other.

The Deathwatch guardsman and Roostaan turncoat sailors moved slowly to respond to the boarding attempt that Jaelik led. He ran among them like a shark in a school of tuna. His rapier flashed, drawing blood repeatedly, battering men down from the sheer force of his blows. They only had one chance.

The waterspout hung over them, chewing at *Rapier's Thrust*'s stern. The force pulled at the grappling lines securing the privateer to the Roostaan warship as well, causing the water-drenched deck to shift violently beneath Jaelik's feet. The Colossus lumbered into view, taking great strides that broke waves across its body.

Jaelik ducked beneath a Deathwatch guardsman's wild swing, took a hand-and-a-half grip on the rapier and thrust, spilling the man's guts to the deck. Alff bashed in the skull of a man to his right. The privateer captain busted another guardsman in the face with the rapier basket, breaking teeth and driving his foe backward. He heard Turkoth as he neared the steps leading up to the aftcastle.

"Turn it back, bitch!" the barbarian leader snarled. "Turn it back, or I'll kill you again!" He stood over Ryla, his sword at her throat.

Jaelik guessed that the power of the Crown of Storms had given the barbarian leader the ability to see and touch the ghost. Perhaps its magic linked it to Slamintyr Lattyrl's daughter in some fashion.

He blocked another sword with the rapier and, still on the move, drove his boot into the sailor's face. He slipped a knife from his boot and left it deep in another opponent's heart.

The waterspout spun across the waves, throwing white-caps in all directions. This time the Colossus slapped its hands again, throwing a wave over the waterspout and temporarily halting it.

Turkoth nicked Ryla's throat with his blade, drawing blood that dripped down her body but disappeared before it hit the deck. "Turn it back!" he commanded.

"Never," she replied. "The Colossus will drag you under."

Jaelik blocked a sword aimed at his face, then seized his opponent's blouse in his empty hand, yanking the sailor from the lower steps of the aftcastle stairs. Another heave sent the man over the side. The privateer captain surged up four more steps before the man hit the water below.

The Colossus continued its approach toward the Roos-taan flagship, staying low to the water to avoid some of the waterspout's attack. The face showed weathering and cracks that had turned the mouth slit into a scarred sneer.

Lowering his shoulder, Jaelik ducked under an attacker's blow and caught the man in the stomach with an elbow, driving him back to the aftcastle deck. He slid the rapier through the man's ribs and heart, then shoved him away.

"Turkoth!" Jaelik roared as he stepped up onto the aft-castle dock.

The barbarian leader swiveled, holding Ryla in front of him. "Who are you?" Turkoth demanded.

"Jaelik Tarlsson, Captain of *Rapier's Thrust*, of Vellak." The privateer captain stood his ground, his blade ready. As always, Alff protected his back, accompanied by three other men from the ship.

Behind Turkoth, the Colossus picked up the closest

Roostaan ship and hurled it into the waterspout. The vessel came apart like kindling, flying in all directions. Wooden shards and splinters struck the flagship and crew as well.

"Did you come all this way to die, boy?" Turkoth taunted.

"I'll not die alone this day," Jaelik countered, moving forward.

"No, boy," Turkoth commanded, drawing his sword more tightly against Ryla's throat. "Stay your hand, or I'll slit this dead wench's throat for her again."

"What wench?" Jaelik replied, gambling.

Turkoth didn't hesitate, pulling Ryla more tightly against him. "Don't think me stupid. Only this woman, daughter of the dead elven wizard, could have told you how to raise the Colossus." He turned her head roughly, baring her throat and showing the line of blood trailing down her neck. "Believe me when I say that I can make this death of hers worse."

Jaelik did.

He stopped.

"Now order your men to throw down their weapons," Turkoth said, glancing at the Colossus wreaking havoc with other Roostaan ships. "And I want that damned creature stopped."

Before Jaelik could refuse, knowing he had no true control over the Colossus and couldn't ask his men to die without a fight, Ryla shifted. The ghost slid her arm into her captor's arm. A heartbeat later, the limb shattered and exploded. Blood and bone lay exposed in the ruin of the arm. Ryla escaped easily, trying at once to pierce the barbarian leader's chest as she got to her feet.

Turkoth's blade flicked out, cutting across the ghost's midriff, drenching her gown in blood. Ryla gazed down in disbelief and pain, unable to defend herself against her attacker's next blow.

Quick as a striking sea falcon, Jaelik threw himself forward, knocking Turkoth away from the ghost. The two men rolled across the deck and the remains of the barbarian leader's ruined arm covered Jaelik's face with blood. The privateer captain struggled to drive the rapier through his opponent's chest. Turkoth's strength surprised Jaelik.

The barbarian leader shoved him back, hooking a foot behind the privateer captain's leg. Jaelik fell, unable to keep his feet under him. The flagship pitched on the roiling waves, keeping him off balance.

Roaring with rage and masked in blood, Turkoth pushed himself up and brought his sword down. Jaelik rolled away, narrowly escaping the blade, and got to his feet. He parried the next blow, riding out the pitching deck, listening to the clangor of steel against steel, feeling the impact shiver along his arm.

Alff, Ryla, and the crew from *Rapier's Thrust* took over the aftcastle, throwing Deathwatch guardsmen and Roostaan sailors back amidships or over the sides. In the near distance, the waterspout had overtaken the Colossus again, grinding against the granite giant and wearing it down, burying it in the sea. The other Roostaan ships circled like sharks, waiting for the way to be cleared to their prey.

Turkoth broke the engagement and stepped back. His wolflike eyes glinted in triumph though he held his wounded arm close to his body.

Jaelik listened to the howling winds and knew that the barbarian leader was counting on the waterspout to destroy the Colossus. He pressed his attack again, meeting Turkoth's expert hand and feeling the unexpected strength there.

"The Crown," Ryla called. "He's tuned himself to it and is drawing strength from it."

Even as Jaelik watched, Turkoth's ruined arm started healing. The bleeding slowed and the flesh knitted.

"You're going to die, boy," Turkoth promised, grinning. "When that waterspout does for your giant, it'll do for your ship as well. You may have delayed the attack on Vellak, but you've not stopped it." He advanced to the attack, keen edge splitting the air.

Jaelik parried a blow, trapping the barbarian leader's sword with his own, sliding his blade down the length of steel so that their hilts met. Turkoth struggled to free his blade, not wanting to retreat. Jaelik headbutted his opponent in the face, resorting to the rough-and-tumble tactics he'd learned in the dockside bars he'd grown up around.

Blood sprayed from Turkoth's broken nose.

Jaelik headbutted the man again, knocking the diamond-encrusted crown from the barbarian leader's head.

"No!" Turkoth screamed, lunging for the fallen crown scooting across the tossing deck.

But Ryla reached the crown first, and at her touch the crown turned to gray-white ash and blew away. At the same instant, the waterspout evaporated and the Colossus rose again. Its huge fists fell mercilessly on the nearest Roostaan ships.

"Bitch!" Turkoth screamed as he drew back his sword and rushed at her.

Fearing that if the man could still see her he could probably still hurt her, Jaelik ran across the distance. The privateer captain stepped in front of Turkoth and blocked his blade, slamming his chest against his opponent's. Jaelik ran his free arm under Turkoth's arm, then turned and twisted and pulled, throwing the barbarian leader to the deck in a wrestling hold. Turkoth scrambled to get back up, but Jaelik recovered first and gripped the rapier in both hands. He swung the blade with all his strength, catching the barbarian leader at the base of his skull.

Blood flew as bone cleaved. Turkoth's head sprang from his shoulders and thudded to the deck. Impossibly, the headless body stood, swaying, for a moment. Then the corpse dropped to its knees and fell backward.

Breathing harshly, Jaelik reached down and picked up the truncated head by the hair. He walked to the stern railing and lifted the head high, blood pouring across the deck at his feet.

"Enough!" Jaelik's voice pierced the sudden quiet that descended over the flagship after the waterspout's disappearance. "No one else needs to die if they're not too foolish to live."

After a brief hesitation, the Roostaan crew laid down their weapons and surrendered.

Glancing beyond them, Jaelik watched the Colossus smash another ship with a two-fisted blow. The rest of the Roostaan fleet sailed for the open sea, quitting the harbor as quickly as they could.

Jaelik flung Turkoth's head over the side and turned to face the ghost. "Are you all right?"

Crimson stained Ryla's neck but seamed to fade even as the sea calmed around them. "Yes." She stepped closer, her eyes anxiously wandering over him. "Are you well?"

"Aye." Jaelik glanced down, surprised at the amount of blood that covered him. Most of it, he realized, wasn't his. He brushed at the filth but knew that it would take a long, hot bath to clean most of it from him. "Is this it, then? The end of your search for your father's artifacts?"

"No." She wrapped her arms around herself. "There's still much out there to be found. And there are a few more things that Turkoth has hidden in this ship that I can sense. I will deal with those."

Jaelik nodded. "You'll excuse me, but I've got two ships' crews to get organized."

Her green eyes bored into his. "You're wrong, you know," she said softly.

"About what?"

"When you put your mind to it, Captain, you can be quite the hero. Not just a pirate or privateer."

Jaelik felt the heat on his face. Not knowing what to say, he turned quickly and headed down the aftcastle stairs.

Alff met him at the bottom, blood matting his whiskers. The quartermaster gazed suspiciously back up at the aftcastle. "Is the ha'nt gone?"

"No." And, surprisingly, the thought of her leaving left an empty spot in Jaelik's heart.

"Now there's a bad sign," Alff commented, scratching the back of his neck.

Drawn, Jaelik turned and looked back up the aftcastle stairs. "Ryla."

"Yes." She waited, lips tight.

"I'd be honored if you'd let *Rapier's Thrust* serve you while she can. If our journeys take us along similar courses."

"An arrangement, Captain?" Her smile was mocking and sad at the same time.

Truth to tell, Jaelik didn't like the idea of her being out there alone in the world even though she'd already been doing it for a thousand years. "Provided I can get a decent night's sleep without you rattling your chains."

She smiled then and nodded her head. "Such a pairing would be dangerous."

"That," Alff said, "would be stupid. One of yer worst ideas."

"The people that hold pieces of Slamintyr Lattyrl's legacy won't be willing to part with them easily," Jaelik pointed out to her. Then he addressed Alff. "Nor will many of them be paupers. For a fine sailing ship and a brave crew, such a course could only result in several chances at treasure."

Alff cursed, but he wore a grin as he marched off to sort out the crew, goods, and prisoners.

Ryla walked down the steps, evidently choosing a more human appearing mode of travel than flying down. "So, a partnership, then?"

"No," Jaelik said. "It's my ship, after all. I'd call this . . . an *agreement*."

"Would you offer a contract?"

"Would you want one?" And as he stood close to her, aware of the heat she radiated, Jaelik could almost forget she was a ghost. But he could never forget that she was a woman.

"It seems to me that there should be something to seal the . . . *agreement*."

"Aye," Jaelik growled, "aye, and there should be." He took her in his arms and kissed her, ignoring the startled stares from the men around him who assumed he was holding nothing but the air.

Alff coughed, barely veiling his disapproval at such action. The ghost returned Jaelik's kiss, long and deep, and held him tightly. He gazed over her shoulder, seeing *Rapier's Thrust* rolling gently on the waves next to the Roostaan flagship. Beyond that, the Colossus stood guard in a flotsam of ruined ships. The sails of the fleeing craft were starting over the horizon in the distance.

Gently, Ryla pushed Jaelik back, emerald eyes searching his, sadness limning the green. "This—might not be easy." She paused, as if searching for the proper words to say. "Not my father's things, not—" She shook her head. "—none of it."

"Lady," Jaelik whispered, smiling, "all I've ever asked from life is a fair wind to fill a ship's sails. Give me that and I'll make my own luck."

DEITIES AND
THE DEEP BLUE SEA

Neptune, Poseidon, and many others have laid claim the title of Deity of the Sea, and not always in a manner that has been the most friendly to our terra-firma–bound ancestors.

From the tropics to the polar reaches, the sea gods extract their duties from those who wish to sail, and sometimes the price is extremely high.

Just ask the survivors of Atlantis—or anyone else who is forced to do business with the gods of the sea.

WALK UPON THE WATERS

BY PAUL KUPPERBERG

THE winds howling off the ocean battered the old sorcerer's lean and tall figure, whipping the heavy cloak
he wore as protection against the cold. His eyes were narrowed against the stinging salt spray, watching the steel-
gray waters roll in to heave themselves against the shore,
sea smashing against land like the fists of a maddened
giant, the land shaking.

It was coming, he knew.

The end was coming and the sea was its messenger.

"All is in readiness, my lord," one of his priests called
from behind him, his shouts barely audible above the scream
of wind and water.

"Yes," the sorcerer said softly, to himself and to the
wind that beat at him. "Let us begin."

He could not tear his gaze from the sea that he had
spent an eternity appeasing. The anger of the One was a
thing alive, living in the pounding surf and raging wind.
There were ceremonies to enact, sacrifices to offer, pleas
to the gods to stay their wrath.

The gods had created man, crawling in some long-
forgotten, primitive form from the rich waters of the sea
to the land. They nurtured humans, giving them the great
magic that had enabled them to shuffle from grunting cave

dwellers to dwellers in golden palaces that soared to touch the sky.

The gods had given the world to the child that came to call itself man. And then the child began to think itself greater than the world that spawned it.

It dared deny the gods, even refusing to believe in their existence.

The gods had given them ample warning. The land beneath them had shaken and erupted, nature's most deadening cold and blistering heat had been sent to plague its recalcitrant children, winds had beaten at the city, the seas had destroyed their fishing fleets, and fire and ice had been rained upon their heads. And still they held, stubborn as only selfish children under rebuke could be, to their ways.

They were man. They were masters of their world.

Those few still holding to the old ways did not fear punishment. They believed that Thalis, Lord of the House of Ghehan, Highest Priest of the Worship, Lord High Mage of Atlantis and the First City, Counselor to the King of the Twelve Houses, would appease the gods as he ever did, would hold their fury and wrath at bay. But the centuries just past had brought change. The gods had fallen from man's favor.

Thalis knew the gods were real. He, who had stood before them, bargained and *warred* with them, knew their love, their scorn, their gratitude, their resentment, and carried still the scars of mind and body that were the fruits of his defiance. But the gods no longer showed themselves to the children of Atlantis and soon the children found something to replace them: the way of their machines and tools. "Science," one young fool insisted, "is sorcery rendered by mortal hands."

Machines, the old man thought with anger. *Toys, curious gadgets of only passing interest to anyone but a child.*

But the One's anger at its offspring's betrayal had bloomed into vengeance. No longer would the deities be satisfied with sacrifices and a few sincerely muttered prayers. The wind's howl was their cry for blood. The sea's rage was their hand come to deliver divine retribution.

Thalis turned at last. His eyes fell upon the massive brazier his priests had erected on the crumbling stone altar at the water's edge. They stood, red robed and grave, around the altar, waiting for him to begin. A goat, shivering from the cold and rain, trembled, staked to the ground before them.

"The gods," the old man said, "are surely laughing." He looked down at the wet black sand beneath his feet. "Do we deserve any less?"

"My lord," said a priest, the old man with the shaved head and the tattoo of Crghas on the right side of his face. "The storm worsens."

"They do not want our sacrifices," Thalis said, shouting now to be heard over the elements. "They will no longer accept tokens, the blood of innocent beasts. They will demand a greater sacrifice from us now."

The priests looked at one another in confusion, then back at their master. "What would they have us do, my lord?" another said, his voice trembling, his eyes wide with fear.

"I do not presume to speak for the gods." Thalis smiled sadly and pulled his purple cloak tight around himself. "I must go ask them."

The cloak was soaked through and made Thalis shiver from with cold.

In the morning, Thalis set sail on the dark waters aboard the *Yar*.

The great ship had first sailed when Thalis was young, apprentice still to Wynsgar, the first Lord High Mage.

Thalis' hair had been dark and full then, his face yet un-
lined with the weight of years. He was young and eager
to do battle with Atlantis' foes, mortal or divine, willing
the ship onward, sailing into whatever lay ahead. He stood
upon the foredeck that first time, the sea breeze in his face,
his hand on the neck of the serpentine figurehead that
arched gracefully out before the ship.

"Where do we go?" the serpent asked its young master,
turning its wooden neck and casting one painted eye on
Thalis.

Thalis had laughed, shielding his eyes from the sun.
"Onward," the young sorcerer sang to the wind, his heart
swelling with the joy of adventure. "Into tomorrow. To
glory!"

He had not sailed alone on that long ago voyage. With
him had been Kahna, warrior priestess of the City of the
Archer, a soldier as fierce and as bold as she was a woman
warm and loving. She would four times in four incarnations be his wife.

And Gith, a gold-maned giant of a man whose life was
pledged to the safety of the young sorcerer who was destined to become Lord High Mage.

And Shanar, a young shape-changing street urchin from
the City of the Twins.

They had set out together on the mighty *Yar*, forty lengths
from stem to stern, fifteen lengths at its beam, with sails
of spun gold. They sailed to defend Atlantis against the
wrath of a minor sea deity. In his youthful arrogance, Thalis
had foreseen only victory and glory. The lives of Kahna
and Gith had been the price for victory and glory . . . glory
was the lie concocted to inspire innocent fools to war. He
had sailed from Atlantis a carefree youth and returned a
man disillusioned, in time for Wynsgar's death.

*   *   *

"Where do we go?" asked the serpent as the *Yar* struggled against the surf and pushed for the open sea.

This time, Thalis sailed alone. Wind and rain battered the ship, the waves tossed it about as effortlessly as a plaything in a child's wash basin. He rode the heaving deck with effort, his feet planted wide on the weathered wooden planks, his staff clutched tight in both hands for support.

"Wherever the sea takes us," Thalis replied.

The serpent coiled its long neck against the buffeting elements. "It would take us to the bottom," the great ship warned.

Thalis nodded. "I should not be surprised."

The *Yar* rode the rolling sea all that day and through the night. Thalis took shelter from the ceaseless storm below deck in his cabin, warming himself over stones he had willed to glow with red heat. Herbal potions warmed over the stones, but Thalis had no stomach for them. The voyage was hard on the old man. "I no longer have the constitution for this," he muttered.

"Nor I," replied the ship in a voice like the creaking of old timbers. "Sooner would I be sailing upon a placid lake, the tromp of children's feet upon my decks."

Thalis smiled at the thought. "Aye," he said, his eyes staring at some faraway place at children who had never been. Kahna was with them, grown older and fuller but beautiful still, patient, smiling mother of a tumultuous horde. They were little and large, boys and girls, an army of children all sharing the same soft, rounded features of their mother and the dark hair, high cheekbones, and slight upward sweep of the eyes of their father.

Here, in this very cabin, upon the unmade berth in the corner, the first of those children might have been conceived on that long ago first voyage. Young, impulsive,

blazing with lust and heat as they sailed into war with a
god, Thalis and Kahna had fallen upon one another. Garments were torn, pulled hastily aside so that the warrior
and the sorcerer could ride one another as their ship rode
the lurching seas. Thalis remembered that time as if it was
yesterday, recalled looking deep into her eyes as they
strained toward release and seeing his soul reflected back
at him. He knew as did she that they were destined for one
another, that their two hearts beat a single song. They would
be together forever.

Of course they were not.

Kahna died two days later. She died as a warrior should,
saving Thalis and Shanar, allowing him the precious seconds he needed to cast his spell and defeat the god's scheme.
But the magic that had finally driven Siroise from this
realm was complex and required great power. Precious moments were lost while Thalis recovered from the effort, and
by that time Kahna was dead.

Thalis long mourned her. Immortality was a cruel gift.
Live forever. Time for everything. Including the death of
every being you ever cared for. Time passes, mortals age,
sicken, dying while you live on, unchanged by the years.
Atlanteans were a long-lived people, but long was not forever and mortals did break so easily. He was left with only
bittersweet memories.

But children. He smiled at the thought. The children of
their children, generation upon generation of them by now,
to comfort him over the countless millennia.

That way he would have known true immortality.

Then he would today have a reason to fight.

Kahna came back to him three more times in the years
that followed: the first time as a young sheepherding nomad,
the second as handmaiden to the Queen of the City of the

Lion, and the third as a blind Amazon archer in the guard of the First City. Centuries, sometimes so many he lost count, separated their reunions, but each one lasted a little longer than the last.

She would be back again.

One day.

Thalis cast a prayer into the night that he would live to greet her, in whatever guise her life took this time.

Thalis!

The wind roared his name, slamming great walls of water at the *Yar*. The ship lurched, swayed, leaned so far starboard that the bulwarks about skimmed the frothing waters.

Thalis! I'm waiting for you, old man!

The serpent bared wooden fangs at the screaming wind and wheeled into it as if to mock its power.

"Ah, Celepha," Thalis nodded in sad acknowledgment at the voice on the wind. "Who else would be sent against me?"

"I hate her," the *Yar* hissed. "Twice has she nearly killed you and destroyed me."

"Thrice tried, thrice charmed," Thalis said.

The wind rumbled like laughter around the ship.

Thalis dreamed of Kahna.

She was the Amazon, tall and muscular, skin the color of burnished bronze, hair braided in a tight tail that hung inches from the floor. She was the most beautiful, the most dangerous, the most desirable woman he had ever known. Even before he saw in her startling sightless gray eyes the same soul reflected back that he had seen three times previously, he whispered, "Kahna," and she whispered, "Thalis," and they were together again.

She stood in his dream on the terrace outside his quarters. The sun was rising and the morning breeze was warm.

Her arms were wrapped across her chest but as the sun rose, its golden light bathing the First City's gleaming towers in a light so brilliant as to be painful, she slowly spread wide her arms, raising on her toes, turning her face to the sun and laughing like a delighted child.

Thalis lay in his bed, watching through the doorway the golden light wash over her golden skin, the silk of her robe shining like white fire in the morning sun.

As he watched, he was content to live forever, if only so the memory of the moment would never, ever die.

At sundown on the second day, Celepha sent three creatures to attack the *Yar*.

They were twice the height of the *Yar*'s mainmast, water-beasts dark and featureless save for gaping, dripping maws lined with coral teeth sharp enough to rend wood and metal. The first of the beasts closed its jaws around the ship's railing, and the serpent roared in rage and pain.

Thalis strode from beneath deck, staff in hand, and screamed an incantation of fire at the beast. The spell surged through him and tore a gash in the fabric of reality that separated this world from the Darkness, releasing a torrent of eldritch fire that turned the raging thing into a howling column of steam. He turned the staff on the second beast, releasing the magical bonds that held the waters to this shape even as it swooped down with its jaws wide to snatch the old sorcerer from the rain-washed deck. The attack died in a torrent of sea water that sent Thalis crashing to the planks.

The third and final beast found its throat caught in the teeth of the serpent, and it bellowed and thrashed as it tried to escape Yar's grasp. The serpent held firm, until the beast decided to return to its primal form rather than face humiliating defeat. It collapsed into water, washing back into the sea that birthed it.

Thalis regained his footing and, wiping the stinging salt of the sea from his eyes, held high his staff to the thundering clouds, and screamed, "I am coming, Celepha!"

Lightning flashed, making night as bright as day. Thunder shook the very air around the ship.

"Celepha mocks us still," growled the serpent, its great head whipping back and forth.

Thalis tightened his fist around his staff. "Celepha toys with us," he said. He knew what she too must know. He was one old man, weary of life and of living. What did a god have to fear from one such as him?

Thalis' staff was carved of the wood of the first tree felled to build the First City.

The gods had gathered members of the Twelve Tribes inhabiting the world and brought them to the place on the edge of the Great Sea and decreed that upon that spot was to be constructed the First City of Atlantis. A craftsman named Argon had taken his ax to the great tree and felled it with twelve blows, grunting the name of each tribe as his blade bit into the wood.

The tree fell. A piece of wood as thick as a grown man's forearm and near three lengths tall splintered off the tree when it fell to the ground. Thalis took up the splinter.

"Here is the nexus of all the magic of the One," Wynsgar nodded in approval at the place the gods had directed them to. "Atlantis shall grow great and powerful here. Its people will spread out across the world, but its heart will ever thus beat here, upon the lands that the gods have gifted us."

Thalis took out his knife and began to carve at the top of the staff the visage of Atlannis, first of the twelve deities.

When he finished the carving, Atlannis smiled out at him. Over the years, the visages of the rest of the pantheon joined Atlannis on the staff.

Now, so many thousands of years later, he feared to look at the staff lest he find the mother of all the gods no longer smiling.

Thalis huddled in a chair in the cabin wrapped in furs and coverlets. He would not, could not bring himself to lie down on the bunk. How could that be right, without Kahna to share it with him?

"Yar," he whispered.

"Yes, Thalis," replied his old friend.

"I cannot sleep," the old man said.

"Perhaps that is best," the ship said softly, in a voice like sea spray through the riggings. "Think of the dreams you will miss."

Thalis closed his eyes.

He saw swimming before him the faces of thousands, of Kahna, of Gith, of Shanar, of Wynsgar, of countless others he had known, had loved, had lost. His life had surged through the ages, bloody with violence and destruction. He had received his share of wounds, had faced death too many times to remember.

. . . but he was still here.

How many had he led into brutal, ugly deaths?

He could count each and every face, passing like specters from the Darkness before him now. Then he would know how many.

His eyes snapped open, banishing the ghosts. He sighed. "Ah, well. There will be time for sleep later."

Celepha next whipped the sea into a screaming, sucking vortex that opened in the *Yar*'s path. The serpent

screamed and reared back, straining with every bit of its
ensorcelled being to turn away from the swirling white hole
in the dark sea. Celepha's laughter was in the wind that
pushed the ship into the ocean's gaping maw.

"I am caught," the serpent roared. Thalis clung to the
mast, his thin arms barely able to hold himself from being
blown away. "The sea has me, Lord Thalis!"

Thalis snarled in defiance. He had at last drifted off into
an uneasy sleep. But his dreams were tranquil, beautiful.
Kahna, this time the delicate, raven-haired handmaiden of
the City of the Lion, tread across the sparkling, reflective
surface of the sea gone utterly calm. Thalis, an old and
weathered man, stood upon the deck of the *Yar*, at peace
with himself and the world and watched her come.

"It is almost time, Thalis," she told him, "for us."

He had smiled at her courtly beauty. Unlike her other
incarnations, this Kahna hated the violence that surrounded
his life, could not bear for herself to lay hands upon a
weapon. But he loved her nonetheless. He learned warmth
and tenderness from her. He learned to reconnect to his
heart.

Celepha had robbed that wife from him in life, using
the sea to take the Queen's royal yacht upon which she
rode. The Queen and her court, more than two dozen in
all, went down with that ship upon placid seas, but Kahna
had been the intended victim. Celepha used her death to
draw him into battle.

Now the bitch goddess of the seas took her from even
his dreams.

"I have bested you twice before," the old man told the
sea. "I have it in me for one more time. Show yourself,
Celepha!"

He gripped his staff in his fists, holding it straight out
before himself, then slowly, his lips mouthing the words

of a spell older than Atlantis, turned the wooden shaft until it was held horizontally. He lifted it slowly, raising it high over his head. The air around him began to glow, to pulsate. It enveloped him in a shimmering blue aura that spread down the length of his body and onto the deck of the *Yar*. From there it spread faster, crackling blue energies radiating from sorcerer to ship, wrapping the tossing, groaning *Yar* in its embrace.

Then, with a grunt, Thalis bid the ship to rise from the waters, pulling free of the sucking vortex that would have otherwise swamped it.

The *Yar* rose until its curved hull was clear of the touch of even the highest waves, and then it began to move forward. Celepha sent winds to slap it back down into the water, but Thalis' enchantment shed their fury like water off a crystal goblet. It slipped past even the strongest gusts until, at last, the vortex lay well behind them.

The serpent sang out in joy. "Thalis," it asked, "why did you not bear us aloft sooner?"

"I am no longer a young man," the mage gasped with his efforts. The *Yar* sank back onto the waves with a crash.

This is the story Thalis told the *Yar*:

"She came back to me the last time almost one thousand years ago. She was an Amazon archer, blind from birth yet trained in the ways of warfare. For her eyes she substituted her ears and other senses, drawing upon the great magic of her mind to compensate for her lack of sight. To see her navigate the streets of the marketplace without incident was remarkable. She could notch and fire her bow in the blink of an eye, always sure of hitting her target. Her name at birth had been Misha, but as soon as we met, I knew she was Kahna.

"We waged war, side by side, Kahna and I. There was

not a warrior alive, man or woman, who could best her in fair combat. With her at my side, I knew I could go anywhere, fight any foe, and never fear for my safety.

"We were together four score plus one year. A plague set upon the City by the pretender King of the City of the Stars ended her life. All I could do was hold her hand and comfort her, watching the sickness slowly steal the breath from her magnificent form.

"The King of Stars . . . his plague was like nothing found in any of the magical tomes. It was nature's creation, he said, discovered independent of sorcery. Because his magic was so weak, he was the first to turn to science, to craft machines that did not draw upon magic for their workings. He was a madman, but there is an audience for even the rantings of madness, I suppose. A thousand years and still the notion of science remains, has grown in fact stronger, until all but a few accept it as their faith."

The *Yar* sighed like the rumble of anchor chain clattering through its anchorage. "I, for one, find the entire idea preposterous," said the ship.

The King of the First City, First Among Equals of the Twelve Cities, came to Thalis' quarters. The sovereign did not often come to his subjects. The young royal's presence in his rooms made Thalis uneasy.

"The Counsel has decided that the City is to leave this miserable place," the king told him. "Why do we stay here, year after year, only to have to fight off the seas that continually batter down our walls and undermine the structures at the city's edge? We can rebuild inland, upon the high ground and at last know some peace from nature's continual annoyances."

The old sorcerer spread his hands before him, confused. "But, my lord," said Thalis. "*This* is the land the gods com-

manded we inhabit. The magic flows through here, beneath
the City. To go elsewhere is to doom Atlantis."

The king smiled indulgently. "Really, Thalis. Magic is
all well and good, but it is not as though we were depen-
dent on it for everything. My engineers can build of metal,
wood, and fabric machines to replace what things sorcery
can no longer supply."

Thalis lowered his hands and shook his head in sorrow.
"Your majesty," he started to say, but the king had already
turned and was sweeping from the room. "It is decided,
Thalis. We break ground for the new city upon the new
moon."

That night, the wind and the sea began their final assault on Atlantis.

The *Yar* sailed into a circle of calm in the heart of the
storm.

Black, angry clouds rose like the walls of a well around
them to the stars. Celepha's magic held the storms at bay,
but no bit of their fury reached Thalis and the *Yar*. The
goddess of the sea had created for them this shelter and,
standing aboard the deck of the serpent ship as it bobbed
easily in the becalmed waters, Thalis could only wait.

The serpent scanned the patch of clear sky above their
heads. "We have traveled far," he observed.

"And we have yet to arrive at our destination," Thalis
said. His staff felt heavy in his hands. Though the night
breeze was cool, he could feel beads of sweat on his forehead. I am too old, he thought, but of course that did not
matter.

Suddenly, the serpent's head snapped up, alert. "Thalis,"
it hissed.

The old man nodded. "I smell it," he said. The sorcery,
the stink of enchantment grew heavy in his nostrils and

then, with the gentle splash of a summer rain falling on a pond, the ocean rose and took form before the *Yar*. She was silver and blue, shades of green and clear water, big enough to fill the sky, the goddess Celepha, mother of the seas.

Thalis, she said, her voice bubbling all about him.

"Celepha," he replied, tensing for combat.

We need not fight, she said.

"We have always had the need in the past," he said.

Those were different times, Thalis, when I acted against the will of the One. Now, I am one of many, the voice of the gods united.

"What do they want of me?" the old man asked.

Celepha seemed to ponder his question. She flowed in the air, enormous and beautiful, the creatures of the sea swimming through her cheeks, her arms, a whale circling lazily in her chest where her heart should have been. When she spoke at last, she said, *We want nothing of you, Thalis. Your work is done.*

"No," Thalis said. "Not while Atlantis yet stands."

A watery hand passed languidly over the *Yar. Atlantis will soon stand no more,* Celepha said softly. *For too long they have denied their gods and our gifts to them. They will quit even the sacred ground that we gave them. They are no more the people of Atlannis, Thalis. By abandoning us, they abandon everything.*

Let their science *save them from our wrath!*

"No," Thalis said again. "I am their protector. I must . . ."

It is decided, Thalis, Celepha said. *The ground shall quake and split, the First City shall tumble and the waters shall wash in and cover it, sweeping its golden towers and spires into the sea. One by one, the rest of the Twelve Cities will succumb to the gods, for without the First City, the heart of Atlantis will be stilled and its time upon this earth ended.*

"You must not . . ." the old man stammered.

It is not for you to decide, the sea told him. *You have left only this choice. We fight . . . until your limbs are numb and your magic exhausted and your soul cries out for rest and I kill you. Or, I grant you three things which you accept and so leave the gods to their business: your life to live out as you see fit, forever unmolested by the sea or any I command and this ship upon which you sail.*

"Three things," Thalis croaked, his heart quickening with anticipation. "You said three things."

Celepha cupped her hands, each greater in size than the *Yar,* and the water of her fingers swam together and then parted and there stood Kahna. The handmaiden, her hair wet and pulled back against her head, but still as dark and silken as the night sky. Thalis' breath caught in his throat.

"Is she real?" he asked.

Celepha smiled and began to lower her hand toward the *Yar.* The serpent thrashed its neck back and forth. "Thalis, no. That which has gone is gone."

This the old sorcerer knew. Though he dreamed of her as she appeared in her lives past, he would dream of her, too, as transcendent of flesh and blood, a woman whose face lacked feature but whose radiance of soul and enormity of heart made her recognizable to him no matter what face she wore. This was not her, not truly, though his heart swelled and he fought to choke back tears as Celepha's hand drew her closer to him. Kahna's lips and eyes smiled at him, Kahna's arms stretched open wide to embrace him.

But it was not her.

This Kahna was dead. That which united their souls had fled the form before him and been back since, as his Amazon archer.

"It is time, Thalis," she whispered. "For us."

The Lord High Mage of Atlantis sobbed once and swung his staff up before him. Through trembling lips he snarled the words to an incantation. Through tear-blurred eyes he watched the thing that called itself Kahna recoil and scream, the porcelain white skin of his lost love peeling away to reveal the sickening purple flesh of some hideous creature from Celepha's depths.

He had fought for an eternity to keep Atlantis alive. He was too old, too tired to fight any longer.

He screamed out the final words of his spell and watched as the night exploded into day, eldritch energies screaming through the air. Celepha cursed what remained of Thalis' life and howled, calling down the winds and storm she had been holding at bay. A wall of water smashed against the *Yar*, washing its deck with a deluge of green water. The serpent made to turn itself into the wind, but before it could move, Celepha's watery hand reached down and snapped its neck with two fingers, throwing the still twitching head into the sea.

Thalis was washed across the deck by the violent seas that broke over the bulwarks. But he never relinquished his hold on his staff and now it lifted him to his feet and propelled him like a vengeful bird of prey toward Celepha.

They are not worthy of you, the sea goddess lamented. Her winds ripped the staff from his hands and sent the length of wood tumbling through the air to shatter against the mast of the *Yar* into a thousand fragments borne away by the wind.

When she struck him down into the sea, Thalis was laughing and crying to the wind, "Time at last to sleep."

*　　*　　*

When the waters came to claim Atlantis, the people tried to repent and called out for their sorcerer to save them. Somewhere, Thalis listened to their cries but was beyond hearing them.

THE SACRED WATERS OF KANE

BY FIONA PATTON

THE swells at Peahi crashed against the beach with an almost constant roar. The two youths who stood on the overhanging cliff watched them for a long time, identical expressions of concentration on their faces.

Kai Malau'a and Makani Kalowai had been friends since they were children. Of similar height and build, both had long, black hair worn loose, copper complexions, and wide, dark eyes. Each wore an identical red loincloth and a necklace of finely braided hair and tiny sea shells, and both had a habit of sneaking off whenever Peahi called to them. But today the surf was in an angry mood.

Frowning, Kai stared at the horizon, carefully noting the shape and movement of each cloud before turning his attention to the surf. The waves were steady enough, but beneath that, he could sense a growing undercurrent. Something was happening to upset the spirits about Peahi. It was nothing he could identify yet, but the sense of it had been disturbing his dreams for days. Growling, he picked up a small, rough-edged weather stone and tossed it over the cliff, watching intently as it hit the waves. Something was happening.

Leaning against a young kukui tree, Makani waited on his friend's word, watching him glare at the waves as if they were deliberately withholding their secrets from him.

Of all the youths on the island, Kai was the most gifted at drawing prophecy from the sky and the sea. He might make a powerful kahuna kilo one day but, as changeable as the ocean itself—one moment calm, the next moment churned into an angry froth—his temper often got the better of him. He'd likely pick a fight with someone today, probably his teacher Alaula, and then he'd feel better. Makani had long since stopped worrying about his friend's mercurial mood swings. Like a summer storm they were over quickly enough.

"So, what do you think?" he prodded finally.

"Twenty-five, thirty feet and growing."

"Too high to risk?"

Kai nodded. "Only the Akua are surfing this morning." If he tried, he could almost see the gods balanced on the water. "Even the whales have gone deep."

Makani squinted at the horizon. His training as kahuna la'au lapa'au involved plants; clouds and waves meant little beyond surfing. "Is there a storm coming?" he asked.

"I don't think so. Something's coming, though." Picking up another weather stone, Kai stared blankly at the pattern of worn markings across its face before returning his gaze to the water below. "There'll be no surfing today," he pronounced bitterly.

"Might as well go to lessons, then."

"You go ahead."

Makani cocked his head to one side. "Alaula will be waiting for you," he tried.

Kai's face twisted into the expected grimace at his teacher's name. "Alaula says he won't teach me anymore," he growled. "He says I'll never be kahuna kilo."

"Alaula says you don't have the *discipline* to be kahuna kilo," Makani corrected. "But then he's always said that. You two have been fighting for years. He'll come around."

"Not this time."

Makani studied his friend's face. "You've had a really big fight, then?"

Kai shrugged. "No bigger than usual. I'm just tired of learning uphill. I read an omen he doesn't see and he sneers at it, I have a dream he doesn't have and he dismisses it. I've studied under him for ten years, and it's always the same. I've had enough."

"You've said that before."

"This time I mean it."

Picking up an ohi'a stick, Makani studied it absently while keeping one eye on the thunderclouds passing across his friend's face.

"So, what will you do then?" he asked finally. "Ask the kahuna nui Po'o for another teacher?"

"No. He'd just take Alaula's side, anyway. I feel . . ." He stared out at the churning ocean, his eyes cloudy. "I feel like I've learned everything I can here, like I'm meant to be somewhere else."

"Where?"

"Leiawa."

Makani blinked. "Leiawa's a myth."

"Nahele say's he's been there."

"Nahele left his mind out on the waves ten years ago."

"He say's there are kahuna kilo on Leiawa who will trade training for the right kind of offering."

Makani expression hardened. "What kind of offering, Kai?"

"Kea limu."

"No."

"Makani . . ."

"No, Kai. We've been through this before. Kea limu only grows in Hamao Bay."

"So?"

"So, it's haunted, you know that. Only the most powerful kahuna la'au lapa'au can go out after kea limu."

"I'm going out tonight."

Makani's mouth dropped open. "*You're* going?"

Kai nodded. "I dreamed about Leiawa last night. To get there I need the kea limu."

"Then ask Okalani to harvest it for you."

"I have. He won't. He doesn't believe in Leiawa either."

"But it's Kane tonight. The lapu and the Night Marchers will be out. We'd be killed."

Kai shrugged. "I'm not asking you to come," he answered with studied indifference.

Makani flushed angrily. "You'd never find the kea limu without me."

"I know what it looks like and I know how far out Okalani goes to harvest it. I followed him last month."

"You don't know how to prepare it, then."

"The kahuna la'au lapa'au on Leiawa will know how to prepare it."

"You don't even know they exist. You're going to risk your life to harvest a night-growing plant in haunted waters for kahuna no one but an addle-minded eighty-year-old fisherman has ever seen because you haven't the patience to listen to Alaula instead of fighting with him?"

Kai rounded on the other youth, his black eyes blazing. "It has nothing to do with patience," he snapped. "Ever since I was a baby, the kahuna kaula have been saying my future was clouded. Alaula says that's because I'm not meant to be kahuna kilo even though all the signs say I have the talent and the mana. He's been saying that from the beginning. He wants me to fail."

"You want it more than he does."

Kai turned away. "I said you didn't have to come."

"Don't think I will. I listen to my teachers when they say I'm not ready, and if you had any sense you would, too."

"So, go listen to them, then. No one's keeping you here. I don't need you. Your fear would probably draw the Night Marchers down on us, anyway."

Makani's eyes narrowed. "Fine. I'll just go and collect your funeral plants instead." With an angry gesture, he turned and headed down the path. Kai watched him go, his expression wrathful then, after throwing the second weather stone over the cliff, made his own way up the path in the opposite direction.

Far below, hidden in the thick layer of sea foam, a creature, part man and part fish, watched the youths' exchange with unblinking silvery eyes. Catching up the weather stone, he scrutinized it carefully, then, breathing a prayer to Namakaokaha'i, he allowed it to sink under the waves. As the Goddess had predicted: it would be tonight.

Slapping at the water with a long pohuehue vine, he called up a wave to lift him toward the shore. As his feet touched the sandy beach, he lost his fishlike appearance and, with one, last glance up at the cliff face, he disappeared into the wauke forest beyond.

That night, Kai slipped away from his family's hut. The air was warm, but the wind was rising; he could almost taste the omens in the air. Something big was coming, and he needed the kea limu to be ready, he could feel it. He wasn't afraid of the Night Marchers or the ghostly lapu. The latter could be frightened away by a sudden noise, and the unearthly processions of Akua and long-dead chiefs and priests were said to be so bright and so loud that he'd have plenty of time to hide.

Stopping before a darkened hut, he waited a few mo-

ments, then made himself carry on. If Makani didn't want
to come with him, he didn't have to. He didn't need him
and he would be well rid of him, anyway. Without a second glance, Kai headed for the nearby beach.

It was much darker than he'd expected. The sky had
grown cloudy during the day and not even the stars were
showing their faces. After stumbling off the path twice,
Kai tripped over a fallen kao branch. Rising with a curse,
he was suddenly aware of a faint light bobbing toward him.
His mouth went dry. His feet were rooted to the ground
and all he could do was stare as the light drew closer but,
just when he expected to see some terrifying lapu floating
toward him, Makani broke free of the trees. He was wearing a large ki leaf about his neck for protection and carrying a stone kukui nut lamp, which he held above his head
to light his way.

Breathing very carefully, Kai leaned against a tree and
glanced at his friend with what he hoped was casual interest.

"What took you so long?"

Makani glared back at him. "Shut up."

With the lamplight to guide them, the two youths made
better time, fetching up on the beach at Hamao Bay a few
moments later. Sheltered from Peahi by a great, sweeping
lava spur, the bay was almost always flat and calm, but
few fishermen dared its waters. It lay just below the island's leina, the cliff edge where the spirits of the dead
leaped off to enter the underworld. At night, those who
had gone before could be seen floating just below the waves,
waiting for their loved ones to join them. Living people
who entered those waters could be mistaken by the spirits
and drawn under to their deaths. Only the most powerful

kahuna la'au lapa'au and kahuna nui Po'o dared Hamao Bay at night. As his feet touched the beach, Makani came to an abrupt halt.

"We shouldn't be here, Kai," he said in a scared voice.

Kai turned. "It's all right. There's no moonlight or starlight. The spirits will never see us." Making his way to the rocks where he'd hidden their canoe that morning, he began to drag it toward the sound of the surf. At the water's edge, he paused.

"Well, are you coming?"

With a deep breath, Makani followed him.

The trip across the bay was made in silence. Makani held the lamp in the front of the canoe, peering nervously into the darkness while Kai paddled. After a time, they could just make out a faint glow in the distance, and at his friend's gesture, Kai brought them up to it.

The glow came from the center of a wide patch of seaweed floating gently on the waves. It was several feet across and, as Kai guided them into their midst, they parted reluctantly, clinging to the sides of the canoe as it passed. In the center, he paused.

"Do you see them?" he asked in a whisper, his words carrying easily across the quiet water.

"No."

Leaning precariously over the sides, both youths peered into the mass of floating greenery, but it was some time before Makani gave a tiny whistle.

"There," he breathed.

Kai joined him.

Nestled amidst a living net of common seaweed, the pale shoots of a dozen magical kea limu plants stretched their delicate leaves toward the night breezes. The glow rose up from their floating roots, illuminating every vein and marking, and they wavered gently on the waves like tiny hula dancers. The two youths watched them, mesmerized by their beauty, until Makani shook himself.

"Do you want me to perform the harvest?" he whispered.

Kai blinked. "No. It's my offering, I'll do it."

"You mustn't touch them with your fingers, or they'll shrivel up. And you mustn't take the biggest or the smallest, and you can only take one."

"I know."

"And you have to pray to both Hina and Ma'iola."

"I know."

"Do you remember the prayer I taught you last year?"

"Yes."

"Did you bring an offering?"

"Yes. Will you *please* be quiet."

Taking a gourd from his belt, Kai poured a fine thread of liquid among the plants. The strong smell of awa filled his nostrils, making him want to sneeze, but his hand never wavered until the gourd was empty. Then he set it carefully in the bottom of the canoe and unwrapped a small piece of bark cloth. As he laid it down on the seaweed beside one of the kea limu, the moon sent down a fine shaft of light to illuminate his work. He glanced over at Makani with a smirk.

"I told you so," he whispered.

"Just hurry up."

Moving deliberately slowly, Kai held up his knife so that the moonlight struck against it and quietly spoke the harvest prayer. Then, without touching the plant, he sliced cleanly through the stalk and let it fall onto the bark cloth, which he folded and tied with a piece of maile vine.

"Done. Maybe I should be kahuna la'au lapa'au instead of you." He straightened.

"Kai?"

The world around them plunged into darkness as the moon passed behind the clouds again.

"What?"

"I heard something."

Far away there came the faintest of sounds. Kai narrowed his eyes.

"It's nothing," he said with as much scorn as he could muster.

"Can we please go home now?"

"Yes."

Picking up the paddle, Kai maneuvered them from the seaweed patch.

They made it back to the beach without incident. Kai tucked the kea limu into a fold in his loincloth while Makani dragged the canoe back to its place in the rock. Then, keeping instinctively close to the lamplight, they headed back to the village. They were almost home when the night was suddenly empty of all sound.

Makani froze.

"Kai?"

"I know."

A faint noise, like a stick banging against a tree, began to make itself heard in the distance. "What is it?"

Kai swallowed. "Birds," he answered finally.

"No, it's . . ." Makani turned, his face pale in the lamplight. "It's drums."

"It's the wind."

"No, it's . . . Kai, I hear chanting."

"No, you don't."

"Yes, I do, it's . . . it's coming from along the path."

His voice rose hysterically, and Kai grabbed him by the shoulders.

"It's birds fighting for nesting sites in the trees," he said sharply. "Now, we have to take the path to get home. There's nothing there, so let's just . . ." He paused.

"Kai?"

"Wait."

"What is it?"

The hairs rising on the backs of his arms, Kai stared into the darkness. All around them he could feel the forest hold its breath as something primordial pushed its way into the world.

"Nothing," he croaked. "Come on."

Dragging Makani by the arm, he took another step, then the night exploded in light and sound. Across the path a huge procession appeared. In front, bearers beating drums, chanted out the rhythm of the march, while at the edges, two lines of huge warriors, armed with long glittering spears, moved easily through the trees. In the center, tall men and women dressed in feather cloaks and brilliant white loincloths walked, their feet floating a few inches from the ground. They spotted Kai and Makani at the same instant the youths saw them.

A scream went up from their midst. Makani dropped the lamp, and both boys bolted, Makani fleeing back down the path toward the beach and Kai plunging into the trees. With wild howls, the warriors gave chase.

Terror propelling his feet, all Kai he could think of was outrunning the horrible creatures bearing down on him. The light from the marchers was all around him, their terrible screaming filling his ears. He felt the whistle of a spear pass close by his shoulder, risked one look back, and ran headfirst into a wauke tree.

Stars exploded in his vision as he was flung backward from the impact. Blood coursing down his face, he tried to roll, then some unseen force caught him up and twisted him sideways. The spear tip aiming at his back took him in the groin. It drove through his loincloth and into the bark cloth around the kea limu. For a heartbeat it pressed toward his skin as the magical plant took the brunt of the ghostly attack, then the warrior was gone and the unseen force jerked him to his feet again. He caught one glimpse of cliffs and sky, and then he was falling down the ragged rocks of the leina.

The last thing he heard was Makani's scream.

It seemed like forever before he came back to himself. Blood had coursed down his face to glue his eyelids shut and pool about his mouth and nose. When he tried to bring his hand up to scrape at it, he almost fainted as the pain of his injuries rushed over him. His left arm, bent at an awkward angle, sent shafts of agony across his shoulders and the place where the kea limu had caught the spear tip burned like it was on fire. Breath hissing through his teeth, he made himself lie still, then carefully forced his eyelids open.

He was about ten feet down the leina, caught within the confines of a fallen hala tree. Below his feet, he could see the dark waters of Hamao Bay, and above him, the night sky. The moon had come out from behind the clouds to sketch long shadows across the rocks and ferns, and it was then that he became aware of a man crouched above him, staring at him with a pair of wide, silvery eyes.

Kai froze.

"Lapu?" he breathed.

Tossing long black hair from his face, the man shook his head. "Aumakua," it answered.

"Mine?"

"Yours, descendant. I am called Kekoa. The Goddess Namakaokaha'i prophesied that you would have need of me tonight and sent me to protect you from the Night Marchers."

The memory of his run through the forest made Kai's breath catch in his throat.

"Makani?"

His ancestor's silver eyes regarded him steadily. "Taken," he answered.

"Taken . . . ?"

"He is dead, descendant."

"No."

"You heard him scream. They tore his spirit from his body. Even with my help, you were lucky to escape them."

Kai closed his eyes. "My oldest friend was killed tonight," he answered woodenly. "How is that lucky?"

"Did you wish to join him?"

The question was sarcastic, but Kai could not muster enough energy to answer angrily.

"No," he whispered.

"Did you wish to save him, then?"

"How?"

"With the waters of Kane."

Kai blinked up at the aumakua. "The waters of Kane are a myth."

"So is the Island of Leiawa."

"Leiawa?"

Kekoa nodded. "Where from a hidden spring flows the waters that restore life."

"I dreamt of Leiawa. I . . ." Kai swallowed. "I told Makani that I was meant to go there."

"And so you are." Kekoa stood. "It's Kane tonight," he observed. "The veil between the worlds is thin. Makani's spirit may still heed your call, but we have very little time. If you don't bring him the sacred waters by sunrise, his spirit will have gone forever."

Kai's expression grew bleak. "It's too far. I'd never get back in time."

The moonlight reflecting in Kekoa's eyes, he shook his head. "There is a way," he answered.

"How?"

"Through the underworld."

"The dead would never allow it."

"They would if you journeyed under the protection of the Akua. Come with me before Namakaokaha'i. Ask for her help. If she allows it, we could reach Leiawa in time."

"Why would a Sea Goddess help me? I have nothing to offer her in return."

The aumakua glanced away for just an instant, but when he looked back, his eyes were unreadable.

"She's drawn to your nature. Offer your worship. If she requires more, she'll name it herself."

Hope granting him new strength, Kai nodded. "All right."

"Then take my hand."

Gritting his teeth, Kai reached out and let the aumakua drag him from the hala tree. Once on his feet, the pain of his injuries made him sway, but then he steadied himself.

"What now?"

"Jump."

"Jump?"

Kekoa nodded. "You stand above the underworld, descendant. Jump."

Looking down, Kai stared into the waters of Hamao Bay. In the moonlight he could just make out the wide patches of seaweed floating upon the waves, the faint glow within their midst revealing the presence of the kea limu. Below that, he could see the faint outlines of the dead. He closed his eyes. And jumped.

*   *   *

The sea closed over his head. Floundering in panic, he felt Kekoa's arms wrap about him, and he opened his eyes.

He stood on the ocean floor, the waves of Hamao Bay far above his head. All around him there was nothing but darkness, but as he stood there, he realized that he could both see and breathe. Before him, a vast forest of black ki trees, their great leaves bent almost to the ground, weaved in the ocean current. Ghostly fish swam, unhindered, through their branches, the glowing light of awareness in their eyes revealing that these were no ordinary creatures, but spirits and aumakua.

About him the water grew suddenly warm and he found himself surrounded by sharks. Their long, sleek bodies brushed against him and their black eyes stared into his as if seeing right through him. As he shrank against Kekoa, his aumakua took his hand.

"Don't be afraid, descendant," he said, his voice drifting toward him like a fine strand of seaweed. "They won't hurt you. They are spirits."

Lifting his head, Kai strained to see beyond the sharks and into the sea of trees beyond. "Is it far?"

"No distance at all and halfway around the world."

"But the sunrise?"

"There is no sunrise here, nor sunset. We exist between the dusk and the dawn. Come." Without looking back, Kekoa led him into the trees.

The way was both steep and smooth. All around him, Kai could hear people singing, but he couldn't see them; the dark forest was too thick. When he turned a questioning glance at Kekoa, the aumakua shook his head. "If you saw them, you would forget all about the living world."

They continued to walk. After what seemed like forever, and yet no time at all, they left the trees and stood before a vast, swirling void. Kekoa paused.

"She is here."

Straining to see into the darkness, Kai shook his head. "I don't feel anything."

"And yet she feels you. Speak her name and you will know her presence."

With a deep breath, Kai opened his mouth.

"Namakaokaha'i."

The word flowed from his mouth on a stream of fine bubbles. They passed into the void and suddenly the Goddess burst into being like an explosion from an underwater geyser. Kai was flung backward from the force of it, then jerked forward as her power surged through him. When she touched the place where his mana resided, he could feel her greed for its living power, made that much sweeter by its presence in the underworld. He almost flinched away from her desire, but at the last moment forced himself to remain still. She reached for his life, and then drew back and he found himself on his knees, his whole body vibrating with the memory of her touch. About him the ocean churned with one question.

Why was he here?

Finding his voice, he told her of Makani; of that night's misadventure, of his friend's untimely death, and his need for safe passage to retrieve the waters of Kane.

The ocean swirled about him and then another question. What would he give for Makani's life?

As Kekoa had suggested, he offered up his worship. The sea grew still, then as quickly as she'd come, the Goddess disappeared. Kekoa stood before him, holding out an empty gourd.

"Take this to Leiawa," he said, "and fill it."

Kai accepted the gourd. "That's all?" he asked.

Kekoa's silver eyes were blank. "For now."

Turning, he walked into the void and, with only a moment's hesitation, Kai followed him.

He lost track of how long they walked, but finally they began to ascend a steep, slippery path grown over by ocean weeds. Very soon Kai's head broke the surface of the waves. The sudden moonlight made him start but Kekoa was already on the beach, standing amidst the rocks.

"Here."

In the cleft between two rocks, Kai found a small stream.

"The waters of Kane?"

The aumakua nodded. "Did you bring an offering?"

Reaching into his loincloth, Kai pulled out the charred remains of the kea limu in its tattered bark cloth wrapper.

"I was going to give this to the kahuna on Leiawa," he said bitterly.

"There are no kahuna on Leiawa save yourself. Give it to the island instead."

Tucking the plant into the rocks, Kai covered it over with a handful of pebbles, then filled the gourd. But, when he stood, he felt a thin trickle of water pass down his arm. Looking down, he saw to his horror that it was cracked.

Mutely he held it up, watching as the water of Kane spilled from a crack in its side. The world seemed to grow suddenly dim.

"Kekoa . . ." he whispered.

"I see it."

"What can I . . . maybe I can fix it with seaweed or maile vine." He began to hunt desperately about the rocks.

"There isn't time."

Something in the aumakua's voice made Kai stare sharply at him. His eyes widened.

"You knew."

"Knew?"

"That it was broken when you gave it to me. Why did you do that?"

"Kai . . ."

"Why!" He grabbed the aumakua by the throat. "Tell me why!"

Kekoa reached up and gently removed Kai's hands as if he had no more strength than a child.

"It was her will," he said gently.

"Her will?"

"Namakaokaha'i. The Goddess prophesied that on this night you would be tested. If you passed, you would become kahuna nui Po'o, the greatest and most powerful of all kahuna."

"That was the change I sensed was coming?"

"Yes. But the Goddess also saw that you would almost certainly fail."

Kai's eyes narrowed. "Why?"

"Because you're arrogant and rash. The Akua sent you a dream spelling out all that was to come. You had only to take it to any kahuna with the talent to read dreams. They would have recognized it for what it was, but you couldn't bring yourself to ask for help so, without council, you risked your life and Makani's, too. He paid the price for your friendship, leaving you to pay the price for his."

"So, what is the price?"

"You."

"I offered Namakaokaha'i my worship."

"Not your worship, Kai, you; all that you are and all that you will be, all your power and all your labor, pledged to her service, and hers alone. Such a pledge, coming from a kahuna nui Po'o, is incredibly valuable to the Akua. For such a pledge she would restore Makani."

"Why didn't you tell me this before?"

"Would you have even entertained the thought of such

a pledge if you weren't desperate?" Kekoa gestured toward the horizon just beginning to show pink.

"So, you trick me into giving her my life, *aumakua of mine*," Kai spat bitterly.

"No, descendant. I *petitioned* her to send me to *save* your life after you brought the Night Marchers down upon your head. She granted my request and asked for nothing in return, neither from me nor from you. And Na-makaokaha'i is no gentle Akua to shower favors for no gain; she's the undercurrent and the tidal wave. That you'd put yourself in the position where you might be exploited by such as she in exchange for Makani's life—which *you* lost—is hardly my doing. I'm simply telling you her price."

Kai stared blankly out to sea. "All that I am and all I will be, all my power and all my labor, as kahuna nui Po'o, pledged to her service, and hers alone," he repeated. He turned back to Kekoa. "No."

"No?"

"No. Such a pledge would increase her power on land and as you said, she's no gentle Akua. I won't labor for that kind of danger to my people. Not even for Makani."

Turning, he crossed the beach and began to climb up Leiawa's steep cliff face. Kekoa watched him, his expression curious.

"Where are you going?"

"To make her another offer."

"What offer?"

Kai looked down at him. "My pledge as Kahuna nui Po'o would be of great value to her, but that's not what she truly hungers for. She hungers for mana. Mine. All that I have and freely given."

Kekoa's silver eyes widened. He began to scramble up the cliff after him. "Without the mana you now possess, you'll never be kahuna kilo, never mind kahuna nui Po'o."

Having reached the top, Kai held up both hands in a shrug. "Without my life to call my own, it isn't worth being either." He glanced down at the water below. "Is this Leiawa's leina?"

"Kai . . ."

"Is it?"

Kekoa glared at him. "Every cliff edge on Leiawa is a leina," he answered sullenly.

"Good." Stepping to the edge, Kai glanced back at his aumakua. "It's a simple choice," he explained. "What does she desire more, the worship of a kahuna nui Po'o, or his mana? I offer either, but my price is Makani."

"Are you mad? You can't give an ultimatum to Namakaokaha'i. She could dash your limbs against the rocks at Peahi in a second."

"Then I'll be back in the underworld before sunrise and she can do as she likes with my broken spirit. Maybe she'll house it in your broken gourd." Kai gave him a flat look. "If this is her will, Kekoa, then we'll let her decide." Turning his back on his ancestor, he flung himself from the leina.

The black ocean of the underworld engulfed him, long tendrils of kea limu rising up to bind his arms and legs. All about him, he heard the laughing and singing of the dead, and then the power of Namakaokaha'i smacked him in the chest like a great wave. It drove straight through him, catching up a portion of his mana, then hurled him from the sea.

The impact of his body hitting the ground sent a shock wave of pain across his ribs. He caught one glimpse of cliffs and sky, and then he was falling. Rocks tore at his hands and feet, his left arm snapped backwards and the crack of broken bones tore a scream from his lips. For an instant he hovered above Hamao Bay and then the branches of the hala tree reached out and caught him. Pain radiating from his arm to throb across his shoulders, he looked up, and saw Kekoa crouched above him. The aumakua stretched his hand out.

"Come descendant, we haven't got much time."

Somehow Kai made it up the cliff. Twice darkness rushed in to claim him, but each time, Kekoa's grip on his arm kept him from completely blacking out. When he finally reached the top, he lay panting heavily, blinking up through a haze of blood at his aumakua. Kekoa gazed back at him with his silvery eyes.

"Can you walk?"

"Do I have to?"

The aumakua shrugged. "The sun is rising and Makani Kalowai lies dead." He held out an unbroken gourd. "Or had you forgotten?"

Too weary to respond to his ancestor's sarcasm, Kai accepted the gourd, feeling the heaviness of the water within it. Painfully, he got to his feet.

He found Makani sprawled across the path. His eyes were wide and staring, and as Kai—his left arm tied tightly against his side with maile vines—limped up beside him, he could sense his friend's spirit fluttering desperately over his body. Shielding him from the dawn sun, he pried his clenched jaw open with his one good hand, then dumped the contents of the gourd unceremoniously down his throat.

A shaft of sunlight broke through the wauke trees. For a heartbeat, Makani was outlined in golden light and then his spirit drove back into his body so fast it burned a path across Kai's cheek. His eyes snapped open. Fingers drawn into claws, he scrabbled at his throat and finally, sucked in one shuddering breath. Then another. And another. After each, his body jerked in convulsions as life reanimated his body. Not daring to touch him, Kai could only watch.

Finally the convulsions eased. Makani's hands went limp, and his head lolled to one side. His dark eyes were dazed, but slowly they grew clear, focusing on Kai's haggard face. The two friends stared mutely at each other, then, with a surge of energy, Makani staggered to his feet. His face was still deathly pale, and he swayed unsteadily. Kai reached out to catch him with his good hand, but Makani jerked back.

"You . . ." he croaked. "Don't touch me. Don't ever touch me. Don't even . . . talk to me . . . ever again." Spinning dizzily about, he stumbled against a wauke tree then, after several deep breaths, began to make his way slowly down the path toward their village. Kai watched him go, then turned and made his own way back up the path to the leina.

Kekoa was waiting for him when he returned. His silver eyes tracked across Kai's face and he nodded in understanding.

"I'm sorry, descendant."

Easing himself carefully to the ground, Kai pressed his back against the rocks and dropped his head into his hands.

"He's alive. That's all that matters."

"He's your friend. He may yet forgive you."

"Maybe."

"It was a foolish offer to make," the aumakua admonished. "Mana freely given is a very great temptation. You were lucky she didn't take it all for your presumption. It will be much harder for you to be kahuna nui Po'o now, but not impossible. With her help, you may yet succeed."

Kai raised his head. "With her help?"

Kekoa shrugged. "You offered her worship. Keep your promise, and she'll aid you as any Akua would do. There's

no weakness in asking for help, descendant." He stepped
to the edge of the leina. "Go to Hamao Bay. You will be
safe in its waters now. Speak her name, and you will know
her presence." He raised his arms.

"Wait? Will I ever see you again?"

The aumakua smiled. "You may have matured this night,
but not so much, I think, that you won't have need of me
again. Throw a weather stone into the surf at Peahi and
call my name."

With that, the aumakua flung himself from the leina.
He changed as he fell and hit the water half-man, half-fish
with barely a ripple to mark his passage back to the underworld. Kai stared at the place for a long time and then rose
and made his way slowly down the path.

His injuries hampering his progress, the sun was already
well past the horizon when he stepped onto the black sand
beach of Hamao Bay. Deceptive in the daylight, its waters
sparkled invitingly and Kai walked into the waves until the
surf swelled against his chest. Washing the blood from his
face and hair, he touched the place where Makani's spirit
had scored across his cheek.

"Namakaokaha'i," he breathed. "Help me mend this rift
with Makani, and I will worship you freely as Akua above
all others. Lend me your strength and your wisdom." His
lips quirked up in a faint smile. "But not your temper, I
have that already."

A strand of pale seaweed caught about his good arm
and he pulled it from the waves and put it about his neck,
feeling it lie wet and clinging against his skin. Then the
island's newest kahuna nui Po'o rose from the surf of
Hamao Bay and retraced the steps he and Makani had taken
so long ago the night before.

CHILD OF OCEAN

BY ROSEMARY EDGHILL

MYKENE was the best pilot from Lordsdeep to Down-below. In the twelve years since she first donned her golden earrings no ship she had sailed on had ever been lost.

The folk called her lucky and captains vied for her presence on their decks. *Mykene has been from the Pillars to the setting sun; she has luck enough to pilot a ship to Lostland if you were mad enough to go.* So they said, in the taverns on the Strand, and it made pleasant hearing of a night's drinking.

But it wasn't true anymore.

"Good weather, Pilot!"

"Good weather," Mykene returned.

The gangway rattled up behind her and the captain received the office to sail. Half-oars was called, and the ship began to move sluggishly out of the harbor. Mykene turned and walked toward the bow. The wind pulled at her short dark hair. Her toes curled against the soft smooth wood of the *Grantine*'s deck. Mykene looked down at the trip-token in her hand, but the cross cut into it was still there.

No one had seen it but her. No one would. She closed her fingers and threw it as far as she could. It flashed as it spun, and then fell into the green glass waters of the bay.

* * *

The *Grantine* passed beyond the harbor mouth. The rowers shipped their oars as the sails filled, and the ship took on her deepwater motion. Mykene straddled the bowsprit, feet stirruped in the coiled bowline. The *Grantine* rocked under her, dancing with wind and water.

Mykene wore a hollow golden dolphin on a golden chain about her throat. The secret of making them belonged to her Guild, as did the right to wear them. She caught the golden dolphin's tail in her teeth and blew; a skirling only a Pilot could hear. One of the Underpeople appeared, dancing in the bow wake.

/What news of the sea?/ Mykene piped, and the sea child sang back to her of fair seas and calm weather.

Her father had been a fisherman who took his small boat out each fair weather day to catch fish in the nets her mother spun. Mykene was a child of six when she ran up the beach to her mother to ask the question that would separate her from her people forever.

"I hear people singing in the water, Mother. Why won't they come and play?"

Remarks of this sort must be investigated, that was the Law—and the honor and remission of taxes in the event of miracle was not to be despised. Mykene's parents went together to the Harbormaster to tell him of their daughter's strange questions.

The Harbormaster heard and agreed. Many ships stopped in Riverrun to scrub and refill their water barrels. It was not hard to find a Pilot to test the netmaker's child.

He would always be the handsomest man Mykene had ever seen. His black hair was braided back and bound with a bright red cloth. His skin was dark, and his teeth were white, and the blue tattoos of completed voyages dappled his arms and chest. There were crosses among the circles, but she was too young then to know what they meant. The gold earrings of a Pilot danced against his neck.

"Well, now, and what would you be wanting with me?" His voice was slurred and lilting with the Lordsdeep accent and his gaze was merry as he tilted Mykene's face up to look into her eyes.

"My daughter says she hears the Underpeople singing," Mykene's father said. His hands rested on her shoulders, blunt and strong with years of setting his will against the sea.

"And do you?" asked the Pilot, speaking directly to Mykene. One hand toyed with a gold pendant he wore around his neck: the shape of one of the Underpeople, curved to leap, with a ring clasped in its jaws.

But Mykene wasn't sure. She turned and hid her face against her mother's apron, and felt her father tense with anger. There was a clash of voices above her head and then the music; beautiful and strange and with nothing in it of the land.

Eyes wide with wonder, she'd turned to look, and the Pilot lowered the golden dolphin from his lips.

"Send her with me," Jarre said, and his smile was for Mykene alone. "She's nothing of yours anymore."

At fifteen Mykene wore the single gold earring of a Prentice and left the Guildhouse to make her first voyage. She wore a silver dolphin whistle at her throat, and sailed with this Master or that as Fortune favored her, learning all the currents, reefs, and anchorages in all the round ocean.

"Good sailing, Jarre!" Her voice was high and happy as she greeted the pilot of the *Orekonos*. Jarre sat upon the prow, staring out to sea, reading wind, weather, and fortune as Mykene had learned to in the years since she first met him. She could hear the Underpeople singing as they danced in the harbor: fine weather as far as the Point.

Jarre turned around as Mykene set foot on the gangplank. "Find another ship."

Mykene stopped, still with shock. She was 'prenticed to Jarre until *Orekonos* finished her voyage. She could not imagine anything she had done to offend him so.

"But—why?"

She heard the thump of callused feet upon the deck, and thump again as Jarre hit the gangplank. He towered over her, face dark and unhappy. "Because I wish you well," he said flatly. "Now go!"

His strangeness terrified her more than anything of wind or weather could. Mykene scrabbled backward until her feet touched the wharf; the next thing she remembered was the musty darkness of the Harbormaster's office, where she stood, sick and trembling, babbling something nonsensical about needing another ship at once.

He went with her back to the *Orekonos*, though she would rather have gone anywhere but there, and when there had been a few words with Jarre in the Pilot's small cabin under the foredeck, it was understood that there would be no other berth for Mykene before voyage's end.

On the third day under sail the *Orekonos* was running close along the coast. Thus far it had been an awkward voyage; Jarre was moody, and distant, and spent most of his time in his cabin and not on the wide white deck between the ocean and the sky. That was left to Mykene, and so she took it.

But now a storm was coming.

Mykene felt it on her skin. The cloudless blue sky mocked her, but her training and her senses did not lie. The storm would come before they anchored for the night.

It would blow up without warning and find the *Orekonos* far from haven.

And Jarre hadn't warned them.

Many things were beyond Mykene's understanding, and that had never bothered her. But this one was beyond her experience, and that did—for a Pilot's experience is all there is to keep a ship and crew safe from the whims of the Gods Below. Cowering inwardly, she went to seek out Jarre.

The tiny cabin smelled of salt, and fish, and the raw pale brandy distilled in a thousand towns along the Coast.

"Storm coming."

Jarre turned at the sound of her voice and set the brandy bottle down. His eyes were the red of salt tears and sleeplessness, and his mouth was taut and bitter.

"Have you never wondered, Child of Ocean, what teine it is that we pay to the Gods Below to move freely upon the surface of their world?" He gazed at the brandy bottle as though he had just discovered it, and lifted it, and drank again.

"Jarre, there's a storm coming—a bad one!"

"Give it this," he said, and tossed a silver disk onto the table.

Of course she recognized it. Mykene had seen trip-tokens in the Guildhouse, where she and other Prentices practiced palming it so that no one saw the luck of the ship but her pilot. Mykene had never understood the reason for such secrecy—all the tokens in the Harbormaster's bowl were the same.

This one was different. Marring each face was an X-shape cut deeply into the metal.

"Have you never wondered what teine we pay?" Jarre asked again, the Lordsdeep music in his voice supple with brandy, and Mykene watched him with wide, scared eyes.

He rounded the table, and took the trip-token back from her cold slack fingers, and fumbled at his neck.

"The Harbormaster said that I must keep my oath—and I will, but in my own good way. This is my ship; mine to pilot—and mine to see home to whatever anchorage she finds. Now do you be giving me that," Jarre added, pointing at the silver dolphin-whistle Mykene wore.

Wondering, Mykene slipped it off. Jarre took it in a white-fisted grip, and removed his golden pendant on its chain.

Graceful sculpted arch, copied from the hard bodies of the Underpeople who skirled in and out of the bow-wave even now. Jarre reached out and tossed the chain over her head, and the pipe lay chill and heavy against Mykene's skin, as if it had not just come from living flesh.

"Now this," he said, and pulled off one of his golden earrings.

One ring for a Prentice, two for a Master . . .

"Jarre! What are you doing?" The prescience of disaster was agony upon her Guild-trained senses; Jarre's madness made it worse. The storm might come at any moment; did he mean her to command the *Orekonos* now?

"Each ship above a certain size carries a pilot, that is the law." He pressed close, busy at her ear, his voice, with mad pedantry, reciting Guild Law above her head. "And each pilot, before embarking, draws a token from the Harbormaster for luck upon Ocean. That, too, is the law."

The sharp pin of the heavy gold circlet pressed through her ear as Jarre slid it home; Mykene felt heat and blood.

"And Guild law and sea-law say that a Master Pilot has the duty to save himself in time of trouble, no matter what happens to his ship. So I'll be in the way of saving the Master Pilot of the *Orekonos*—they can hardly say it's the wrong one, now, can they? Can you cry aid on that, do you think?"

The song to call the Underpeople to aid was the first one a Prentice learned. Mykene clutched the golden pipe. "Of course, Jarre, but what—"

"Come then, Child of Ocean."

But Jarre had left it too late.

When they reached the deck the squall-line was a black whip against the horizon. The Underpeople had vanished from the bow-wake, heralding the storm. Jarre swore with tears in his eyes, but no matter how hard he played "Aid to Mariners" on Mykene's silver pipe, the Underpeople would not rise to his music.

He stood and stared at her sick-eyed, and Mykene realized at last that Jarre would not give warning, had never meant to give warning, that somehow the marred trip-token in the cabin below meant that *Orekonos* must do as best she could without her Pilot's skill.

She opened her mouth to warn them in his stead, but any sound she might have made was drowned out by the captain shouting, aware at last of his peril. The ship bowed sharply as the leading edge of the storm hit, and then *Orekonos* was climbing a wall of furious air, decks awash, and there was no more time to do anything but try to survive.

Mykene's bare feet slid on the pitching deck; her nose and mouth were full of the cold salt sea. She felt the captain turn *Orekonos* and try to run before the wind, and Mykene, knowing the coast, struggled to reach the helm. *Orekonos* must be put to deep ocean for safety, and there was no one left to tell her captain so.

There was a boom like the sound of a drum; a grating felt as intimately as broken bones. The mast whipped forward and broke—Mykene was swept overboard in the first

instant; she struggled above the water just in time to see
the *Orekonos* torn neatly in half upon the reef.

Mykene gasped for air and took water instead. The sea
whirled her away from the *Orekonos*. Her last sight of it
was of the deck, separated from the hull, sliding with crazy
slowness beneath the surface.

Take me! Take me and let the others go! she cried silently.
But if the harsh gods of wind and water answered, Mykene
did not hear.

Of the crew of the *Orekonos*, Mykene the Lucky was
the only survivor. It took her half a year to find her way
home again, and learn the last lesson of her craft.

Sixth day, and Mykene stood in the gull's-height calling soundings down to the helmsman, her voice a sea-bird
cry. *Grantine* ran close along the coast for shelter, and the
rocks here were treacherous. When the sea ran low, they
were visible and easy to miss, but the sea ran higher every
year—higher and not high enough to save the wooden hulls
of the ships that plied these waters. Without a pilot, no
ship would dare to sail.

But a pilot's luck must be paid for, and the Gods Below
must have their teine. In the twelve years since the death
of the *Orekonos* Mykene had never questioned that wisdom, and for that loyalty the gods had given her luck—in
all her years at sea she had never drawn the barred token.

Until now. Now the teine that Jarre had paid was hers
to pay as well. One ship in fifty, chosen by lot, to pay for
the luck that let the others through. One ship and all it carried, to pay the Gods Below for their forbearance, and the
Underpeople for their help. One ship, and its pilot must
bring it to its doom, no matter how.

Jarre had been lucky. He'd had to do nothing but give his ship to the storm.

But Mykene must do more.

Not a shadow of peril had clouded *Grantine*'s journey. Tomorrow sunset, if this went on, she would lie safe and whole in Rammage Harbor. But *Grantine* had been promised to the Gods Below, and less than a day remained for Mykene to accomplish the lot that had fallen to her in the Harbormaster's office.

Mykene was a Master Pilot; she knew the thousand several ways to doom a ship. Fire, lies, poison to the crew, a dark night's weakening of the hull and a myriad other shifts—all that the Gods Below might have their due sacrifice. Fire was the easiest, so they had told her at the Guildhouse—fire, and the Underpeople waiting by to bear the pilot alone to safety from the doomed and burning ship. For a Pilot, so said Guild-law and sea-law, must save himself, no matter what happened to his ship.

From this height the waters of Ocean were clear. Pale blue dappled with the shadows of reef and fish shaded to the glistered gray of the northern deep. Mykene feared what walked beneath its surface with all her superstitious heart. The Gods Below were real. And by tomorrow's sunset they would be paid—or cheated.

Mykene slipped the gold chain of her calling-pipe over her head. She held pipe and chain in one glittering handful for a moment before she spilled them into the ocean. She understood Jarre now as never before. This was her ship. She would share its fate.

Whatever it was.

Grantine rode at night anchorage. Mykene curled, sleepless, in the prow. The Starharp hung before her in the night sky, a whorl of stars upon the horizon, and phosphores-

cence streamed from the reefs like ribbons of light. Tomorrow *Grantine* would be in sight of Rammage Bay; the
voyage would be over, and with it all her choices.

Cheat the Gods Below—and doom all the ships along
the round ocean that trusted their pilots to see them safe;
for wouldn't the Gods, thus served, withdraw the luck that
led mariners home?

But even with pilots and their luck, weren't more ships
lost every year than could be accounted for in the paying
of the teine? The pilots who survived tattooed a cross where
a circle should have gone—she had seen them in the taverns, their skins patterned like a God's game of naughts
and crosses where Mykene's skin held naughts alone.
Shouldn't the Gods, who took so many ships not meant for
them, be willing to let this one ship go?

Had any Pilot before her had wondered these things?
Had any of them dared to act upon their thoughts? There
was no way for Mykene to know—any more than she knew
the will of the gods.

She fell asleep near dawn, and dreamed of Jarre.

Rammage was a simple enough harbor; there was only
one way in or out; a deepwater channel that shifted constantly. The locals took crabs and shellfish from the bay's
shallows, and set brightly-colored glass floats at the edges
of the channel. No pilot was needed to navigate Rammage Bay.

Still Mykene sat in the gull's-height and watched—for
the sea-people had sung this dawn of a storm at Rammage.
The storm always shifted the channel, and now, as she
looked down from the gull's-height, she could see that there
were no floats to show the way in.

By the time the helm saw what she could see, it would
be too late. The captain trusted her. Keep silent, and she

would drown the *Grantine* in sight of land, as the gods and her luck intended.

She felt Jarre standing behind her, a ghost ghostly silent, waiting for her to make her own sacrifice; the appeasement prescribed by generations of custom and ritual.

But if the gods must be appeased, it must be because they held power. If they held such power . . .

"Clear!" Mykene bellowed. "Steer clear! *There's no channel!*"

The gull's-height whipped back and forth as the *Grantine* heeled over. Her foredeck rails cut a spangled scarf of foam from the water until she righted, her timbers keening sea-songs, turning out to sea again away from the treacherous haven. Mykene clung to the mast, bleeding from the blow it had dealt her, and laughed and cried like a madwoman.

It took eight hours for Mykene, in a shallow fishing boat with a pole several fathoms long, to mark the new channel and lead *Grantine* down it. The fisherfolk came out to help her, but the pilot of the *Grantine* was the one who set the last marker and poled out of the way to watch her ship slip in to dock.

The Harbormaster came to meet her as she stepped from her fishing boat to the beach.

"A thousand pardons, Pilot—you should never have to do such work!"

Mykene stared at him with new serenity. Jarre's storm had blown itself out at last, and her memories of Jarre could rest.

"She's my ship, Harbormaster—mine to see safe home."

This time, and every time—for as long as skill and Pilot's knowledge could win against wind and water.

If the gods wanted their teine, let them *take* it.

THE SEA GOD'S SERVANT

BY MICKEY ZUCKER REICHERT

AN ocean breeze wound through Luzare's docks, thick with the odors of salt and bracken. It tossed back the hood of Alzon's cloak, spilling a thin mane of chestnut hair. He threaded leisurely through the masses, ignoring the coarse exchanges of dock hands and sailors, the creak of riggings, the flap of unsecured sails, and the dull thunks of clamps against masts. He clutched his satchel with both arms, pinning the fluttering blue-and-white fabric of robe and cloak against his chest. The wind still plucked at the hems and floated tendrils of hair in his wake.

Ships rocked in their moorings. Alzon scanned the horizon for the multicolored sails of the ketch, *Salty Rainbow*. Gulls screeched, wheeling gray shadows against the vivid sapphire of the sky. The sun blazed golden, without so much as a momentary wisp of cloud to obscure it. He found the *Salty Rainbow* without difficulty and adjusted his course toward it. With any luck, they would reach the port in Vitargo in two days. There, he hoped to secure a job as the staff mage for the Vitargan jewelers' guild.

Alzon tugged his hood back into position. He lowered his satchel to his side, exposing the symbol emblazoned on the chest of his cloak. The white unicorn of the goddess Telmargin reflected the fiery glow of the sun into his eyes. A few of the sailors stepped aside as Alzon approached, and he felt their stares at his back. Wizards were rare and, as such, mistrusted by simpler folk, such as those who manned the docks. He had chosen a path that did not allow for the privacy other users of magic took for granted. The Wizards of Telmargin were as much initiates of the goddess of vows, magic, and moonlight as users of the sorcerous arts.

When Alzon reached the *Salty Rainbow*, he found a short line of sailors and passengers boarding under the watchful eye of Captain Melix. Tall and broad, features scoured by salt, the captain stood with his arms folded across his chest. Pale eyes studied each man as he crossed the gunwale. Passengers and workers alike seemed intimidated by that stony gaze. They lowered their heads and shuffled silently on board, as if afraid any break from routine might earn Captain Melix's wrath.

Alzon held back, watching the others file onto the *Salty Rainbow*, seeing no need to hurry. When the last traveler boarded, he would follow, his arrangements already secured. He had a cabin below decks and planned to spend every moment studying there. The rock and toss of ships ill-suited him, and he had no intention of interfering with the sailors' routine. He preferred them fully attendant to getting them all safely across the massive and dangerous ocean into Vitargo. Anything he did would only distract them.

A child of about ten years scurried on board, apparently a cabin boy. Finally, Alzon stepped to the side of the ship.

Captain Melix ran his gaze from the top of Alzon's blue hood to the tips of his cloth-shod feet, lingering longest on the unicorn emblem. He cleared his throat. "So you're the wizard."

Alzon shifted his heavy satchel from one hand to the

other. The comment required no response, yet silence seemed insolent. "I am," he finally replied.

The captain spat in the water. "Two things unlucky on a ship."

Alzon returned the captain's stare, certain what one of those unlucky things would turn out to be. "I paid for my passage and my cabin. Deal's been struck."

Captain Melix continued as if he had not heard. "Women and wizards."

Alzon drummed his fingers on the satchel, irritated. "Are you refusing my fairly bartered passage?"

"No." The captain's attention fell to the satchel, though he did not challenge its contents. Beyond him, on the deck, several sailors casually formed a semicircle, some clutching lines. "But I know we'd all feel more comfortable if we knew you weren't going to use any of that jiggery-higgery stuff on the *Rainbow*."

Alzon sighed. He had no intention of practicing magic during the journey, but he hated promises for a viable reason. True vows uttered by a Wizard of Telmargin could not be broken at the risk of losing all magic. Every one held the weight of the goddess behind it, and oath-breakers got no second chances. Nevertheless, if he missed his passage, he could not reach Vitargo in time. He would lose any chance at his ideal job and the reasonably normal existence it offered. He had put his life on hold to pursue magic, and the time had finally come to settle down, find himself a kind and clever wife, a winsome lot of children. "I can agree not to work any spell on the ship or its crew for the duration of this trip."

Captain Melix seemed unswayed.

"And," Alzon continued routinely, "as a Wizard of Telmargin, I cannot break that promise once made." He gave the captain a searching look, as hard and flat as the seaman's own, though he knew his huge brown eyes would soften it. "But that limits me fully, despite the situation. Even should a man topple overboard, I cannot save him." It was not precisely true. Alzon could breach the vow at the price of his magic and clericy; but his words might as well be god-spoken. He would die rather than endure the rest of his life without his powers; and, if he would spend his own life for them, he could not hesitate to give up a stranger's.

Captain Melix looked from the unicorn symbol to Alzon's face. Then he turned to his crew.

A ragged series of nods swept the shipboard men. The captain's glance sent many scurrying to duties left untended.

The oath-bond of Telmargin's wizards seemed renowned enough to Alzon. Yet, if the captain did not know of it, his word might mean nothing.

"Make the vow," the captain grunted.

"As you wish." Alzon shrugged. "I vow by Telmargin, my mistress, that I will work no magic on board the *Salty Rainbow* for the duration of this trip."

A dense silence followed.

The vow weighed heavy on Alzon, a deep, primal expectation. To the others, however, it might seem nothing more than words.

"Welcome aboard," the captain said with none of the cordiality the greeting implied. He stepped aside. "Your cabin is ready. Below. Third and aft."

"Thank you." Though flooded with relief, Alzon kept his tone as gruff as the captain's own. Stepping around the larger man, he leaped lightly to the bulwarks. Gently grasping the shrouds, he sprang to the afterdeck.

The sailors scattered to their jobs, securing sails, casting lines off cleats, and setting ballast. Melix moved like an enormous cat, bounding to the deck and shouting or-

ders simultaneously. "Shore up those lines, sailor, and prepare the tillerman! You know *Rainbow* carries strong
weather helm!"

As Alzon entered the darkness below, footsteps hammered above him, and the captain's orders wafted to him
as muffled and meaningless noise. It would have taken an
instant to kindle a magical light; but, true to his vow, he
fumbled with a hanging lantern, oil, and his tinderbox instead. Balancing the heavy satchel, he lit the lantern. His
every movement cast flickering shadows on planking.

The first door aftward lay open, revealing piles of rope,
seized with twine wrap to diminish unraveling. Sails tumbled across piles of extra rigging, tabled with boltropes and
stiffened with battens. Cleats and belaying pins, nails and
a hammer, oar rests and rudder gear lay spread across the
floor.

Lantern light bobbing in an irregular circle, Alzon continued past the second, closed, door to his cabin. As he
tripped the latch and pulled, the ship lurched. Tossed sideways, he crashed, shoulder first, against the frame. Instinctively, his grip winched tighter on the lantern. Driven
from his grip, his satchel slammed onto his foot. Incapac-
itating agony shot through his toes. He jerked backward
with a howl, half rage and half pain. Bullying through the
discomfort, he wrestled the bag inside, hooked the lantern
on its gimbal, slammed the door, and hurled himself on a
straw ticking covered with a stiff, woolen blanket. Jerking
off his cloth shoe, he clutched his toes in his hand, rocking against the pain.

Gradually, it dulled to a raw ache. Alzon examined his
toes, cautiously flexing them. Finding them intact, he managed an ironic smile at his own clumsiness. Replacing his
shoe, he studied the cabin. Small and windowless, it contained only the bed, a battered desk, a wooden chair, a

chamber pot, and a chest. A washing pan balanced on the chest, shifting slightly with the now-smooth movement of the ship.

Alzon studied the scarred wooden surface of the desk. Water rings intertwined across it, and gouges marred it like valleys. Crafted of wood several shades darker, the chair clearly bore no intended relation to it. Its high-slung seat would bunch his legs against the bottom of the desk. With a deep sigh, he lay back on the ticking for a nap before his studies. He had spent much of the night negotiating his passage. Certain the sailors would like to keep him below decks as much as he wished to stay there, he knew he would have all the time of the journey to read. And the desk did not seem the most comfortable place to do it.

Closing his eyes, Alzon settled into the peaceful rock of the ship. The steady flap of the sail and the chaotic music of shackles tapping mast lulled him to sleep.

Alzon jolted awake in inexplicable panic. Beneath him, the ship bucked and rolled. Footsteps slammed on the deck, and a vivid curse wafted through the boards.

"What—? How long—?" He struggled to his feet, immediately thrown to the floor. He still felt exhausted. Too little time had passed for the weather to change so drastically. Then, something hard slammed the deck, shaking the ship as if to shatter it. Using the cabin wall for support, Alzon managed to rise again, now recognizing the rhythmical clatter of hard rain. Thunder cracked through his hearing, and a flash of light leached through the cracks. The lantern flapped on its gimbal ring, rolling frantic shadows through the cabin.

Wildly bewildered, Alzon fought his way up the gangway to the hatch. He shoved it open into a darkness deep as pitch. Rain hammered him, a cold barrage of pinpoints that penetrated his cloak and sent a shudder through him. "What's going on?" he shouted over the din.

Lightning flashed a web across the heavens, revealing a dense network of clouds. Thunder rang a moment later.

A sailor blundered past, chasing a whipping line. "Fires and smoke! Came out of nowhere."

Wind howled through the riggings, and the sails thrashed frantically, battered by a nonsensical squall. Instantly soaked, droplets pelting his face, Alzon stood stunned. Waves whipped toward them, massive as dragons and howling as madly. The ship swerved fiercely, controlled more by the ocean than human hand. The sailors scuttled across the deck, shouting to one another as they flailed for lashing lines and repositioned ballast.

Slammed unexpectedly from behind, Alzon fell to his knees. A sailor huffed out an unconvincing apology, followed by an explanation. "Got to secure the hatch."

"Aft! Aft!" Melix bellowed, fairly throwing a passenger toward the stern. "Rethalin, man the helm. Lessiv, did you forget the sacrifice?" It sounded more accusation than question.

A thin man lunging for the back stay replied. "I was generous, sir. Very generous. No reason for Merathe's wrath, sir."

A swell rushed under the *Salty Rainbow*, sliding it from crest to trough. Thrown free, the rudder failed. The ship yawed violently.

"Slow!" The captain turned his ire upon a new victim. "Ease the wind." Water arched over the stern, hurling spray and pouring through the scuppers. Melix fought against a surge. "Ease the damned wind."

The spars creaked dangerously. The hull fishtailed, thrown broadside. The captain froze. A single curse left his lips.

Alzon glanced around the ship. In defiance of logic, water came at them from every direction. The bow bobbed, as if to drink deeply of the ocean. The hull shuddered, and the stern swung airward.

"She's going to pitchpole!" someone shouted.

For a terrified moment, the ship seemed to hang sideways, frozen in time and place. Alzon tumbled, rolling across the quaking deck. Spray flew, high and blinding. He struggled to stand as the ship pitched suddenly backward, flinging him to the deck. He lurched into a clumsy stagger that carried him aft, driving him against the taffrail. Breath dashed from his lungs, and he sagged. Someone crashed against the rail beside him. Gasping for air, Alzon twisted his head to a brawny sailor. The man's green eyes flashed with sudden understanding. "It's you, Wizard. It's you Merathe wants."

The words seemed utter nonsense. Alzon had no dealings with the god of the ocean, no skills for or experience with the sea. Before he could say so, a colossal wave smacked the ship broadside, sending it into an uncontrolled spin. Most of the crew now lay on the deck, thrown there by motion that defied even the most experienced sea legs. Captain Melix clutched the savagely pitching tiller in white-knuckled hands, praying fervently into his beard.

As if in answer, the waves ceased their relentless pummeling of the *Salty Rainbow*. Clouds separated like ink in water, admitting a spare beam of sunlight that lanced straight into Alzon's eyes.

Blinded, Alzon dropped his gaze.

"Get him!" Melix shouted.

The abrupt stillness of the ship seemed every bit as disorienting as its pitching and yawing once had. Footsteps rushed toward the wizard. Hands seized his cloak from every direction. He blinked away the brightness, his vision

suddenly filled with arms and bodies. "What— I'm not—"
The need to use his magic became all-consuming, but his
promise just as fully doomed him.

Alzon found himself airborne over the sea, rescued from
his vow but in imminent danger. "No!" He scrabbled for
a pocket and the feather always hidden there. He pawed it
free, screaming the words for the flying spell, and his uncontrolled fall became a graceful swoop. Pointing his head
toward the dark sky, he glided upward.

A sailor shouted. At first, Alzon assumed, at him. They
had betrayed him for prejudice, branded him the cause of
their misfortune, rather than a freakish storm. Then, a mon-
strous wave shot toward the heavens directly in front of
him, surging far over his head, then curling down to swal-
low him.

Alzon scarcely had time to choke out the words of a
water-breathing spell before its very component, salt water,
closed over him. It struck like a club, slamming him deep
beneath the water. The world churned and frothed, driving
him in crazed spirals that stole all sense of direction. He
opened his eyes to a blinding white mass of bubbles and
debris, completely unbalanced. Bits of shell cut his eyes,
and he jammed them closed. Uncertain which direction to
go, he surged what he believed was upward.

For what seemed like hours, Alzon fought the boiling
sea, finding nothing but water in any direction. He knew
he struggled, submerged, less than a quarter hour, however.
Otherwise, his spell would have failed and he would have
drowned. His legs felt like lead weights, and his arms ached
from a battle that had become worse than futile. He gasped
in full pants of water, his magic alone keeping him alive,
and realized he had to stop. The duration of the water-
breathing went by number of breaths, not time. The harder
he worked, the shorter he had.

Though it went against every instinct, Alzon forced himself still. The water no longer seethed around him. He opened his stinging eyes to slits. His vision granted him a splendid panorama. Pale green stalks clambered upward from a vast plain of sand. Rocks rose like mountains from the sea floor, and multicolored fish glided past without a glance in his direction. The realization of position filled him with excitement and despair. He now knew which direction to swim, also aware he could never make it in time. Already, the substance funneling into his lungs thickened. He would have to hold his breath or risk the magicked air turning back into the reality of sea water in his lungs.

Gasping in one last lungful, Alzon prepared a desperate surge for the distant surface.

A shadow fell over Alzon. He whirled to face an enormous creature, half fish and half man. Green hair swelled in the tides around a dark face and eyes that seemed all white and pupil. The other had gill slits where a man's nose would sit and a wide mouth with a human arrangement of teeth. It had arms like a man, but its torso ended in a flatly scaled fish tail. Alzon recognized the mer-figure at once: Merathe, god of the ocean.

Alzon gasped in a thin stream of water, then choked savagely. His consciousness dulled. *It's a hallucination. I just need air.*

No, the merman replied in his head. *I'm very, very real.*

Alzon's thoughts blurred and spun. He closed his eyes and waited for death to close over him. The one spell he could work underwater was already failing him. He lacked the energy needed to perform it a second time.

Alzon, Wizard of Telmargin, promise yourself to me as my servant, and I will save you.

Darkness enveloped Alzon. His lungs spasmed. Without air, he would die in moments. *Death or a life in bondage.*

The choice was none at all. *I promise,* he sent with all the force left inside him.

By Telmargin.

By my mistress, Telmargin. Then oblivion overtook him.

Alzon awakened on a straw ticking covered with a stiff, woolen blanket. *A dream. Thank the gods, it was only a dream. But what a nightmare.* He sat up, opening his eyes.

Craggy pinkish walls framed an irregularly shaped room with an oval window. Water streamed past, and Alzon glimpsed an occasional fish. He wondered what kept the water from pouring into the room, though he felt too relieved that he did not consider the matter for long. The furniture consisted of two chests and a stool, all constructed of shells. Instead of his usual cloak with its unicorn symbol, he wore a scratchy tunic and trousers, tannish-green in color, ugly as well as uncomfortable.

I'm a servant. Merathe's servant. Thoughts of escape crowded Alzon's mind, immediately banished. He had chosen enslavement over death, and he always knew he would rather die than lose his magic. He had made a vow. Mental or spoken, he could not break it. He belonged to Merathe. For eternity.

Alzon lowered his head, his shaggy chestnut locks, stiffened by salt water, falling against his cheeks. He placed both hands over his face. The job he would lose in Vitargo seemed meaningless, an insignificant point in an existence that no longer had purpose. All the things he had put aside until he finished learning magic: a job, a family, a home, a life; these were no longer within the realm of possibility. Freedom, once taken for granted, seemed the ultimate gift. In the space of a few heartbeats, his time, his desires and dreams, became impossible fantasy.

A shy knock sounded on his door.

Alzon opened his eyes into his palms. He saw the sandy floor through the cracks between his fingers, a desolate plain of gray. "Yes?"

The door opened a bit, and a blue eye studied him through the gap. Wisps of blonde hair floated around a middle-aged, female face; but he saw no feet.

A mermaid? The features appeared too human. Then, Alzon realized water filled the corridor beyond his room. It did not matter whether she had feet or a tail; while swimming, her parts would not touch the ground. He raised his head and dropped his hands. Whatever trick of the sea god kept the water from rushing in his window apparently kept it in the hall as well. "What do you need?"

The stranger's head withdrew momentarily, then dipped inside his room. "I'm Laina, a maid. I just . . . just wondered if . . . you needed . . ." Her nervous pauses trailed to silence.

Alzon did not feel like company, but this woman appeared innocuous, a good person from whom to learn the lay of his new home. "Come in. Close the door behind you, please. That hovering water makes me dizzy."

Laina smiled weakly. "You get used to it." She swung her legs inside and did as he had bade. Small and slight, she appeared more like a girl than a full-grown woman. She wore her hair in short feathers that already looked dry. She wore a simple shift of the same homely fabric as his clothes. It did not cling to her as he would expect from wet linen. At her belt, she carried a duster and a scraper. "You're new here."

"Brand new," Alzon admitted. "How long have you been here?"

"Twenty years, almost." Laina glanced around the simple furnishings. "Nothing bad could ever happen to a sixteen-year-old with my grace, so I thought. Danced on

Father's bowsprit and fell right off. Hit the undertow and sank like a stone."

"So Merathe didn't *take* you?"

"*Take* me?" Laina crinkled her features in bewilderment.

"Off a ship."

"Oh, no." Laina pulled the duster and waved it at an imaginary cobweb. Alzon found it difficult to imagine spiders or dust could penetrate the ocean. "I fell. I'd have drowned for sure, but he saved me. Brought me here."

Alzon rose and sat on one of the chests, gesturing for her to take the more comfortable position on the bed. A person who had lived here for two decades would probably know all about serving the sea god. "How many servants does he have?"

Laina shrugged. "Varies. About a hundred, usually."

"Where do they come from?"

"Ships mostly." Laina gave Alzon a comforting smile, clearly intended to put him at ease. "Fall off. Sometimes thrown. Lost in storms. Occasionally they're just fools who tried to swim in rough water. Even know one who tried to kill herself." She grinned ironically. "She's tried since. Not much luck, though. The master makes us all able to breathe, first thing."

"Breathe underwater?"

"Oh, yeah." Laina shifted forward. Apparently, his conversational style put her at ease as well. "Couldn't live here without that. He keeps our rooms air-filled, for comfort, I think. Rumor was his first servants went mad without it. But the rest's all water here."

Alzon's thoughts kept returning to how he got into Merathe's service. "Does he ever . . . take people off their ships or the shore? Against their will?"

Laina leaned back again, curling her feet onto the edge of the pallet. "I've heard of one or two times. If the person's got something ... like a skill ... he really wants. That's how we got our doctor. Master just swept his little boat right under."

Alzon tried to process this new information, though it scarcely mattered. He strove to funnel his questions in a more pertinent direction, but Laina beat him to it.

"Aren't you going to ask what it's like here? How hard it is to serve the master?"

Alzon forced a smile. "I was just getting to that."

"It's not that bad," Laina offered helpfully. "The work's hard, but it ends at sundown." She flushed. "At least, I think it does. We don't actually see the sun."

The off-hand comment struck deep, dragging under-standing to Alzon's core. He would never see the sun again, the stars, the moon. The simple beauties and pleasures of human existence would forever elude him before he had a chance to fully appreciate them. The years he had intended to spend pursuing the dreams he had forsaken for knowl-edge became lost in a moment.

Oblivious to Alzon's turbulent thoughts, Laina contin-ued. "We're really too busy to worry much about what we're missing. He's strict but reasonably fair. We eat all right." Her grin turned lopsided. "Hope you like seafood. And he doesn't beat or rape anyone, and—"

"Anyone ever escape?"

Laina stopped speaking and swallowed hard. "I wouldn't suggest you try."

Alzon shook his head. "Wasn't planning to. I can't. Bound by an oath." It was not exactly true. He had never promised not to attempt escape, but Telmargin frowned on weaseling around promises with semantics. He doubted he could escape with his magic intact.

"Oh." Laina studied him. "Well. Not too many have

tried. I know one who did. He stayed free for a while, but the day he dared get near the ocean again, he drowned."

Alzon nodded, recalling the unearthly storm that had attacked the *Salty Rainbow*.

"Anything else you want to know?"

Alzon felt certain he would have many questions; but, for the moment, he could only verbalize one. "What happens next?"

"To you?"

Alzon gazed at Merathe's maid, hoping he did not sound selfish. It was difficult to contemplate others' fate when his own lay in the balance. "Yes, please."

"The master will call for you, give you your assignment. Spell out the rules." Laina's features softened, even more sympathetically. "It's a bit intimidating but not too awful. At least you know the expectations ahead of time. It helps, rather than trying to bungle through things hoping for the best."

A harder knock sounded through the room. Laina rose and whispered. "That'll be Luke. He'll take you to the master." She shrank back on the pallet, as if afraid to be caught with him. "Good luck."

Alzon rose and walked to the door, keeping his body between the newcomer's line of vision and Laina, just in case she had done something wrong by visiting. He opened the panel to a wall of water and flinched instinctively. But the water continued to flow leisurely past him, as though held from his room by an invisible barrier. Beyond it floated a stout, pink-cheeked man, his dark hair cut to stubble. The tide yanked at a tunic and trousers that perfectly matched Alzon's.

"My name is Luke," the man said formally. "Come with me."

Instinctively, Alzon started a water-breathing spell, then

stopped himself. Laina had said he would be able to breathe, and he saw no reason not to try. Nevertheless, when he stepped into the water, meeting no resistance from whatever barrier kept it out of his room, he caught himself holding his breath.

Luke took little notice. He spun, carving a wake of bubbles, and glided down the corridor.

Alzon followed, finally taking a slight, experimental breath. The water glided in, as silken and natural as air. He followed Luke in silence, kicking his feet behind him, occasionally touching the bottom for momentum or purchase. Fish drifted through the current, and crabs scuttled amidst the billowing clouds of sand churned up by his toes. The walls glimmered with chips of abalone and quartz, and the motion of the water carried their glow and sparkle through the hallways.

At length, Luke stopped in front of an enormous set of double doors and knocked. It sounded distant, diffuse, beneath the ocean.

"Come in," Merathe's voice called clearly.

Despite the pressure of the water, Luke pulled open the leftmost door easily, revealing another air-filled room. This one contained a large window, beyond which floated sea life of myriad types. A school of seahorses glided past, accompanied by a mass of tiny, black-striped amber fish. Several plush chairs lay in a semicircle facing the ocean view, one occupied by the merman/god who had doomed Alzon to servitude.

Lowering his feet to the floor, Alzon entered the room. The abrupt transition from dense water to open air sent him staggering. He fell to his knees before his master. The huge door swung soundlessly shut behind him.

Merathe's gaze swiveled from the view, to the door, then to the floor. "Kneeling isn't necessary. You've done nothing that displeases me." He gestured at one of the chairs, and Alzon noticed that the sea god's fingers were fused, like flippers, and opposed by his thumbs. It reminded Alzon of having permanent mittens.

Alzon rose and took the proffered chair. He expected to feel awed, intimidated. Instead, he found his hands balled to fists at his sides. He would not dare to insult a god, but he saw no reason to kowtow, either. "My lord, what do you want from me?" Even as he asked, he knew the answer. The ocean god had selected him for a reason, the only true talent he possessed. *My magic.*

"Your life here will not be hard," Merathe began a speech that sounded rehearsed. "I don't demand—"

Alzon could not bear to listen. "I made a vow, my lord. I have no choice but to honor it."

The merman smiled. "Very wise."

"But the others . . ." Alzon thought of Laina, how quiet and haunted she seemed, her life stolen at the age of youth and beauty. ". . . couldn't you . . . I mean . . . wouldn't there be some . . . advantage to . . . rotating them? My lord?"

Merathe blinked, apparently stunned silent by Alzon's impudence, no matter how carefully worded. Then, he laughed. "I need a servant with spunk. At least one who's going to wield as much power as I plan to grant you."

Alzon ignored the compliment, and the revelation, awaiting an answer.

The god lashed his tail. "You mean, toss aside my experienced servants for new ones I have to train from scratch every few years?"

"Yes, my lord."

"Why would I want to do that?"

"Variety, my lord." Alzon kept his head low. Though he challenged Merathe, he knew better than to do so with open rudeness. "Your servants might work better if they know you reward the best with freedom, and they won't feel as if you've stolen their entire lives."

A scarlet cloud covered Merathe's face, then seeped onto his features. "Have my servants been complaining?"

Worried he might place Laina in danger, Alzon shook his head. "It was just an idea, my lord."

"I rescue my servants from certain death. I grant them lives when they would otherwise have none. Are you condemning me for this?"

Alzon loosened his fists. Merathe had an inarguable point. "No. No, my lord. I have no right to judge. I am only your servant." His thoughts returned to the storm. Merathe had thrown him into danger, not saved him from it. He may have granted the others mercy, but the god of the oceans had plundered Alzon's autonomy with clear and deliberate foresight. The very mastery to which he had dedicated his life, the skill for which he had sacrificed so much, had made him valuable to Merathe. And cost him his independence for eternity. *He wants my magic.*

That thought triggered another, and Alzon smiled. He stood and made a fervent bow. "My lord," he said, "What services shall I perform for you?"

Merathe's features returned to their natural green-tinged brown, and he settled back into his seat with light flicks of his tail. No doubt, he chose this room for the comfort of his air-breathing visitors and new servants, not himself. "Alzon of Telmargin, my powers are massive, as they pertain to the sea."

"Indeed, my lord. I've had a taste of them."

Merathe managed a closed-mouth grin. "But I'm otherwise quite limited. I would like you to provide the little magics I need other times and places. Messages sent. Favored sailors flown to safety. Act as my whim beyond the confines of the sea."

Alzon now realized that Merathe had not picked him solely for his magic, but also for the vow that would hold him to his servitude even while beyond the sea god's realm.

"My lord," Alzon said, springing from his chair to bow before his new master. "I wish to swear you an oath."

Merathe's smile became more friendly, and he waved Alzon on with a flipperlike hand.

"Today, I am your loyal servant. Tonight, I vow to Telmargin, my mistress, I shall have my freedom."

"Only if I grant it—" Merathe started, then broke off with a squawk of realization. "What have you done?"

Alzon stepped back, no longer obsequious. "Placed my magic, my very life, at your mercy."

"No." Merathe's massive tail smacked the sand. "No!"

"If you still have me tomorrow—"

Merathe understood, "It will be sans magic, for you will have broken your oath. You've stolen what I've waited decades for. You've stolen my wizard!" His eyes narrowed. "I have no use for you now."

Alzon knew he had played a mighty gamble, yet he had to take the risk. His freedom, he discovered, meant as much to him as his magic, perhaps defined his very desire for it. The power that came with magic granted a level of independence few knew.

"I should kill you."

Alzon had worried about that, but the fact that the god had not already done so suggested he was willing to bargain. "And you could. But, if you spare me, if you grant me the freedom to keep my magic, I will still work for you. Only now, I will do so willingly."

Merathe stared at the fish window in silence, still but for the smooth back and forth movement of his tail. Gradually, a light dawned in his iris-lacking eyes, and his features lapsed into an easy expression. "You'll run errands for me?"

"Reasonable ones," Alzon agreed.

"Say, once per moon cycle?" Though surely unused to haggling, Merathe added. "I'll let you keep the water breath. I can use a clever . . . a clever . . ." He broke off, obviously uncertain what to call their new relationship.

"How about 'friend'?" Alzon suggested boldly.

"How about 'envoy'?"

Alzon laughed, his dreams of the future restored in an instant. "Can't blame a man for trying."

OCEAN'S ELEVEN

BY MIKE RESNICK AND TOM GERENCER

*W*OODS *Hole, Massachusetts, AP—Worldwide panic continues to intensify today, amid confirmations of reports that the North Atlantic Ocean has either "dried up" or "simply vanished overnight." The disappearance took place Tuesday at approximately 12:40 AM (EST) according to a spokesman from the National Oceanographic and Atmospheric Administration, where speculation rages amid...*

...meanwhile, the President has urged citizens in coastal communities to remain calm. "After all, we're talking a trillion tons of seawater, boats, and fish," the Chief Executive Officer said in an emergency address this morning. "It didn't just get up and walk away."

But of course, that was precisely what it did.

It was 2:00 PM when the North Atlantic Ocean sloshed into Bob Zellinski's cubicle and stood dripping on the rug.

"You need a towel?" asked Zellinski.

"I need a job."

Zellinski stared at his visitor for a long moment. "I thought you *had* a job."

"I was an ocean two hundred million years ago. I was an ocean five thousand years ago. I was an ocean last Tuesday. There's no advancement."

"What would you want to advance *to?*" asked Zellinski.

"Something more challenging."

"Isn't it challenging when you have a typhoon or a tidal wave?"

"*You* may call a tidal wave awesome and challenging," said the ocean contemptuously. "*I* call it projectile vomiting."

"So what kind of position *are* you looking for?" asked Zellinski.

"I think I'd make a really top-notch dishwasher," it suggested, leafing through his *Anthony Robbins' Page-A-Day Inspirational Desk Calendar* and soaking all Bob's files. "Or maybe a fireman. And I have years of experience working with urchins." When this got no response, the ocean tried a different tack. "This *is* Intellitemp Employment Services, isn't it?"

"Well, it was when I showed up this morning," said Zellinski.

"And you're an employment agent?"

Zellinski nodded affirmatively. "That's me—and believe me, at times like this it isn't easy."

"What's your name?"

"Bob."

"Good name, Bob," it said, shaking his hand with a prehensile starfish. "Very buoyant sounding. Very flotational."

"I'm glad you approve."

Several seconds passed. Finally Zellinski managed to speak again. "You're the Atlantic, right?"

"Yeah, well, North Atlantic, actually," said the ocean, slumping slightly. "What gave it away? Was it the kelp, or the tang of salt air?"

Zellinski merely stared at it.

"It's the kelp, isn't it?" said the ocean with a tragic sigh. "It's always the goddamned kelp."

In truth, the kelp had been a factor in the failure of the ocean's thin disguise, but other features had contributed as well. (Like what, we hear you ask? Well, like the offshore drilling platforms, the telltale intercontinental trade routes, and the singular proliferation of porpoises frolicking in its bays.)

"Anyway, I'm sick of being an ocean and I never want to be one again."

Zellinski continued staring. "Jesus wept," he whispered.

"Jesus was under a lot of strain," said the ocean. "Just like me. So what about that job?"

Zellinski explained that he would be happy to help the ocean in any way he could, but he was having trouble understanding how it fit into his cubicle, which was admittedly spacious by company standards, and yet not nearly big enough (or so he would previously have thought) to accommodate an entire ocean.

"I'm not the whole Atlantic," said the ocean irritably. "I'm just the *North* Atlantic."

"Even so . . ."

"I've been working out," explained the ocean. "Dieting, too, though I'll probably gain it back, since most of it was water weight. It's Hollywood's fault, really," it added petulantly. "All those stupid movies I've been in . . . I mean, hell, the camera adds fifteen pounds at least."

"So how is it that an ocean can speak English?" asked Zellinski.

"Correspondence classes," said the sea. "Although I'm still having trouble with the diphthongs. Squid?"

It held out a thrashing cephalopod, but Zellinski begged off, citing a recent lunch break and a hastily-ingested burrito.

"Suit yourself," said the ocean. "But squid are very low in cholesterol." There was a brief pause. "So can we get down to business?" said the ocean. "I'm really in a bit of a hurry. My rent is due this Friday."

"Rent?" repeated Zellinski. "You pay rent on the ocean floor?"

"Of course not. I told you: I'm through being an ocean. I'm renting a little efficiency apartment on Fifth and Periwinkle until I get settled."

The ocean then proceeded to tell him, while Zellinski held tightly to his desk for the sense of reality it gave him, that it was very sorry about the medical waste it had just washed up on his printer.

"No problem," said Zellinski, deciding that the very best thing to do was find the ocean a job as quickly as possible and get it out of his office. "What experience have you had? Besides being an ocean, I mean."

"I was a line cook. But I didn't enjoy it much."

"When was that?" said Zellinski, trying to picture the North Atlantic grilling steaks or even flipping pancakes.

"About a month ago," said the ocean. "At the Burger World franchise over on Park Street. Oh, I got the sullenness and the mumbling down pat, but the paper hats kept getting soggy. And the manager was always yelling at me for putting seaweed in the burgers."

"Why did you do that?" asked Zellinski, curious in spite of himself.

"It's healthier—but they don't seem to care about that at Burger World. And when I tried to substitute some nice, fresh calamari in the fishburgers, the manager complained, even though the customers liked it."

"They did?" said Zellinski, since he thought it sounded doubtful.

"Well, either that or *it* liked the customers," said the ocean thoughtfully. "Sometimes it's difficult to tell." It shrugged, drenching Zellinski in a less-than-fine salt spray, then regarded him for a moment with its many eyes—whale, fish, otter, and hurricane. "So anyway," it continued, "they put me on the drive-thru after that, which went fine until I shorted out three headsets . . . and then this one lady in a Buick got attacked by a hammerhead."

"Is she okay?" said Zellinski, alarmed.

"The hammerhead?"

"The lady."

"She's fine, physically," replied the ocean, "but they say she'll never be able to look at a cheeseburger again without screaming."

It suddenly seemed out of things to say.

"So can I get a job?" it concluded after a brief pause.

"Well, we had a request yesterday for a parking lot attendant."

The ocean shook its head. "That was my second job."

"And?"

"Salt water doesn't mix with fine Corinthian leather." It grimaced. "And I can't drive a stick shift."

"Too bad," said Zellinski sympathetically.

"And then one day I stayed home sick in bed, you know, with one of those really strong neap tides, and the bastards just fired me."

The ocean further told Zellinski it had gone through no less than eight other failed jobs since its first foray into the world of humans, including positions in data entry (during which a woman from the secretarial pool was bitten by a flounder), bookkeeping (all the ink ran off the ledger pages), farming (which it summed up with the telltale phrase: "Pigs do not float"), and an ill-conceived position as a lifeguard at a public pool.

"I would have thought you'd make an excellent lifeguard," offered Zellinski.

"I thought so too," agreed the ocean. "But a low-pressure

system moved through one day during kiddie-hour, and all these preteens wound up on the roof of the food court."

Zellinski listened to all of this with equanimity. In the end, falling back upon his training, he had the ocean fill out an aptitude questionnaire, which it had trouble with, since it kept dripping on the pages and a cuttlefish ate two of the pencils. But eventually it finished and Zellinski tallied the results.

"Well?" it asked eagerly. "What does the future hold for me? Test pilot? Third baseman for the Red Sox? Hollywood superstar?"

"According to this," replied Zellinski, "you are best suited to being an immense body of salt water somewhere between North America, Europe, and the Ivory Coast."

"Yeah? What does it pay?" said the ocean, perking up— but it calmed down again when Zellinski informed it that this was the very position it had so recently vacated.

"Maybe I could show you my portfolio," the ocean suggested, suddenly disgorging several hundred pounds of fish and mammals. "That dolphin there is some of my best work."

"Get this thing off me!" said Zellinski, referring to the large and ugly creature that had him by the shirtsleeve.

"Yeah, I'm not very proud of the monkfish," admitted the ocean sadly. "I should've put more effort into it, but I was going through some personal problems at the time."

" Look, you're an ocean," said Zellinski, trying to keep his temper under control. "You may not like it, but then I don't like the fact that I'm short and fat and bald and come last in the alphabet. According to what you've told me, you've had ten jobs and screwed up each of them."

"Hercules had twelve labors," noted the ocean.

"Hercules pulled them off," was the answer. "You didn't."

"You really know how to get to a guy," said the ocean sullenly.

"Look, I'll make you a deal," said Zellinski. "I'll place you in one job. That's it. I'm not going to waste my time when we both know that what you're really good at is being the North Atlantic Ocean."

"What's the deal?"

"First things first. I want your agreement that if you fail at this, you'll go back to being an ocean."

There was a long, thoughtful pause. "All right," said the ocean at last.

"Okay," said Zellinski. "McNair & Sons needs an electrician. You've worked with electric eels. What do you think?"

"I'll take it!"

Two days later all the power within a fifty-mile radius of the local electric company's generators went dead. Zellinski didn't even have to ask anyone what had happened.

Zellinski looked up as the Amazon River entered his office.

"What can I do for you?" he asked.

"I'm so tired of flowing downstream," whined the river. "I don't care what kind of job you find for me, but it has to go upstream."

"Funny you should stop by at this time," said Zellinski. "I just happen to have an opening for an aggressive automobile salesman who specializes in DeLoreans. Nobody knows them; nobody knows you. It'll be a perfect fit."

"Do DeLoreans go upstream?" asked the Amazon.

"On those rare occasions that they go anywhere at all."

"It sounds promising."

They went over the details of the job—the pay, the sick

days, the vacation days (and Zellinski promised to request four days a year for its silt to settle after the spring rains)—and finally they shook hands, with Zellinski barely avoiding losing a finger to a piranha.

Then, as the Amazon River went off to meet its new employer, Zellinski cleared his desk and prepared for his meeting with the Sahara Desert, which was adamant about relocating to a cooler climate.

Science Fiction Anthologies